IT TAKES TWO to MANGO

CARRIE DOYLE

Poisoned Pen
PRESS

Published by Poisoned Pen Press, an imprint of Sourcebooks
P.O. Box 4410, Naperville, Illinois 60567-4410
(630) 961-3900
sourcebooks.com

Library of Congress Cataloging-in-Publication Data

Names: Doyle, Carrie, author.
Title: It takes two to mango / Carrie Doyle.
Description: Naperville, Illinois : Poisoned Pen Press, [2021] | Series:
   Trouble in paradise! ; book 1
Identifiers: LCCN 2020048785 | (paperback) | (epub)
Subjects: GSAFD: Mystery fiction.
Classification: LCC PS3604.O95473 I87 2021 | DDC 813/.6--dc23
LC record available at https://lccn.loc.gov/2020048785

Printed and bound in Canada.
MBP 10 9 8 7 6 5 4 3 2 1

For Liz, who is always my first reader, second reader, third reader, and so on. I would never be able to publish a book without you.

CHAPTER

1

PLUM LOCKHART SAT AT HER desk on the twenty-sixth floor staring down at the blaze of neon lights illuminating Times Square. It was only four thirty, but it was already dark outside and as cold as it could get without snowing. *A pity,* thought Plum. At least snow would have made the filthy streets look pretty. The endless frigid winter days had blended together, and it felt to Plum like it was the forty-seventh day of January, yet it was only the first week. The weather matched her mood: gloomy, negative, and uninspired.

It had been a particularly grim afternoon. Plum had been forced to lay off Gerald Hand, her art director, and he had made a scene (predictable) and accused Plum of being "an opportunistic cold-hearted wannabe" (uncalled for) and was escorted out by security (not her idea). The entire editorial staff was now on edge and regarded Plum with weariness and suspicion, which she resented. She felt they should be grateful to her for keeping them employed in this treacherous market. It was no secret that *Travel and Respite Magazine* was hemorrhaging money—the entire publishing industry was collapsing—and downsizing was inevitable.

There was a knock at Plum's door, and she swiveled her chair around and espied Steven Blum through the glass wall. She motioned for him to come in, although he was already halfway through the door. Seeing as he was her boss, he really didn't have to wait for permission.

"How did it go with Gerald?" asked Steven, taking a seat across from her.

"Brutal."

Steven nodded. He was squat, bald, overweight, and hardly fit the profile of head of the magazine group at the glamorous Mosaic Publishing, but he was a numbers guy who had been promoted from accounting.

"It couldn't have come as a shock to him. The magazine is doing terribly."

"He has an inflated sense of self," sighed Plum, taking a sip of her white chai latte. "But people are delusional."

"Yes, I have often found that."

"He really didn't have to take it personally. He was very catty and churlish. He could have at least left with dignity."

"Yes, that's the way to go. Take your leave graciously."

"Well, what's done is done," she said and began flipping through some of the files on her desk. "The good news is that I finalized the feature on Mongolia. I'll actually be heading there myself for ten days. I ordered all of my horseback riding paraphernalia online. If you look over there, you can see a box of whips... Just to clarify they are for riding, not—"

"Plum..."

"Yes?"

"We need to talk."

"What's up?"

"*Travel and Respite* is basically a pamphlet these days."

"And I choose to see that as a positive. It is easier for people to pop in their suitcase and bring with them when they travel."

"We are shutting it down," Steven announced.

"Completely? Not even turning it into a website?"

Steven shook his head. "It's done."

Plum had suffered enough disappointments in her thirty-five years of life to quickly adapt and turn setbacks into opportunities. She folded her perfectly manicured hands and placed them on her desk. Once, she had skipped a manicure and a nasty editor at a competing magazine asked if her nails were jagged because she had scratched her way to the top. While it was true that she was ambitious and had succeeded, she had done so through hard work and plunging ahead when the chips were down. She was proud of her efforts. And she had kept her nails perfectly polished ever since.

"All right, then. What's the plan?" she asked brightly.

"No plan. As of this afternoon, everyone is released."

Plum glanced sideways out the glass doors at the remaining skeleton staff.

"We can't move them over to another magazine?"

He shook his head.

"How about *Panda Love*? I heard the plushie market is brisk."

"No. When we shut down *Mansions and Hovels*, we put the editors there."

"Steven, if there is one favor I ask of you, and only one, it's to find them jobs. My team means a great deal to me. I want to do what's right by them."

"Okay, but it's unlikely."

"This will be a blow," she said. "Where will you move me?"

Steven stared at her without saying a word. His mouth formed into a sort of flat line, the crude type that a child would draw when first putting pen to paper. "Nowhere."

"Nowhere?" asked Plum. "Enough joking. Seriously."

Steven didn't respond.

"I thought you were grooming me to take over one of the bigger magazines?"

"You thought wrong."

"Are you telling me that I'm...laid off?" she asked, her voice rising.

"Yes."

A thought occurred to her. "Steven, if you were going to fire me, why did you have me fire Gerald? Why didn't you do it?" she asked, looking up and blinking through her trendy fake eyelashes.

"I knew he would make a scene. I didn't want to deal."

"He hates me now!"

Steven shrugged. "Calm down, he'll get over it."

She glared at him. "I find it very insulting when men tell women to calm down."

"Just act like a lady."

"I am a lady, and this is how we act."

"Now, don't you make a scene," cooed Steven, as if speaking to a toddler. "Didn't we just say not to be churlish? To take your leave graciously?"

Plum felt as if her head were about to spin off and go flying all the way down to Broadway. She imagined it splattering right at the feet of some tourists from Des Moines who were on their way to see *Phantom of the Opera*. Then they would really have something to tell their friends back home.

"What does grace have to do with this? This is my livelihood we are discussing. I have financial responsibilities."

"Like what? You're single, no kids."

"True," she conceded. "But I sponsor an animal shelter in Long Island. I don't know what they would do without my assistance. There are a lot of abandoned older dogs, hard to find homes for..."

"You're whining about animals? Let's not be a drama queen."

Oh, really, thought Plum. She would show him a drama queen. She instantly recalled the way women on reality shows handled their rage, which was flipping over tables, so she rose and put both of her hands under her glass desk and tried to hoist it on Steven's lap. But sadly, the desk was so heavy that she couldn't even lift it an inch and merely exerted a tremendous amount of useless effort in her attempt. After awkwardly huffing and puffing while trying to lift the table—while Steven watched with amusement and contempt—Plum finally sank into her chair, certain she had caused blood vessels to pop in her brain with her futile endeavor.

"Just go," she said sadly. "I need to process this."

"Unfortunately, it is you that needs to go."

Plum glanced up and saw that two security guards had miraculously materialized at her door. "You're throwing me out?"

"You can take your whips and riding helmet with you."

Ten minutes later Plum found herself standing on the chilly streets of New York, holding boxes of impractical crap, being jostled by throngs of people clutching Playbills and briefcases, and waiting for her Uber. And of course, now it was starting to rain. She was bristling from the indignation of being escorted out and not being allowed to say goodbye to her beloved team. The looks of horror she received as she teetered by in her high heels would haunt her forever. It reminded her of her childhood when she was unjustly accused of throwing gum in Brad Cooke's hair on the school bus. She was summoned to the principal's office during science class and had to walk past all of her snickering classmates. She had been set up by a vicious girl named Mandy Garabino—one of her popular classmates, who was renowned for her indoor pool. But that was another lifetime ago, when she was poor, shunned, and ostracized. She was not that girl anymore.

By the time her Uber came, the rain was teeming, and she dove into the sedan soggy and dejected. Her phone buzzed, and she pulled it out of her pocket optimistically. It was a text from Benji, the IT specialist she had been on a date with the night before. They had met on Connect—one of the many dating apps Plum subscribed to—and had engaged in lighthearted cyber banter before converging at a dimly lit bar on the Lower East Side. It wasn't a promising location (Benji chose it for the craft beer), but Plum was determined to be more open-minded in her forays into the dating world. It was her New Year's resolution, in fact. She glanced at the text.

> Yeah, got your message. It was fun last night, but I don't think I want to see you again. You were giving me a cold, stuck-up vibe. We're not really a match, so let's defriend and move forward. Cheers.

He was dumping *her*? Benji, with his wispy goatee, wrinkled pants, and predilection for using *literally* and *like* in every sentence, was defriending her? And signing off with the word *cheers* even though he wasn't British? What a poser! He couldn't be serious!

For the second time in an hour, Plum's blood boiled. She quickly sent Benji back a text telling him exactly what she thought of him (homunculus; infantile; wannabe) and then pressed on the dating app Connect to start swiping through prospective guys. She zeroed in on a handsome surgeon named Manish and was about to swipe right on him when she realized they had gone on a date the previous year and he had never called her back. She had thought it had gone well, which was the odd part. Whatever, next case. There was Jeremy, a lawyer. But then Plum remembered she had exchanged emails with Jeremy, and although it was initially promising, he ultimately told her she sounded too high-maintenance for him. After several minutes of swiping, Plum was inundated with rejection. How could she have not noticed that her dating life was a disaster? Had she been so consumed with her job that it didn't matter?

By the time she had returned to her apartment and opened a bottle of white wine, Plum was engulfed in self-pity, which after a few large pours turned into anger, an emotion better suited to Plum because it fueled her into action. She had always been resilient—she hadn't had a choice, considering her gloomy childhood. Raised in a dingy house in a small town in the middle of nowhere in Upstate New York, she had the two most indifferent parents the world had ever seen. She was an only child; her parents had been old when she was born and always seemed surprised they even had a daughter, whom they promptly neglected. They worked full time, disappeared to casinos on the weekend where they squandered their small salaries, and often forgot to feed or buy new clothes for their daughter, which subjected her to much derision and ridicule at school. She knew at a very young age that she would have to fend for herself, and her dream was to escape to the city, land a prestigious job, and travel the world. And Vicki Lee did just that.

Yes, Plum's birth name was Vicki Lee. She had selected the name Plum when she read an article about a fashionable author named Plum, who said it was short for Victoria, as Queen Victoria was known for her love of plums. She quickly ditched Vicki Lee and reinvented herself as Plum (short for Victoria) Lockhart.

And now Plum blinked around her sparsely furnished living room and knew she couldn't waste any time. She had to get ahead of the news that she was laid off and secure a new job before she was irrelevant. She fired off emails to everyone she knew in the publishing world and went to bed feeling productive and hopeful.

The next week passed in an eerie quietude. After that first morning, Plum had awoken with cheerful optimism and rushed to scan her emails, confident that someone would want to hire her. But it was a steady stream of rejection and deference. "We're not hiring," or "We're downsizing," appeared to be common refrains. The worst was, "I'm also looking, any ideas?" If she had any ideas, would she be writing them? The few remaining publishing folk with any sort of hiring capabilities were mysteriously silent. She tried to ask people to lunch, to coffee, to drinks, but everyone refused. The few friends Plum reached out to appeared to have vanished with her job. She had never felt more alone.

The once desired snow materialized and dumped six feet on the ground. Plum barely ventured out, and because she had never learned to cook, she was basically subsidizing the local overpriced Chinese delivery restaurant, dining on a steady stream of soy sauce dishes that kept her ankles bloated and her bank account low. Last year at this time, she was in Kenya on safari, consorting with giraffes and flying in hot air balloons. How quickly life had changed.

On a gray Tuesday morning, Plum awoke at eleven thirty and wandered into her bathroom. She caught a look at her reflection in the mirror and almost didn't recognize herself. Plum knew that her looks were polarizing. She was tall—five foot ten—and had long, red ringlets, pale skin, and high cheekbones. Her one serious boyfriend, Jake, had remarked long ago that she was "a Botticelli painting come to life," and she chose to perceive herself as such. But her detractors considered her too chalky white, too tall and Amazonian. She would have to agree with them this morning. Her hair, which she usually took pains to blow out straight or at least get coiffed, was a complete frizz ball, sticking out all over the place, as if channeling Nicole Kidman circa 1990. The dark circles under her eyes were tinged blue, and there was a nest of lines popping up on her forehead. Her fake eyelashes were hanging by a thread, and she had no choice but to peel them off. Due to the fact that she barely moved off the couch, her body was unusually flabby, and the elastic on her pajama pants was tight. *This won't do*, Plum thought. She at least had to make an attempt to keep up appearances.

Plum was tweezing her eyebrows when her phone rang, and she was so immersed that she absentmindedly answered, forgetting it was the first call she had received in a week.

"Plum? It's Jonathan Mayhew. How are you, darling?" came the posh British voice through the phone.

"Oh, hi," said Plum without enthusiasm. A week ago, Plum had been dodging calls from the likes of Jonathan Mayhew, who ran an eponymous luxury villa rental agency on the Caribbean island of Paraiso. It wasn't that the resort was not fashionable or exclusive—it simply had been covered in magazines a million times over, and there were so many other exciting destinations.

"I'm thrilled I finally got you," Jonathan cooed. "You are as hard to connect with as the Queen herself. Rather harder, I say. I did tell you that the Queen recently visited our little island…"

"You did. But wasn't that seven years ago?"

"Was it that long? You have a wonderful memory."

"I know."

"I'm still hoping that you will come down and visit us again. They've just opened a new tapas restaurant at the resort, and we now have a pickleball court! And business is booming. I am actually expanding; the demand is so high, I am hiring associate brokers right and left. I also should mention…"

"Before you continue, I should tell you that I am no longer at *Travel and Respite*," announced Plum. It was the first time she had actually said it out loud, and it hurt more than she thought it would.

"Oh? Where are you now? Which competitor was able to lure you away?"

"No competitor."

"No? You went to a fashion mag?"

Plum yanked a large eyebrow hair out and yelped in pain. She stood upright and stopped what she was doing. "I am currently retired. Sorting out my next move."

There was deathly silence on the other side of the phone. Plum was certain Jonathan was scheming about how quickly he could get off. But his response surprised and irritated her.

"Oh well, dear, brilliant. Here's a thought, why don't you come down here and work for me? I'll put you in charge of the publicity, throw you some accounts…"

Plum quickly cut him off. "That's a nice suggestion, Jonathan, but I have lots of irons in the fire and am not quite ready to move down to oblivion."

"I see." Jonathan sniffed. "All right, then. Good luck in your next endeavor."

The nerve of him, thought Plum when she placed her phone down on the counter. Did he really think she would want to hock villas on an isolated island? Surely, she wasn't that desperate.

The miserable winter days continued on without any leads on the job front. The most harrowing aspect for Plum was that she no longer had a plan.

On the last weekend in January, Plum made a trip to her local drug store to pick up milk (no longer organic, she had to save money). As it was ten o'clock on a Saturday night and everyone she knew would be out at a fancy restaurant, she didn't bother to put on any makeup or reattach her fake eyelashes, and she threw her untamed mane under a wool hat. Her coat was almost long enough to cover her pants, so there was no use changing out of her pajamas. She stopped to peruse the feminine hygiene shelves and had just deposited a large box of Super Plus tampons into her basket when she heard someone behind her.

"What happened to your hair? Did you stick your finger in an electric socket?"

She spun around.

"Gerald."

Her former art director stood looking at her with sneering eyes. Gerald Hand was shorter than her, which allowed her an excellent view of his prematurely balding head, but other than that, he was well put together and attractive, albeit with somewhat of a pointy nose. He had a white cashmere scarf casually knotted around his neck and a sky-blue anorak coat with a snug fur collar. Appearance was crucial to Gerald, and Plum could see his palpable disdain as he slid his gaze up and down her body. She cursed herself for not changing into something decent.

"I'm surprised to see you, Plum. Word on the street was that you'd put your tail between your legs and hoofed it back to whatever hole you crawled out of."

"Now, now," reprimanded Plum.

They had always had a volatile relationship, with extreme highs and bitter lows. When the magazine was doing well, they were best friends. They would have long, liquid eight-course omakase lunches and gossip about the industry. There was even one night that Gerald became teary and confessional about his nasty breakup with his on-and-off boyfriend, Leonard—a choreographer—and Plum cheered Gerald up by promising to help him enact revenge on Leonard. But toward the end, when things were winding down, their friendship had become tense.

"Do you feel guilty for being such a bitch when you fired me?" he asked.

"It was hardly my choice."

"But you were nasty. You always put yourself first."

"Well, if I didn't, no one else would."

"Yet how quickly you got your comeuppance."

"I wouldn't call it that. More of a life restructuring."

"You know your problem? You are blinded by ambition and unable to feel emotion."

"I don't think that's true."

He gave her a skeptical look. "Right."

"What are you up to now?" she asked, attempting to change the subject. She did feel a twinge of guilt at how she had fired Gerald. He was sort of a friend.

"I'm freelancing, doing some consulting."

Huh, she thought. Gerald was also still unemployed. "How great," she said. "Me too."

Normally she would have asked him to be specific, but if he turned the tables on her, she would have no response.

Gerald's eyes narrowed. "I heard that you sent out your resume to every magazine on the planet and you've been shut out."

Plum's cheeks flamed with mortification. She was about to deny but then thought better of it. "Don't be stupid, that was just on a lark. I have other plans. I'm actually making a big, dramatic move."

"What is it?" He leaned in eagerly.

"You'll see."

He nodded and gave her a patronizing look. "Just as I thought."

"What?"

"You have nothing. No prospects."

"Not true."

"Oh, really? Then what?"

Plum's mind raced. And before she even knew what she was saying, she had blurted out a response.

"I'm moving to the Caribbean to work in the luxury rental market. Jonathan Mayhew has tapped me as his heir apparent. He made me an offer I couldn't refuse. So long, cold New York winters. Hello, sunshine."

CHAPTER

2

BEFORE SHE HAD EVEN LEFT the airport, Plum was assaulted by the humidity. She could feel her hair rising and curling as she moved along the customs line. What had she been thinking? The tropics were no place for a pasty-white redhead like herself. She was practically courting melanoma.

As she inched along pushing a giant luggage-filled cart with bent wheels and clutching her passport, she began to feel sorry for herself. Yes, it was strange. Here she was in literal paradise, and she was sad. Rather than a new beginning, it felt like an end. Plum's self-esteem had derived from her ability to ascend the ranks of the publishing world despite unloving parents, an unhappy childhood, and no useful connections or fancy schools or anything that would have given her a leg up. And yet, the demise had been abrupt and short. Hadn't she played by the rules? Worked her ass off? Made her career the focus of her life? True, her manner was a bit brusque and abrupt, but if she were a man, it wouldn't be an issue. And now she was cast out to some godforsaken island with no idea of what was to come. She promised herself it was only temporary. She would use this as a hiatus and continue her job search in Manhattan. This steamy island was not her destiny.

Matters didn't improve when she reached the front of the line and the customs agent told her she would need a tourist card before she could proceed.

"What's that?" she snapped with impatience.

The woman pointed to an office on the other end of the building, where yet another line stood.

"But I'm moving here. Do I need a tourist card?"

"*Sí.*"

"This is a very inefficient system," Plum burst out with exasperation. "There was no signage telling me that I needed to go there first."

"Thank you. Next, please," said the customs woman before waving to the next customer to proceed.

After twenty minutes procuring a tourist card, which cost thirty-five dollars, Plum returned to the long customs line—increased by a plane's worth of tourists from Chicago—to finally venture into Paraiso. Hot and exasperated, she scanned the throngs of people holding welcome signs to find one with her name. She finally located it in the fingers of a chubby man in his sixties, with clear glasses and a big smile.

"That's me," she said, motioning to the sign.

He shook her hand enthusiastically. "I am Enrique. I am pleased to welcome you to Paraiso."

"Thank you."

"You are very tall."

"I am well aware."

He laughed mirthfully and took her cart, and she followed him out of the airport and into the blinding sunshine. She blinked around at the diesel-fumed entrance and felt strange that this was her new home. Would she one day return here and experience that warm sensation of arriving someplace beloved and familiar? She briefly conjured up the image, which quickly dissipated when she was almost run down on the crosswalk by two men in a junky car, who waved cheerfully as if they didn't even notice they had almost killed her. No. This was not her home. This was a working job search until she found better employment back in New York. A paycheck to provide for the animals at the shelter.

She attempted to make small talk with Enrique, but he spoke limited English, and she spoke no Spanish. She had not foreseen this as a problem and couldn't help grumbling to herself how irritating it was that all of these people in the hospitality industry did not speak English. Well, she decided, she would have to learn Spanish. How hard could it be?

They coasted along past the twinkling, blue Caribbean Sea, which was a color so bright, it looked almost fake, before they veered into the center of the island to cut through to the western side. The drive to Las Frutas was eye-opening. When she had visited last time, years ago on a press junket, she had been chattering in the car with editors from other magazines and tapping away at her smart phone. She had barely taken the time to glance out the window until they rolled through the sturdy gates that enclosed the breathtakingly beautiful Las Frutas Resort. But this time she scanned her new homeland with curiosity. The roads were narrow and lined with small houses as well as storefronts selling produce and sodas. When they ventured through small commerce areas, women with baskets of chips, bananas, and bottles of water came forth to proffer their wares. The cars drove slowly, but mopeds with helmetless passengers weaved through them at dangerous speeds. Kids were playing soccer on the side of the road. Everyone was smiling and happy. It was a marked difference from the streets of New York, where people scowled and pushed and shoved their way along, in that "every man for himself" sort of way. It puzzled Plum. And made her suspicious.

"Do you think you could turn up the air-conditioning?" she asked. Her linen pants were becoming sweaty and sticking to the leather seat. Not to mention her fresh, new eyelashes were peeling off due to the humidity.

"It's on the maximum," he replied.

"Really? How unfortunate."

She hoped she had brought enough lightweight clothing with her, though she couldn't be certain, as she had packed up so quickly. It had been surreal to shove all of her winter duds into a storage unit in the Bronx that cost an arm and a leg. In the end she realized it would have been more prudent to give them all away and buy an entirely new wardrobe when she returned.

"We are now here," said Enrique as they drove up to the white-walled fortress and presented their passports and IDs to the guards at the reception. They scanned Plum's passport and took a picture of her. *For posterity?* Plum thought. After what seemed like an endless process, the guards finally said, "Welcome."

As the gates parted, Plum experienced a religious sensation, as if she were entering heaven. The explosion of vibrant colors and fragrant flowers engulfed her. They drove along the quiet, paved road, shared with guests in golf carts, bikers in bathing suits, joggers and tennis players jauntily meandering. The paths were shaded with palm trees, and flowering, pink bougainvillea had unfurled on every whitewashed wall. No one seemed in a hurry, except the brightly colored birds flitting from bush to bush. People were moving slowly. *This new pace could be very peaceful,* Plum thought. Or it might really irritate her.

Jonathan Mayhew Caribbean Escapes was located in Golf Villa Twenty-Four, a low-slung building that doubled as a residence for the proprietor. Plum had refreshed her memory of the resort when she accepted the job and read all of the information available online. She knew there were twenty-five golf villas, all dappled around the links course, and the majority of them were rented out to visitors or locals who used them on weekends. The resort had one hundred guest rooms at the main hotel and then about two hundred more villas of varying shapes, sizes, and value scattered all over the rest of the former sugar plantation's five thousand acres.

"I'm so pleased you made it," said Jonathan, who came out to the porch to greet her. A slim man, in his sixties, with little hair, a glib face, and a mouth full of bad teeth, he carried himself with a certain elegance that felt posh to the people he interacted with. Jonathan was known for his well-tailored white suits, and today he didn't disappoint, adding a light-blue checkered shirt underneath.

"Yes, here I am," said Plum. For better or worse, she wanted to add.

"You're lucky with the weather."

"Oh, really?" she asked, glancing around at the cloudless sky. "Was it raining?"

Jonathan chuckled. "Of course not, I'm joking. The weather is always like this. You're in paradise, love."

Enrique was instructed to take her belongings to the town house that Jonathan had secured for her while Jonathan introduced her to her new colleagues and showed her around the agency.

Plum's first impression was not favorable. She entered a dusty room with three desks tightly nestled together and fitted with ancient desktop computers, the likes of which she had not seen in several years. The walls were adorned with maps and posters of the resort, and filing cabinets were stacked along the wall. There were several open windows, mostly obscured by giant ferns that lurked outside in clay pots. There was no air-conditioning, and the only cooling system appeared to be the languid overhead fan that produced about as much air as a baby farting. It felt claustrophobic.

A plump, motherly woman of about sixty with silver hair cut neatly into a bob and a heavily lined face rose to greet Plum. She had large round eyes behind even larger round glasses that made her appear wise and comforting.

"Welcome to Paraiso," she said in accented English. "We are very happy to have you here."

"Thank you."

"I'm Lucia. The office manager. Please let me know if you need anything."

"I will."

"Lucia is the backbone of Jonathan Mayhew Caribbean Escapes," Jonathan quickly added. "She makes sure everything runs smoothly. Organizes all of the paperwork, and she's in charge of billing and reservations as well. We wouldn't get on without her."

"I don't disagree," concurred Lucia. She winked at Plum.

"Excellent," said Plum with approval. "I love efficiency. It takes people of all levels to make the system work. Corporate synergy."

Plum had taken an endless number of management classes in an effort to improve herself and liked to throw out the buzz words.

"Yes," said Lucia.

Plum could see Lucia's eyes appraising her from behind the thick lenses of her glasses.

"Damián Rodriguez is not here right now," said Jonathan. "He's wooing a new client. He's a real go-getter, as you Americans like to say. You'll meet him soon, although he is rarely in the office, mostly out and about promoting us."

"Sounds good," said Plum.

"He sits over there," said Jonathan, pointing to the desk in the corner.

Plum nodded and noticed that there was a tub of hair gel on the edge of his desk alongside a small vanity mirror. On the wall next to it hung a calendar with a scantily clad blond. It wasn't hard for her to suss out what Damián was like.

Jonathan led her through the room and opened a door on the side, revealing a small work area. There was an oversize mahogany desk, more framed posters of the resort, and a large coat rack with various straw hats perched on its pegs.

"This is my office. Plum, I want to make sure you know I have an open-door policy, so whenever you need anything, do not hesitate to knock."

"Sounds good," said Plum, scanning the room. She noticed that Jonathan's ceiling had an industrial-strength fan.

"So that's it," he said, plopping into his rattan swivel chair. "Lucia will fill you in on what needs to be done."

"Great. And where is my office?" she asked.

"Your office? Why, your desk is out there."

"Out where?"

Jonathan rose and strode out to the large room from whence they came.

"That's yours."

He pointed to a desk that abutted both Lucia and Damián's desks. It stuck out at such an awkward angle that Plum would literally have to suck in her stomach and plaster herself against the wall to ease into it.

Plum felt the bile rising to her throat. "I'm sorry, there must be some mistake."

"No mistake. We do an open plan here at Jonathan Mayhew Caribbean Resorts. Like the tech companies in Silicon Valley."

"That will not do."

"What do you mean?" asked Jonathan, his friendly demeanor sliding.

Plum could see Lucia pretending very hard to be engrossed in her computer screen in an effort to stay out of the fray.

"I mean that I was the editor-in-chief of a famous magazine. You lured me here with all sorts of promises. Working in a common area doesn't befit my stature."

Jonathan puffed out his cheeks. "Your stature? Plum, you have a wildly inflated sense of self, if I do say."

"I'm doing you a favor, Jonathan."

"Plum, I hired you because no one else would, despite the fact you have a reputation as a tyrant, despite the fact I would have to train you, as you have zero experience in renting villas, and despite the fact you don't speak a lick of Spanish."

"But I have great contacts, excellent taste, and I am able to elevate crap hotels and resorts and make them seem like the most desirable destinations on earth."

"You asked me for the job."

"To help your little business."

"Well, if this doesn't befit your so-called stature, then you are free to leave."

"I just might."

"That's your decision. But you will be missing a great opportunity."

Jonathan turned on his heel, walked into his office, and closed the door. Plum was reeling. She spun around to see if Lucia had heard (which of course she had, it was a tiny office) and was mortified to observe a gorgeous man standing in the doorway. And from the look on his face, he had heard everything as well.

This was where Plum's innate resilience came in handy. Rather than collapse into blubbering idiocy, she smoothed her blouse, strode over to the man, and put out her hand.

"Hello, I'm Plum Lockhart, the newest senior advisor," she said, using the title she had insisted upon during her contract negotiations.

The man had movie-star looks—thick, black hair, strong tanned face, gleaming white teeth. He was younger than she was—about thirty years old, fit and muscular, and most certainly aware of his effect on women. He glanced up at Plum—who was a couple of inches taller than he was—and gave her the once-over.

"I'm Damián Rodriguez," he said, taking her hand and holding on to it a little longer than one usually does, all the while maintaining strong eye contact.

"Oh, the owner of the hair gel?" she motioned toward his desk, and his eyes followed.

"I always like to look my best. Especially when there are beautiful women around."

His eyes slid down her body unctuously. Plum ultimately extricated her hand and felt her pulse quickening. She sized him up in a hot minute—egotistical, misogynistic, aware of his own good looks, a giant red flag. On his dating app profile, he would undoubtedly feature a picture of himself shirtless to display his abs and command potential dates to "impress me." And yet, despite that knowledge, he was still able to incite a small flutter inside Plum that made her want to leap into his arms and have him carry her off into the sunset. She repulsed herself.

"I heard you complain about the location of your desk, but I must assure you that I am very pleased with the new arrangement," Damián said smoothly.

From behind him, Lucia emitted a chuckle but then quickly regained composure.

"Oh, really? How will we get any work done?" asked Plum.

"True, it will be hard for me to work with such a beautiful woman as yourself next to me."

"Okay, let's stop with the 'beautiful woman' bit."

Damián feigned offense. "You question that?"

"I don't like to be patronized."

He put his hand to his heart as if to protest. "I meant you no insult."

She didn't wait for him to finish. "The problem is that you and Lucia will be so close that we'll be able to hear the person on the other end of the phone."

"Ah, I do not talk often on the phone," said Damián. "I prefer to meet my clients in person. I think communication is best when you can look into the other person's eyes, *no*?"

Plum turned her attention to Lucia. "Jonathan had said that business is booming and he had recently hired a gaggle of people. Where's the rest of the team?"

A spark of amusement flashed across Lucia's face before she answered diplomatically, "Business is doing very well. Damián and

I are grateful to have you here to help us achieve the next level of success."

Plum frowned, realizing that she had been lured here under false pretenses (and completely forgetting that it was she who had pursued the job).

"Yes, business is very strong," said Damián, lowering himself into his desk chair and putting his feet up. "It will be helpful to have someone else to answer my phone and do my paperwork. Lucia can only do so much."

"Excuse me?"

"I'm no good with clerical work. I will need you to do that."

"I'm not a secretary," said Plum sharply. She folded her arms and moved toward his desk, where she could stare down at him.

"I do not follow titles. I know you are here to help me."

"Incorrect. I'm here as a liaison to the real world. To save Jonathan Mayhew's company from oblivion."

"You have no experience. It is better to watch me and learn…"

"I ran a major magazine. I'm sure it's not rocket science."

Damián smiled but Plum noticed a quick spark of hostility flash across his face. "The art of renting villas is not easy."

She rolled her eyes. "Nothing has ever been easy for me. I'm pretty sure if you can do it, I can do it better."

Damián's eyebrows rose, and a mischievous glint entered his eye. "I admire your confidence. And as a welcome offering, I will present you with Casa Mango. It is a beautiful four-bedroom villa. The owner lives in Switzerland and wants us to manage it. Why don't you see if you can rent it out for Presidents' Day weekend?"

He slid a manila file toward her.

"No problem."

"Damián, she just arrived," said Lucia disapprovingly. "And Casa Mango…"

"Don't worry about me, Lucia," said Plum. "I managed a staff of fifty. I'm not scared of a challenge."

"This is more than a challenge," murmured Lucia, shaking her head.

"Ah, yes, perhaps this former editor-in-chief is not ready for a challenge," teased Damián, pulling the folder back toward him.

"Of course I am," said Plum, snatching the file from his fingers.

"You think you can rent out Casa Mango?" asked Damián.

"I don't see why not."

"*Dios Mio*," whispered Lucia, making the sign of the cross.

"How hard could it be?" asked Plum.

"That sounds like a bet," said Damián.

"That's not how I do business, Damián. Professionals don't tend to be degenerate gamblers."

This only made him smile wider. That annoyed Plum to no end. She no longer considered him even remotely attractive and felt nauseous that she had thought so.

"Very well. You do not have to make a bet with me if you are scared."

Plum sighed. "This is amateur hour, and we are not in fourth grade. I'll rent out the casa, do the work that you are unable to do, and then allow you to buy me a glass of white wine."

"Okay. And what will you buy me if you are unsuccessful?"

"That won't happen."

CHAPTER

3

THE ONE-BEDROOM TOWN HOUSE THAT Jonathan Mayhew had secured for Plum was modest. It was located north of the main road that cut through the resort, in the hillier area near the tennis center. The pungent smell of the ocean faded as she ascended and was replaced by the heady fragrance of the tree lilies. The plantings were lusher, but the neighborhood felt less beachy and more like a jungle. Not to mention it was more remote, despite the fact there were several other town homes scattered around the cul-de-sac.

Plum was relieved to find that the furnishings of her new home were adequate, although the bathroom and kitchen were in dire need of renovation. Even though this was a temporary situation until she found another job, she did not want to lower her standards. Therefore, she would have to do something about the artwork, which consisted of oversize, splashy canvases of palm trees and crude wildlife that appeared to have been rendered by children who had access to neon paint. The curtains and comforters in the bedroom would also need to be chucked out as well and replaced with a color palette that reminded Plum less of vomit. Lastly, she would have to procure air-conditioning as soon as possible. She was okay with sweating pounds out in a sauna or at the gym (although, truthfully, she rarely stepped foot in a gym), but she did not need to do that in her living quarters.

She immediately unpacked her clothes and shoes, aligning her high heels by style and height—stilettos, kitten heels, pumps, sling-backs, and platform shoes. The two pairs of flats were relegated to the back, next to the sandals and a lone pair of flip-flops for when she got a pedicure. In New York, Plum had subscribed to a fashion curator (as did all editors of glossy magazines) who would select seasonal designer clothing for her to wear to work and events. Unfortunately, Plum had been fired in the winter, so she had not received her latest spring collection, and now that it was no longer subsidized, she had canceled the service. That meant her wardrobe was lacking in the tropical clothing department. She wasn't completely discouraged—she still had plenty of suits and knits, but when she studied them in her Caribbean closet, they appeared very formal. She sighed, noting that she had no choice but to make do.

Plum had not eaten all day and was uncertain what to do for dinner. None of her colleagues had offered to take her out on her first night, which she thought inconsiderate. She had always hosted large get-togethers at four-star restaurants for the arrival of whatever staff she had poached from a competing magazine. And here she was, in a foreign country, and no one had even asked to take her to drinks. Although she had made a truce with Jonathan (by pretending nothing happened), he had not extended any sort of welcome invitation. Fortunately, Lucia had been nice enough to stock Plum's refrigerator with the basic essentials: bread, eggs, cheese, milk, fruit, and Diet Coke, so she set about making an egg sandwich before situating herself on the small sofa.

Plum glanced at her phone, prepared to dial someone and say she had arrived in Paraiso, but then realized she really had no one to call. Did she really have no friends? She had filled her life with work dinners and travel junkets and had failed at cultivating friendships. Those took time; she had been so focused on her career, she told herself, that she couldn't afford that luxury. But deep down she knew her insecurity had caused her to hold people at arm's length. Despite the fact she had ascended the ranks in the magazine world, she had always felt like an impostor. She knew that no matter how she changed, she was still Vicki Lee Lockhart, the gangly poor kid whose own parents wanted nothing to do with her.

She decided not to dwell on that. Instead she turned on the television. After clicking through all of the channels several times, she was dismayed to discover the programs were in Spanish. In frustration, she shut it off. She tried to go online on her computer but discovered the internet was not working. How would she amuse herself? This isolation was unexpected.

Well, I can resume my life as a workaholic, thought Plum. Having a singular goal was comforting. She would make oodles of money through commissions and laugh her way back to a high-powered job in Manhattan. She opened up the file Damián had given her on Casa Mango. It was an ugly villa that appeared to have been decorated in the 1970s. The entire house (bedrooms as well as kitchen and baths) was covered in a dingy, off-white linoleum floor with dirty, gray grouting and nary a throw rug in sight. Plum could just imagine trotting from one end of the villa to the other and finding the soles of her feet coated in filth. The kitchen had dark-brown wood, not at all befitting a Caribbean vacation house. There was very little furniture in the living room—only an armchair and a sad, sunken sofa. Plum had thought the fabrics used in her current abode were outdated, but Casa Mango's decor took it to an entirely new level. There was a blizzard of stripes that appeared to have been ripped off a circus tent and cut up to make drapes and comforters outfitting the bedrooms. Every surface was bursting with unusable and kitschy knickknacks like porcelain clam shells and aquamarine figurines. And one look at the grimy pool and

Jacuzzi had Plum instantly shuddering and imagining the wildlife that used it as a crash pad. It was just so wrong.

However, Plum was not deterred. She had spent a lifetime poring through magazines and studying everything and everyone she thought exhibited class. Her powers of observation were excellent, and she noticed even the smallest details that could make a place more desirable. If Damián had thought she would be intimidated by this challenge, well, he was surely mistaken.

After a fitful night's sleep, during which Plum found herself being attacked by invisible mosquitoes that buzzed in her ear but disappeared whenever she turned on the lights to catch them, she set off to work at seven forty-five, ready to confront the day. She lathered herself in sunblock and donned a light-blue suit and cream blouse. She hesitated about what footwear to pick. Her feet were expanding in the heat, and she wanted to slide into her flats (or even sandals!) but knew it was more professional to have some sort of elevation, so she compromised with a pair of slingbacks with a kitten heel. As she floored the golf cart Jonathan had provided for her down to her office (which had it traveling at a frustrating twenty miles an hour), she glanced up at the cerulean sky and felt optimistic. *It is kind of nice not to wake up in freezing New York*, she thought. Flowers were blooming, and a soft breeze caressed her face. *Perhaps this is more my speed*, she decided.

When the rest of the office appeared two hours later, Plum had gone through all the stages of grief, anger, rage, and desperation and was quite certain this was not her speed. Her fury was compounded by the fact the internet was as slow as snails and her silk blouse was clinging to her overheated armpits.

"Where were you?" she bellowed at Lucia, who was the first to arrive.

Lucia gave her a quizzical look then went to put water in the coffeepot. "I dropped my grandson at school."

"Well, maybe you should have alerted the team."

"Why?"

"So that we were aware that you would be late."

"I'm not late. I always take my grandson to school."

Plum wanted to make a big show of glancing at her watch, but she did not wear one. There was not a clock on the wall either, which she was certain was by design. She pulled out her phone and held up the screen. "It's almost ten o'clock!"

"It is? That is incredible."

"Yes," Plum concurred. "You realize now—"

"I never get to work at nine forty-five," Lucia interrupted.

Plum nodded. "It's very late."

"I'm early," said Lucia, pressing the button on the coffee bean grinder. "I usually arrive at ten."

The rest of the day transpired in a similar manner. Everything took longer, and everyone moved slower, and Plum was quickly learning that the favorite word among locals was *tranquilo*, which meant that everyone should remain calm and things would happen in the distant future. Her patience was wearing thin.

Plum ascertained where Casa Mango was and set out to pay it a visit. Electronic navigation systems didn't work at the resort (bad coverage), so she had to clumsily balance a resort map on her lap while steering her cart. She found herself going in the wrong direction more than once and had to submit to that annoying beeping sound the cart made when backing up. She felt like she was living in the Dark Ages. How she wished for an Uber to take her around.

The villa was on a cul-de-sac near the heliport, surrounded by thick vegetation, untended flower beds, and rotten mangoes that had fallen from the trees. It was as dire as she had thought. The place had a neglected, dirty air and reeked of mildew. The backyard was no better: the lawn was faded with patchy grass, and the pool looked toxic. She was not discouraged, though. When she had started her journalism career, she had worked for a beauty editor, and one of her jobs was to find the woman on the street to make over. She learned which ladies would make good candidates due to their bone structure, and now she could use that skill on Casa Mango. She made a careful list of everything she would need to spruce it up and called furniture vendors, painters, and landscapers and implored them to start the work as soon as possible.

By the end of the workday (four o'clock), Plum was so fatigued from begging and wheedling craftsmen that she needed a glass of wine. She asked Lucia if she wanted to head to the bar at the beach, but Lucia mumbled something about picking up her grandson. Jonathan was off to dinner at the hotel manager's and didn't extend an invitation. She was desperate and lonely enough to consider asking Damián, but he never returned from his last appointment. Undeterred, Plum set off alone to explore her new neighborhood.

Playa del Sol, the resort's beach, was buzzing with activity, Plum noted as she slid her golf cart into the parking lot next to dozens of other carts. She alighted from her vehicle, walked down the pebbled path, and took her first real look at the Caribbean since she had arrived. Bathers were frolicking in the crystal-blue water, lounging on floats, zipping around on the banana boat, and lying on the chaises. The smell of sunscreen permeated the air. Music drifted out of curious rocks in the ground that Plum ultimately grasped were speakers. Beach boys raked the sand and offered towels and drinks to guests.

As she made her way to Coconuts, the beach bar, she could hear people speaking in many foreign languages. It made her feel at home. Which made her feel jolly. She slid into a wicker stool at the bar and ordered a glass of white wine. The bartender tried to talk her out of it—insisting that the fruity concoctions were better—but she was not interested. She downed the treacly wine quickly. It had a bitter aftertaste, but it didn't bother her. She ordered another, forgetting that she had not eaten anything since the morning.

By six o'clock Plum found herself quite drunk, as did those

around her. She was slurring her words to the bartender, and when she attempted to talk to the couple next to her, everything came out in gibberish. She thought that the way to tackle the language barrier was to speak as loudly as possible, which only produced alarmed glances from those around her. The bartender tried several times to coax her into eating something by placing tortilla chips and guacamole as well as the menu in front of her, but in her inebriated state, she decided it was best to skip some meals in order to attain the type of beach body she saw flaunted around her. She had gained some weight in recent weeks and felt the need to fast in order to rebalance.

A man in a light-blue blazer and tie sat down on the stool next to her and spoke. It took Plum a beat to understand that he was addressing her.

"*Señorita*, are you a guest of the resort?" he asked, in a deep, unaccented voice.

Plum stared at him. He was somewhere in his early forties, with a full head of graying black hair, chocolate-brown eyes fringed with thick lashes, and dark eyebrows. There was something so masculine and assured about his manner that Plum felt instantly off-balance. She thought him the best-looking man she had ever seen. And in her drunken state, she felt it important to tell him as much.

"You know, you're very handsome."

He smiled. "Thank you. I appreciate the compliment."

"There are a lot of handsome guys here," said Plum, taking a swig of wine. "In New York, they're unicorns."

"You're from New York?"

"Yes. And the men there don't like me. Why don't they like me?" she asked plaintively.

"I'm sure that is not true."

"It is! They say I'm high-maintenance and bossy. Like it's a bad thing! An insult. I think it's good to know what I want and to be assertive, don't you agree?"

"I do," he said. "I appreciate a strong and confident woman."

"Thank you. It's just like this," she said, her head bobbing with all the alcohol inside it. "I'm a sensitive person. I have feelings too. But I am not a pushover."

"I think that's admirable."

"Are you just saying that?"

"No. I don't like to say anything I don't believe," he said, becoming serious. "I come from a long line of strong women, and I would not be who I was today if not for their resilience."

She adored that he answered her question that way. He was growing handsomer by the minute. "Do you think I could be lovable?"

"I'm sure you could. I'm sure you are."

"Because, yes, I'm ambitious, but that doesn't mean I don't have feelings! People don't understand that about me."

"I'm sure."

"And I have a lot to give to the right person. And I want someone to love me," she slurred.

"May I ask, how long will you be staying with us at Las Frutas?"

"I would have said temporarily a few hours ago, but now that I met you, maybe longer," she said, gesturing with her hands in the air. It caused her to spill her wine. "Oopsy."

"I'm so happy you enjoy our resort. But if I may say this delicately, perhaps you should cease your celebration for the evening. Maybe we can entice you with some food from our restaurant?"

Plum was watching the man's mouth as he talked but couldn't decipher what he was saying. "You have beautiful lips."

"Thank you."

She stuck out a long finger and touched them. "Fleshy, nice."

"You are too kind."

Plum started to move towards him, but the effort was too much, and she began to slowly slide off her barstool. The man caught her in time.

"Will you allow me to take you back to your room?"

"Why, I don't even know your name!" she said, doing her best Scarlett O'Hara imitation. "Frankly, my dear, I don't give a damn!"

"My name is Juan Kevin Muñoz," he said, as he put his arm under hers and helped her stumble through the sand toward the parking lot. There was a golf cart with the resort's name and SECURITY emblazoned on the side. He hoisted Plum into the passenger seat.

"Are you arresting me?" she slurred.

"No. I am merely returning you to your room."

"My town house."

"Your town house. Now do you know where it is?"

"Um...it's...by the tennis courts."

"Wonderful. Do you know what street?"

She vigorously shook her head. "I can't remember. Oh well. I'll have to sleep in your bed!"

He smiled. "I think it's best if I take you back to your house."

"Why, are you married?"

Plum suddenly had a passionate hatred for this man's wife.

"I'm divorced," he said.

"It's great that you're tall. So many men are too short for me."

"That's good to know." He picked up a walkie-talkie. "I will call the front desk and find out where they booked your house. What's your name?"

"My name is Plum Lockhart, but I didn't book through the hotel. I live here!" she squealed. "I have moved to Paradise!"

"Really?"

Plum suddenly felt queasy. She crumpled into her seat and leaned her head on his shoulder. "I work for Jonathan Mayhew. He rented me the town house."

"Oh, you're the American! I heard about you. I know where you live."

He started the cart and set off. Plum's eyelids became heavy, and she found herself dozing off. She felt a surge of vomit in her throat but quashed it down. The rest of the night floated by like the scrambled visions in a kaleidoscope. She could see hazy patches of her town house, the man giving her water and toast, and the ceiling fan in her bedroom, though it was as if she were not in her body but outside, looking in. She fell asleep in her clothes and did not wake until the sun was streaming through the windows.

CHAPTER

4

THE MORNING AFTER PLUM'S EVENING of drunken debauchery caused her great mortification. When she rose, she walked all the way down to the beach to retrieve her golf cart and was dripping in sweat by the time she made it there. It must have been at least three miles. The humidity had caused her hair to frizz and stick out all over the place, but fortunately the beach was still deserted, save for a man pulling a boat out of the water.

The heat was beginning to rise off the water, the air was heavy, and the tantalizing blue sea seemed irresistible. Plum glanced around. The man with the boat was dragging it to the other end of the beach. No one would notice if she quickly slipped off her dress and went for a dip. And besides, her bra and panties were matching and could pass for a bathing suit. She quickly discarded her clothes, leaving them on a beach chaise, and waded in, avoiding the pebbles that dotted the powdery sand.

The water was calm and soft, and Plum felt as if she were swimming in liquid velvet. She dunked under and then did the breast stroke all the way to the rocks that enclosed the wading area. Even though it was deep, it was clear enough that she could still see her feet swarmed by tiny, incandescent fish. *This is what the doctor ordered*, she thought, glancing up at the puffy clouds skimming along the sky. This was exactly why she had moved here.

She dressed, collected her cart, and returned home to change into an embellished tweed minidress with a mandarin collar, epaulettes, and a gold waist chain before heading to the office. Arming herself in a power outfit gave her the semblance of control. As the day wore on, the toll of the previous night returned. Plum suffered greatly from the paranoia that comes with a hangover and was suspicious of everyone who addressed her, as if they knew what had occurred. She also had to make frequent trips to the bathroom to splash her face with water. On one such trip, she heard a man's voice out in the hall. It sounded somewhat familiar, so she opened the door slightly. When she spied the security guard from the night before, she quickly shut the door, heart thumping anxiously. Plum stared at herself in the mirror, and her mind raced. She did not want to see this guy, not when she looked like this, not ever. It was not like Plum to lose control. What must he think? She waited what seemed like an eternity until he left and then sauntered out of the bathroom.

"Juan Kevin Muñoz stopped by to see you," said Lucia.

Mercifully, Damián was out of the office and did not witness her face turning beet red.

"Who's that?" asked Plum, feigning ignorance.

Lucia gave her a quizzical look. "He is the director of security at Las Frutas. He said he met you last night."

"What else did he say?" asked Plum, practically lunging towards Lucia.

"Nothing else. He came to see how you were adjusting to Paraiso."

"That's all?" asked Plum suspiciously.

Lucia nodded. "Did you expect something else?"

"No, no," said Plum, sliding into her chair. "He's the director of security? Not just a guard?"

"That is correct."

"It's an usual name. *Juan Kevin.*"

"His father is from Paraiso, and his mother is Irish. He grew up here on the island."

"Oh, nice guy?" she asked casually.

"Very nice," Lucia said before adding, "single."

Plum pretended to be busy with her work, but when she glanced up, she saw Lucia eyeing her curiously. She was about to ask a follow-up question when Jonathan returned and asked to meet with Plum to discuss publicity plans. She went through a list of publications she was reaching out to, but all she could focus on for some reason was the director of security. She could barely remember him—she had been very drunk after all. And yet, he left an impression on her. He was gallant and had really sexy eyes.

After a day of fantasizing about having a wild affair with the dashing Juan Kevin Muñoz, Plum returned to reality and the work at hand.

Plum decided to lay low the rest of the week. She spent her nights at home, lamenting the lack of delivery food options and her inability to cook, and subsisted mainly on scrambled eggs. (The only bonus was that she had dropped the pounds she gained during her unemployment.) She found herself watching Spanish game shows out of boredom. She downloaded the Spanish for Beginners app on her phone and started to learn the language.

During the day she spent every hour that Jonathan was out of the office sending out her resume and trying to engage with potential employers. She updated her LinkedIn profile countless times. Now that she had embarrassed herself with the director of security, she was more eager than ever to return home. In the meantime, she threw herself into renovating Casa Mango.

Plum was excited at the transformation. It was amazing what a few coats of paint, some fresh bedding, new curtains, and a thorough cleaning could produce. Not to mention a gardener who had transformed the outdoor area. Because she was short on time and couldn't fix everything, she had ordered large clay planters that she scattered around the house atop every cracked surface and in every dingy corner. The result was a success. She took Lucia with her for the final inspection, and while her colleague marveled at her work, Plum commissioned a photographer to take some glossy shots and then uploaded them to the Jonathan Mayhew Caribbean Escapes website.

Her excitement was palpable as she eagerly awaited queries through the website.

"Anyone rent Casa Mango yet?" asked Damián, what seemed to be every hour.

"Mind your own business."

"I knew it would be impossible for you."

"I am juggling many interested parties," Plum retorted, although that was a lie.

There was no interest. The silence was deafening. Plum dropped the price. Nothing. She became creative with her descriptions of the "idyllic" villa, promising that it boasted "dramatic" art work and "a shimmering garden with flowering trees and ample room to work on your tan." A few people reached out, but no one booked. Lucia kept giving her more and more sympathetic looks.

"Call my friend Charlie Mendoza. He's in charge of all of the entertainment at the resort. Maybe he has musicians coming to perform that need accommodations," said Lucia.

Plum called Charlie, and he was very nice, but he said that he'd already reserved a villa for the band and ballet troupe that were booked for Presidents' Day weekend. He very generously promised he would definitely reach out to her next time. But next time would be too late for Plum.

She dropped the price again. At last she received a query and burst into Jonathan's office with excitement. She was extra thrilled to note that she was interrupting his afternoon tea with Damián. It riled her that she had never been invited to partake.

"I have a client who wants to rent Casa Mango for Presidents' Day weekend!" she said gleefully.

"Brilliant," said Jonathan.

"You better get the paperwork before they change their mind," sneered Damián.

"I already sent off the contracts," she said smugly.

"Contracts? Plural?" asked Jonathan.

"Yes."

A wicked look flashed across Damián's face. "Do you mean more than one person is renting the villa at a time?"

"Yes, is that a problem?"

"Definitely," said Jonathan in his clipped tone. "It is our policy to only rent villas to single families. It's why we are the most exclusive broker on the island."

"I'm sure these people are reliable," said Plum, although she had absolutely no proof of her contention. "It is a groom and his two groomsmen coming down before the wedding."

"It's a bachelor party!" roared Damián, before gleefully spewing out phrases in Spanish.

Jonathan shook his head. "No, we cannot do it. Simply cannot."

"I don't understand. What's the big deal?"

"Bachelor parties or group rentals that visit our beautiful resort do not take care of our properties," said Jonathan patronizingly. "They trash the houses, and the cost to repair by far outweighs the money we make."

"Well, first of all, Casa Mango is hardly a marquee property," insisted Plum. "And I am happy to ask them to sign some additional insurance forms to prevent that from happening."

"Jonathan, I told you that she doesn't understand this business," Damián said as if Plum were not even in the room.

"You may be right," conceded Jonathan.

"Are you kidding? This is unprofessional. Damián—you're intentionally sabotaging me."

His eyebrows shot up. "*Mi amor*, I would never do that."

"Oh, please."

"Calm down," Jonathan said.

This made Plum even more irate. What was it with men telling her to calm down? She stood up. "Fine, I will find someone else to rent it to. But for the record, this is ridiculous!"

She saw Jonathan and Damián exchange conspiratorial looks, which incensed her. As she made her way out of the room, Damián yelled to her, "And remember, by Presidents' Day or you owe me a drink!"

"You're not my boss!" snapped Plum.

❦

Plum did her best to find someone else to rent Casa Mango, all the while keeping the bachelor party dangling in case she was able to change Jonathan's mind. She approached him one more time to beseech him to reconsider his policy but was met with an abrupt dismissal. It was clear he regretted her presence. To make matters worse, her proximity to Damián's desk was increasing her frustration as she could see the scoundrel looking over her shoulder and eavesdropping on the phone conversations where she was pitching travel agents.

"I am sorry you failed in your attempt to rent out Casa Mango," said Damián one evening. He was on his way out; a buxom brunette stood waiting for him at the door.

"I still have time."

Damián snorted. "The weekend approaches. You will find no one."

Plum was unable to think of a snappy comeback. When he had left, she glanced over at Lucia, who was watching her carefully.

"Don't let him bother you."

"Oh, he doesn't. He's quite…pedestrian."

"He doesn't think with his brain."

"Lucia, how bad would it really be if I rented it out to a bachelor party? No one would have to know."

Lucia shook her head. Behind her glasses, her eyes looked worried. "Don't do it."

"But why?"

"It will lead to trouble."

"There's only three of them, how much damage could they do?"

"They could make trouble," Lucia warned. "I have a bad feeling."

"I'm not governed by bad feelings."

"Don't do it," pleaded Lucia.

But in the end, Plum did it. She had no choice. It would've been unbearable if Damián had won this challenge. Plum told Jonathan she had found a nice family to rent the villa, and Damián looked at her askance and interrogated her, but she dismissed him. Lucia remained quiet, but Plum could see she was distressed. *Oh well*, thought Plum. You don't become a success without risk.

On Thursday at noon, the door to Golf Villa Twenty-Four banged open. Everyone was at lunch, which would be followed by a long siesta, another aspect of Paraiso work life that annoyed her to no end. Plum was so engrossed in writing a query letter to an online media company that was seeking an editorial director, she didn't even glance up until she heard someone clear his throat.

"I'm here for the keys to Casa Mango."

One look at the wiry, pasty man in front of her and all Plum could think was that a trip to the Caribbean was just what the doctor ordered. In his early thirties, with brown hair, eyes shielded by large, impenetrable wraparound mirrored sunglasses, he had beads of sweat gathering on his forehead. There was an air of impatience that engulfed the pale man.

"Oh, you're Nicholas Macpherson?" Plum said, standing and extending a hand, which he took with reluctance. "I thought your group was coming in tonight!"

"Yes, well, plans changed," he mumbled.

"I'm sure this will be a fun last hurrah before the wedding."

"Yes," he said flatly.

"You said it was your friend Jason who's getting married?"

"That's right."

Plum quickly gleaned that he was disinterested in small talk (he didn't even remove his sunglasses!), so she opened her desk drawer and retrieved an envelope with the keys and information on Casa Mango.

"Here's everything you need. Would you like me to escort you to the house?"

He cut her off and swiftly jerked the envelope out of her hand. "That won't be necessary."

She was slightly disappointed, as she would have been proud to show off the renovation and have someone applaud her hard work.

"Of course. Well, do you need anything else?"

He shook his head. "No."

He left without saying goodbye. Plum sunk back into her seat, wondering if she had made a mistake.

Lourdes Viruet arrived early Saturday morning to fix breakfast for the guests at Casa Mango. The house was quiet, and she was not sure what time they would arise, but she set about preparing the coffeepot and slicing fresh mangoes, papaya, pineapple, and passion fruit before placing them neatly on a platter. She covered it with cheesecloth so the flies wouldn't get to it. It wouldn't make sense to start the eggs or toast until she saw a sign of life, so instead she made her way out to the living room to tidy up. There were some empty beer bottles and a bag of chips that she gathered and deposited in the trash, all the while fluffing pillows and straightening the items that had been displaced on the coffee table. Nothing seemed out of the ordinary until she went out the back to the pool area and noticed a big clump of clothing lying next to the Jacuzzi. She picked up a towel by the screen door and went to gather the clothes, only realizing at the last minute that it was not clothes but a person.

"*Señor?*" she asked hopefully.

He did not move. He was a big man with unkempt, sandy hair, who lay facedown on the concrete. Lourdes assumed he was drunk, and she was unsure what to do. She couldn't leave him, but would he be angry that she had woken him? She was paralyzed by uncertainty. The sun was already strong, and his white skin seemed susceptible to burning, so she became emboldened.

"*Señor?*" she said louder.

Once again, he remained immobile. She looked closely. It appeared he wasn't even breathing. Lourdes touched his shoulder with hesitation, but he didn't move. She shook it but again incited no reaction. She slowly turned him over and recoiled in horror. His face was bloated and contorted, and there was blood trickling from his forehead. Lourdes backed away with her mouth agape. She was seized by a desire to escape as quickly as possible, and she ran through the hedge to the neighbor's house, where her friend Nina worked. Lourdes was so hysterical that it took a minute for her friend to calm her down and find out there was a dead man lying in a heap at Casa Mango.

CHAPTER

5

PLUM ALMOST FAINTED WHEN SHE received the call. It was her worst nightmare come true. She was sorry the man had died, but that was eclipsed by her rage that Damián and Jonathan Mayhew had been correct. Not to mention this would blemish her career.

"Something bad?" asked Lucia, reading her face when she put down the phone.

Plum could only nod.

"Casa Mango?"

"You were right," whispered Plum.

"I always am," Lucia replied, matter-of-fact. "I'll go with you."

There were several cars and golf carts parked in the driveway of Casa Mango, and people were coming and going. A cluster of both uniformed men and women and people whose jobs were unidentifiable stood chatting in the entryway, and at one point, a woman burst out in laughter. The festive atmosphere didn't match the dread that Plum felt.

Lucia followed her as they made their way out to the pool area. The sun was strong, and the birds were carrying on as if nothing had happened, singing their songs to whomever would listen. A crime scene photographer was snapping pictures, and a couple of official-looking people stood to the side, smoking. Two medics were setting up a stretcher. There was a man in a blazer who stood in the middle with his back to her, and when he moved to the side, Plum's eyes flitted to the ground in front of him, where the lifeless body of the deceased lay. She felt despondent. When she glanced up, Plum was horrified to realize the man in the blazer was Juan Kevin Muñoz. Her first thought was to jump behind a bush, but a quick glance around revealed she wouldn't have time to dash away. And Juan Kevin was moving toward her. She would have no choice but to pretend she had never laid eyes on him before.

"Hello, Lucia," he said, greeting her colleague warmly, and Lucia did so in return. Then he turned his attention to Plum.

"Miss Lockhart. How are you today?"

"Obviously not great," she retorted with condescension. Unfortunately, that was her fallback tone when she felt defensive.

"Yes," he said. "I can imagine."

"Do we know who died?" asked Lucia.

"It was the best man, Nicholas Macpherson."

"He's the one I met." Plum sighed. "Too bad, he looked very stressed out. He really needed a vacation."

"I suppose now he will rest in eternal peace," said Juan Kevin.

Plum wanted desperately to avoid eye contact with Juan Kevin, but she could tell he was gazing at her with a penetrating look. She met his eyes and saw a flash of amusement behind them, which irritated her. She did not want this security guard to think he had something on her or that they were somehow buddies just because he had escorted her home when she was drunk. She purposefully forgot she had harbored romantic fantasies about him for twenty-four hours.

"What happened?" she asked briskly.

"The police say that it appears he slipped and fell."

"That's terrible," she said.

"Yes," agreed Juan Kevin.

"Think of the liability. For sure his family will sue us," lamented Plum.

Lucia gave her a sympathetic look. "Don't jump to conclusions."

"According to his friends, he had too much to drink," added Juan Kevin.

"Really?" asked Plum, perking up. "Do you know where they are? I'd like a word with them."

"They're inside," said Juan Kevin.

Plum rushed into the villa. She had to contain this situation before lawsuits erupted. If she could get some statements from people that Nick Macpherson was out of his mind on booze, a sympathetic judge might toss a potential civil case. A similar situation had arisen when she was on a travel junket in Peru. A journalist with whom Plum had been rooming (and had despised on sight as she had taken the better bed and refused to trade, despite the fact Plum's magazine was way more prestigious) had collapsed and been hospitalized, and the rest of the group's ascent to Machu Picchu was in jeopardy. But when Plum had informed the trip coordinator that the journalist hadn't taken her altitude sickness pills despite Plum encouraging her to, the group was able to carry on.

Plum found the remaining bachelors huddled in the corner of the living room, talking in hushed tones. Introductions were made, and the men were identified as Jason Manger and Deepak Gupta.

"This is a nightmare," whispered Jason, the groom. He was a very fit man, medium height, in his midthirties, with dark-brown hair closely cropped into a buzz cut and a prominent square jaw that a caricaturist would certainly accentuate. There was an intensity about him that Plum was sure existed even before his best friend had died.

"I'm sorry for your loss," said Plum.

"It's so annoying…typical Nick to get drunk and end up dead. He didn't know when to stop," said Jason with irritation. "That was his problem with everything."

"Yeah, but Jason, he's dead, let's not bash the guy," said Deepak, in a decidedly British accent that sounded fancy to Plum. He was taller than his friend, dark-skinned, and slight, and he appeared absolutely stricken. Already there were shadowy bags forming under his eyes.

"He agreed that this would not get out of control, and sure enough, he partied himself to death," complained Jason.

Deepak shook his head with sorrow.

"It was terrible telling his girlfriend…" said Deepak. "She was so upset."

"I can imagine," murmured Plum.

Juan Kevin appeared in the hall and motioned for Plum. She called for Lucia and asked her to sit with the men before excusing herself and following Juan Kevin out to the courtyard, where he stopped in front of a short, bowlegged man.

"This is Captain Diaz. He's with the police," said Juan Kevin.

"You are the owner of this villa?" Captain Diaz said in an unfriendly tone.

"No, but I represent the owner. He lives in Switzerland, and I have full authority to act on his behalf."

They stared at each other cautiously. He was a severe-looking man—completely bald, with pockmarked skin and black eyebrows shaped like two upside-down Vs. Despite the fact that Plum was taller than him, he exuded a menacing presence. She thought he looked not unlike the villain in a *Saturday Night Live* skit about a Spanish soap opera.

"We have not removed anything from the scene, and I am confident no one has touched anything, other than to ascertain if the victim had a pulse. We do not have a warrant yet, therefore we need your permission to search the premises. It will most likely be perfunctory; it appears our victim was intoxicated and fell and hit his head."

"Of course," said Plum.

"We will look in the rooms, and then we can remove the body," Captain Diaz said.

The two policemen parted and walked in opposite directions, finally affording Plum a good look at the deceased. His position was contorted, as if twisted into a pretzel, with one leg dangling over the edge of the Jacuzzi, the other near the edge of the adjacent pool. There was a crushed highball glass next to his hand, a murky, brown liquid spilling out of it. A small umbrella that one would place in a fruity drink lay crushed a few feet away. Plum's eyes swept up toward his face, and she gasped.

"That's not him!"

Everyone froze and turned towards her.

"What do you mean?" asked Juan Kevin.

"That's not Nicholas Macpherson!"

Captain Diaz's eyes flared. "What are you saying?"

"There's been a mistake."

Captain Diaz stared at her for a moment before he quickly went inside and returned instantly with Jason and Deepak, who were followed by Lucia. He pointed at the victim.

"Is that your friend?"

Deepak glanced quickly at the body and looked away. Jason's eyes remained on the body. "Yes," the groom said.

"That is Nicholas Macpherson," repeated Captain Diaz.

"Yes, that's him," repeated Jason.

They all looked at Deepak, who nodded. "It's Nick."

Everyone turned and looked back at Plum. "It's not him," she insisted.

Captain Diaz sighed impatiently. "*Señorita*, his own friends have identified him."

"I understand…maybe it is Nicholas Macpherson," she said slowly. "But that's not the person who came to my office to retrieve the key and said he was Nicholas Macpherson."

"How can you be sure?" asked Captain Diaz.

Plum pointed at the victim. "This man has thick, blond hair. The man who came to my office had short, brown hair. And this—Nick—is a big guy. Looks like a rugby player. The man who identified himself as Nicholas Macpherson was thin and wiry."

"Do you know who she is talking about?" Captain Diaz inquired of Jason and Deepak.

They both shook their heads.

"The house was open when we arrived," said Deepak. "Nick never even went to get the keys."

"Then who was it?" asked Plum.

Jason shrugged. "All I know is this is our friend Nick. The other guy...well, I don't know who that was."

"There was an impostor?" asked Juan Kevin.

"What did his passport say?" asked Lucia.

"I didn't look at his passport," Plum confessed.

Lucia's eyes bulged. "When he checked in, what ID did he produce?"

"None."

"You just handed him the keys?"

"Yes. He said he was Nicholas Macpherson, and I gave him the keys. Was I supposed to ask for proof?" demanded Plum. "I honestly didn't think that someone would pretend to be my client."

Lucia clucked disapprovingly, which made Plum defensive.

"No one told me I needed to get his ID."

"This tragic accident has made you confused." Captain Diaz sniffed. "This was the man you gave the keys to. This is Nicholas Macpherson. You are mistaken."

Plum bristled. "Not so fast, *señor*. Maybe something sinister is going on."

"Nonsense." The captain bridled. "Nothing sinister happens in Paraiso."

CHAPTER

6

AFTER THE CAPTAIN'S PRONOUNCEMENT, CASA Mango quickly cleared out. Jason and Deepak went to their bedrooms to rest, Lucia went back to the office, the police officers dispersed, and the body was taken away. Only Plum and Juan Kevin remained. Now that she was alone with him, she again felt a deep wave of embarrassment over the fact that he had carried her to bed and wished he would get lost, but he didn't seem to be in a hurry to leave.

They both stood contemplating the spot recently occupied by the body of Nicholas Macpherson.

"We are thinking the same thing," announced Juan Kevin finally.

"And what am I thinking?"

"About our night together."

"What? We didn't have a night together. That's slander," said Plum crossly.

He cut her off. "I'm kidding. But I felt I should acknowledge it."

"I don't think that was necessary. I was obviously suffering from food poisoning, and it affected my ability to walk and talk. I appreciate you taking me home, but I don't want to revisit that again."

Juan Kevin smiled. "All right, then. I hope you are feeling better."

"I am. I have chosen to stay away from local fare."

"Ah, yes—the food. But as I recall, you hadn't eaten anything."

"Were you taking notes?" she snapped. "Or is this a mean-spirited attempt to make me feel bad?"

His expression changed. "I apologize. That wasn't my intention. I was trying to make you feel more comfortable with me, but I failed."

"I'll accept your apology," Plum acquiesced. *A man who apologizes is refreshing,* she thought before moving her mind back to business. "And, since you are not a mind reader, you should know I'm thinking this is very suspicious and that police captain of yours is completely inefficient."

"He is being thorough."

"He's being lazy, in my opinion."

"That is a bold statement."

"I am full of them."

Juan Kevin appeared concerned. "You believe someone deliberately caused Nicholas Macpherson's death?"

"Look, I'm not a detective, but I know that this at least is worth looking into. This smacks of something bad, and I think we are standing in the middle of a crime scene."

"How's that?" asked Juan Kevin.

She gave him a haughty gaze. "I'm sure I wasn't the only one who noticed his face. It was bruised and mangled, as if Nicholas Macpherson—if that's really who he was—had been attacked by a frying pan. It was not the sort of bruising one gets from a fall."

Juan Kevin shifted his stance but nodded. "His injury appeared almost…personal."

Plum's eyes flitted around the area where Nicholas's body had lain. "And look at these marks."

She pointed to where the body had been, then she stepped off the slate patio and continued down to the row of palm trees and bushes lining the fence that separated Casa Mango from its neighbor. "The path I just walked has flattened grass and disturbed stones. It looks as if he was murdered near the trees separating Casa Mango from the neighbor's house and then dragged so it seemed as if he fell by the Jacuzzi."

She bent down and scanned the lawn. There was a cigar, almost completely unused, lying in the grass. She pointed to it.

"It's Cuban. Expensive and illegal to buy in the U.S., not to mention disgusting."

"Disgusting is a matter of opinion. But yes, I agree it's unusual that it was discarded."

Plum walked back toward the Jacuzzi.

"And we should find out what he was drinking. There's a beer over here by the pool, and look at this." She picked up a tiny, squashed umbrella, the sort one finds in fruity cocktails. "Someone had a daiquiri. And then here, this highball glass"—she picked it up and sniffed it—"smells like rum. Why didn't the police take it to be tested? Maybe it was poisoned."

Juan Kevin smiled with amusement.

"Why are you giving me that odd look?" Plum bristled.

"I am impressed with your theories."

"They are more than theories. They are..." She was about to say something, but a glint of something deep in the frothing, blue Jacuzzi water caught her eye. She slipped off her heels and waded down the steps of the hot tub.

"Are you going for a dip?"

She gave him an infuriated look. She bent down and ran her hand on the bottom of the Jacuzzi. Her fingers scraped around the floor until she grasped what she had been looking for. She held it up.

Juan Kevin squinted and moved closer. "An earring?"

"Yes."

It was a dangling, turquoise earring. *Not expensive*, thought Plum.

"Doesn't necessarily mean anything, could have been there before."

"Juan Kevin, I made sure this place was immaculate when I leased it. I can assure you there was no earring in this hot tub when we rented it to these men."

"Perhaps they had friends over before this happened."

"Perhaps," conceded Plum. She stepped out of the tub, her long legs glistening with water, and slid her feet back into her shoes. She glanced up and saw Juan Kevin staring at her legs. She was instantly self-conscious about their chalky-white appearance. She mentally put purchasing self-tanner on her to-do list.

"But you think it is somehow connected?" asked Juan Kevin.

"My problem is this doesn't make any sense. There was a guy claiming to be Nicholas Macpherson, and then Nicholas Macpherson ends up dead? At the very least, that should be cause for alarm. But the police don't seem interested in thinking this is anything other than an accident."

"Miss Lockhart, I think what you say has value. But you're new to the island and don't yet understand the nuances. Unfortunately, in the travel and resort community, anything suspicious is bad for business."

"What will happen? It'll get brushed under the rug?"

Juan Kevin studied her carefully. "There's a saying here in Paraiso that it's best to let sleeping pigs lie."

"We have that saying also, but it's with dogs."

"Why would you let sleeping dogs lie?" asked Juan Kevin.

"I don't know. But why would you let sleeping pigs lie?"

They paused, musing over the weird idioms until Juan Kevin continued, "Look, I love my island and my people, but sadly sometimes those in government or power make choices I do not necessarily agree with."

"Are you saying you think this might be murder?"

"I'm not saying any such thing. Because it doesn't matter what I say. Everyone involved will want this declared an accident. At the end of the day, Paraiso relies on tourists. We need them more than they need us. And if we endanger that relationship, they will not return. Captain Diaz may want justice, but he knows foreigners can make that difficult to attain."

He gave her a disapproving look, as if including her in that group, and it gave Plum pause. She gazed at the empty spot where the victim's body had so recently lain in repose. She felt as if the world were dividing, and she had to make an ethical choice. The truth or her career. And then she thought, *Hell, what career?* It was always better to be on the side of lawfulness. Plum was a rule follower. She would make the honorable decision.

"As the representative that brought these men to the island, I think it is my responsibility to find out what happened," said Plum with conviction.

A small smile formed on Juan Kevin's face. "Even if it means putting your travel business in jeopardy?"

"I am a moral person," Plum announced, not quite sure that was true. "I must do the right thing."

He nodded, looking both pleased and surprised. "Then I'll help you."

"Captain Diaz!" said Plum, breathless from running to the front yard. She had thought herself fit (for no particular reason at all), but the humidity on the island sapped her energy. She also realized she had not been doing as much walking as she did in New York and would have to make an effort in order to stay in shape.

The captain was watching the EMTs load the body into the ambulance. He turned and gave her an unfriendly look.

"I know you don't want a scandal, but I think we need to look into this death further. I'm not sure it was an accident. We owe it to the victim's family to investigate."

Captain Diaz's nostrils flared, but he replied with studied courtesy.

"*Señorita*, I always follow protocol. This death will be scrutinized. There will be an autopsy."

"Good," said Plum with relief. "Then you also suspect it may be murder?"

His tone became stern. "I didn't say that."

"But you plan on conducting an investigation, right?"

"I did not say that either."

"Then what are you going to do?" demanded Plum. She folded her arms crossly.

He stared at her long enough to test her patience. Finally, he spoke. "*Señorita*, you are a villa broker. I am sure you do your job well. And now I will appreciate it if you leave me to do my job. Which I also do well."

He turned to walk away, but Plum spoke.

"Well, *are* you going to do your job?" she asked loud enough that even the EMTs glanced over at her in surprise.

Captain Diaz turned slowly back to her. "I always do."

"Good," she said. "Then what about Jason and Deepak?"

"Who?"

"Nicholas's friends. Are you just going to let them fly home? What if they killed their friend?"

"I cannot detain them."

"But you can strongly suggest they stay," said Plum. "It is not a unique situation. You don't have to tell them they're under suspicion, you can just tell them there is more paperwork to fill out before they leave. It will buy you some time."

Captain Diaz paused and started to say something before stopping. A smirk crept across his lips. "I will ask them to stay a few more days, here in this villa, as your guests at the resort, *señorita*."

"But isn't this a crime scene?"

"Once again, I did not say that. We do not have crime scenes at Las Frutas. I will humor you, but you can be certain: this was officially an accident, not murder."

"Thank you," said Plum, before adding, "you should probably have a police officer guard the house, in case. I think everyone would feel safer."

The captain shook his head in disbelief. Plum could have sworn he mumbled "Americans" under his breath.

Plum moved toward her golf cart. It was early enough in the day that most guests or residents would still be at the beach or playing golf or tennis. There were a few landscapers blowing leaves and clipping hedges on the neighboring properties, but it was mostly quiet. She felt almost tranquil for a moment, forgetting the grisly scene. She lifted her face toward the sun and sighed. She knew she would be rewarded for doing the right thing.

CHAPTER

7

JONATHAN MAYHEW WAS APOPLECTIC TO say the least.

"What? You did what?" he demanded, his eyes ablaze.

"Look, it's not such a big deal that I didn't check his ID," she asserted.

"It certainly is!" roared Jonathan. His normally cool appearance was ruffled. "You may have let a criminal into Casa Mango. Who knows who he was or what he did?"

Plum put her hand in the air as if waving this information away. "The point is, I've asked the police to look into this as a potential murder. That way we're not liable."

A vein in Jonathan's forehead started pulsing. "Plum, what if it was a murderer you gave the keys to and he was responsible? And you requested that the police investigate? They were more than willing to write this off as a tragic accident, and now you've put our company in danger?"

"You can't think of it that way," she insisted, although her confidence was fading. When Jonathan put it like that, he did have a point.

"I'm of a mind to fire you this instant!" he said.

"I'll sue you."

"You have no grounds to do so. You haven't even made it through the three-month trial period we agreed upon. Not to mention that you were insubordinate. I clearly stated numerous times that you were not allowed to rent to a bachelor party, and you did just that."

Plum had a habit of becoming enraged when people were angry at her. It was a defense mechanism. Therefore, even though she was slowly grasping that she was completely at fault, she would not tolerate the accusations. She rose and made for the door.

"I will take care of this, Jonathan," she said. "Don't worry. This will all be settled efficiently."

"Why should I believe you? And why should I not throw you out right now?"

"Because…" Plum's brain worked quickly. "Because I've just had confirmation that the *Market Street Journal* is sending a team down to feature one of our properties and our resort in the next couple of weeks. It's one of the most prestigious travel sections, as you know, and any luxury rental company would give its eyeteeth to appear in it. But if you want to fire me, I will just call it off…"

"No!" yelped Jonathan quickly. "Is this true?"

"Absolutely," confirmed Plum. She mentally crossed her fingers.

Jonathan sighed deeply. His mood had decidedly improved. "Well, in that case, just take care of this mess with Mango."

"I will."

"Do everything you need to do without getting our agency's name bandied about."

"I will."

"Then we can forget it ever happened."

"My thoughts exactly."

When Plum left Jonathan's office, she found Damián at his desk, a smirk on his face.

"I think you owe me…" he began.

"Oh, shut up!" she snapped.

Jason and Deepak had placed an irate phone call to Plum's office. They were furious that they were not allowed to evacuate the island immediately. Plum had been patient initially, but when their whining and complaining escalated into threats and accusations, she hadn't acquiesced and instead hurled her own accusations at them, questioning their loyalty to their friend. That had temporarily placated them, and they had all agreed they would calm down and regroup at Casa Mango later that evening. Plum had been wearied from persuading the so-called bereaved and felt that there was something about the service industry that didn't quite reconcile with her disposition.

"Lucia, any chance we can move Jason and Deepak to another villa?" asked Plum, hoping that would relax them.

"All of our properties are booked, and the hotel is as well," said Lucia. "It's Presidents' Day weekend, one of the most popular times of the year."

"That's unfortunate. Please keep checking and let me know if anything comes up."

"I will."

Plum was perspiring, and her blouse was sticking to her chest. "This fan doesn't work at all. Will Jonathan ever invest in air-conditioning?"

Lucia smiled. "I doubt it. But don't worry, you'll get used to the heat."

"Never."

"Maybe a word of advice? You always look lovely, but you don't need to dress so…big-city professional?"

Plum frowned. She glanced down at her sleek Valentino pantsuit that perhaps had a bit too large a thread count for this weather but still looked sharp. "No, it is important to maintain a professional appearance. I like to dress for success."

Lucia nodded. "True, but dressing for success here and dressing for success in New York are quite different things."

"I acknowledge your opinion, but I was mentored by the editor of *Vogue* for many years, and I think I will take her lead."

Lucia smiled. "Of course."

Juan Kevin offered to accompany Plum to the unofficial interrogation that evening. Her first instinct was to dismiss him. She was still humiliated that he had seen her inebriated and assumed he felt that he had the upper hand. But she relented when she thought it over and decided to put business before personal issues. It could be useful to have them tag team Deepak and Jason. Plum devised a plan that they would try to "chat" with each of the men separately and then compare notes. Perhaps they could coerce a confession. That would be exciting, particularly if she were the one to wheedle it out of the killer. How hard could it be to crack a crime? Plum's mother used to read dozens of mysteries, and as they were the only books lying around and Plum had nothing to do, she read them after her mother discarded them. Plum had a knack for guessing the killer halfway through the book. She would apply that same skill here.

Plum nodded to the policeman who lingered outside the entrance of Casa Mango. He shrugged in return. She was not at all impressed by him, seeing as he didn't even question her identity or her reason for visiting Casa Mango. No wonder people were being killed on the island. *Such a disgrace*, she thought, completely forgetting she had also neglected to check the fake Nicholas Macpherson's ID and was possibly responsible for people being killed on the island.

Deepak Gupta opened the front door tentatively, still unshaven, blinking as if he had been sleeping.

"How are you doing?" asked Plum, striking a concerned tone. She was purposely a few minutes earlier than the time she'd agreed upon with Juan Kevin.

"As well as can be expected," Deepak responded before moving aside to allow Plum entrance.

She glanced around the living room and could tell that Deepak and Jason had been holding their own type of wake. There were two empty Jack Daniels bottles, several cans of Coke, and half-eaten bags of Cheetos strewn around the surfaces of the room. Pillows were askew as if perhaps someone had slept on them, and towels lay in heaps on the sisal rug.

"Would you like something to drink? I'm having a beer."

She followed him into the kitchen. He opened the refrigerator and offered her a Presidente, but she refused. He shrugged and opened one for himself.

"Juan Kevin will be here shortly. Where is Jason?"

"He'll be out in a minute. He's on the phone with his fiancée." Deepak ran his hand across his burgeoning beard and shook his head. "This sucks," he said, his voice trembling.

"I'm sorry again for your loss," said Plum. She slid onto the stool at the counter.

Deepak sighed deeply and stared at the ceiling. "I'm so mad at Nick for allowing this to happen. It's like I wish I could go back in time and stay awake and not let him keep partying. Then he wouldn't have slipped and fallen."

"Is that what you think happened?"

"Isn't it?" asked Deepak, confused. "That's what the cops said."

"What do you think?"

Deepak shook his head. "I don't know. He was pretty drunk."

Plum nodded. "Did he often party alone?"

"He wasn't alone."

"What do you mean?"

"He was with some woman."

Plum's ears pricked. She almost leapt off her stool. "Who?"

"I've no idea. We had been at the bar at the beach. We had run into some acquaintances from New York—AJ Thompson and his girlfriend, Lila Donovan—and ended up having drinks with them. But Nick was all over the place, chatting up different ladies. It got late, Jason and I wanted to go home, but Nick wanted to stay. We left him."

"And how do you know he was with someone?"

"Late at night I heard the front door open and heard a high-pitched female giggle, then I pulled the pillow over my head and fell back asleep."

"Would you be able to identify the women he was with at the bar?"

Deepak shook his head. "I mean, there were a bunch; they came and went. Some blonds, some brunettes. It was always that way with Nick. He loved the ladies."

Plum gave him a quizzical look. "Didn't you say he had a girlfriend?"

Deepak arched his eyebrow. "Yes."

"I see."

"He wasn't the most faithful guy," he said with a shrug.

"Granted, I only saw him postmortem, but he didn't seem like much to look at."

"You're awfully blunt."

"Thank you," she said, choosing to take it as a compliment.

"Nick possessed tremendous charisma. Life-of-the-party sort. Not to mention he was a big spender. That always produces a gaggle of admirers..." His voice trailed off sadly, as if the realization that his friend was dead was just hitting him.

Sensing Deepak's fragile state, Plum kept the questions coming before he could dissolve into tears.

"Then last night wasn't unusual?"

"The night before was the same story. We were at the beach bar both nights. Jason didn't want to even talk to other women, so I stayed with him while Nick did the rounds."

"Jason's devoted to his fiancée?"

"Sure," said Deepak, quickly taking a sip of his beer.

Plum straightened up. "You don't sound so sure."

A strange look passed over Deepak's face. "No. He's devoted. You could say that."

"Well, I could, but would you?"

Deepak laughed and stared at his bottle of beer. "Very clever."

"What do you mean?"

"Coaxing everything out of me."

Plum leaned toward him. "Is there anything you shouldn't be talking about?"

He chuckled. He seemed about to say something but then stopped himself. "Let's just say, Jason wants to marry Kirstie. And nothing will stop that. If he has to avoid other women for a while…he's willing to do that."

"And if he didn't have to avoid other women?" prompted Plum.

Deepak's face was grim. "I don't think he would. But that doesn't matter. Kirstie's family has made it clear."

"Are they the threatening sort?"

Deepak shrugged. "I don't think Jason feels threatened by them."

"Did Nick have enemies?"

"Loads. Nick pissed a lot of people off. He would do things like borrow money and never repay it. Not to mention his string of angry ex-girlfriends. The list is long."

"Enemies who hated him enough to follow him to Paraiso and kill him?"

"I doubt it," said Deepak. "I mean, everyone has enemies. And besides, the cops don't think it was murder. I'm not sure why you do."

Before she could answer, they heard the doorbell ring, and seconds later, Juan Kevin followed Jason into the kitchen.

"Sorry, I didn't think I was late," said Juan Kevin.

His hair was damp as if he had just showered, and he smelled of some fruity cologne. Normally Plum loathed scented men, but there was something appealing about it on Juan Kevin.

"You're only five minutes late, but I prefer to be ten minutes early," said Plum.

Juan Kevin's eyebrows shot up. "I see. That's probably a good idea."

"They polled the CEOs of the Fortune 500 companies, and they agreed that punctuality is essential to success. I like to take it a step further," said Plum.

"I agree," said Jason. "If one of the guys working for me is even a minute late, I can him. Everyone is replaceable. People need to put their best effort forward."

"Absolutely," said Plum. She would have definitely hired someone like Jason. *Although you don't see that type in the publishing business*, she mused. Perhaps that was why it was collapsing.

"Did you ask them about the earring?" Juan Kevin inquired. He pulled the turquoise piece out of his pocket and held it up.

"Whose is it?" asked Jason.

"That's what we want to know. It was in the hot tub," said Juan Kevin.

Deepak and Jason moved closer to examine it, and both shook their heads. "I don't recognize it," said Deepak.

"Me neither."

"Do you remember any of the women that Nick talked to wearing something like this?" asked Plum.

"I don't think so," said Jason.

"That's not something I notice. I'm not a jewelry guy," added Deepak.

"No wonder you're single," said Plum.

Before he could respond, Juan Kevin spoke. "Perhaps Deepak can show me around the villa. I want to make sure everything is secure."

"Certainly," said Deepak, who swiftly followed Juan Kevin out of the room.

Jason poured himself a shot of tequila and downed it. "When do you think we can leave?"

"I can't answer that. But we hope to be able to find out everything about Nick's death so we can provide a conclusive answer to his family."

"They said it's an accident. What would take long?"

"They probably have to do paperwork," said Plum. She didn't want to admit she had asked the police to detain them.

"Everything on this island takes forever," lamented Jason.

"I don't disagree."

"How can you live like this? It's dysfunctional. I would go nuts."

Jason is a kindred spirit, thought Plum. Most people were put off by demanding and aggressive New Yorkers like Jason, but Plum felt like she was finally speaking the same language to someone for the first time in a month.

"It's been challenging to acclimate to the local culture, but I am looking at this as a time of temporary restoration and health. Paraiso's low-pressure way of life can be healing," replied Plum.

"Tell that to Nick," muttered Jason.

"Yes, obviously that is an aberration," agreed Plum.

"I really wish he hadn't drunk so much. But he wouldn't listen to us! He was stubborn. And it always ended up a mess, just like Kirstie warned me."

"Your fiancée?"

"Yeah. She begged me not to let him come this weekend. She knew it would end badly."

He stopped speaking abruptly.

"Continue," prompted Plum.

But Jason's moment for sharing had ended. He shook his head. "Obviously she didn't think he would die."

Juan Kevin returned to the kitchen with Deepak. It was evident the men were done talking and ready for them to leave. Plum fired one last question.

"The man who came to my office to retrieve the keys to Casa Mango referred to himself as Nicholas Macpherson. Do you have any idea who that man could have been? Why he would have wanted keys to the villa?"

A less observant person would have missed the quick glance that Jason shot Deepak, but Plum saw it. And if she were a betting woman, she would have sworn Jason slightly shook his head as if to warn his friend.

"No," said Jason firmly. "I have absolutely no idea."

"Me neither," confessed Deepak.

Plum gave both men a probing look. "Are you sure?"

"Positive," they both said in unison.

"I think we ascertained some valuable information, but we are not close to solving the murder," said Plum, when they had stepped out into the balmy night. They walked down the path toward the driveway and stood near Juan Kevin's car. The sun was sinking in the horizon, and the sky was streaked with twilight. A police offi-cer sat on a chair at the end of the driveway, looking totally bored.

Juan Kevin gave her an amused look. "We still don't even know if it was murder. His friends seem convinced it was an accident."

"They could be covering. Maybe they murdered him."

"It's possible."

Plum sighed. "I honestly thought we would get more out of them."

"There's a reason professionals handle this."

Plum furrowed her brow. "The police? Please. It's up to us." She motioned to the officer staring at his phone. "You think that guy is going to crack the crime?"

Juan Kevin smiled. "You definitely seem more motivated than he is."

"I am. I don't have a good feeling about this. And I don't know why everyone is so eager to accept this as an accident. You saw his face." Impulsively, Plum added, "Maybe we should go to the bar and ask around? One last push. The bartender might know who the women socializing with Nick were."

Juan Kevin glanced at his watch. "It's a good idea, but I can't."

Despite her desire to keep their contact professional, a wave of extreme jealousy throttled Plum. "Why, you have a hot date?" she blurted out before thinking.

Juan Kevin smiled. He held her gaze before responding. "No. I need to check on a villa. There was recently a fire there, and the owner is returning to the island tonight. We agreed to meet at six thirty."

"Oh," said Plum, with palpable relief. Then to cover it, she quickly asked, "Are there a lot of fires here?"

"No," replied Juan Kevin. "This was a silly instance of someone forgetting to blow out their scented candles and no fire alarms in the villa. There was one in the front hall, but the batteries had died. That's why I was glad to see you had not just one but two in every bedroom at Casa Mango."

"Right. Well, I suppose I'll head to the bar without you. We do have a ticking clock."

Juan Kevin paused, his perceptive eyes studying her. He finally spoke. "I will meet you there in an hour and a half."

Plum brightened. "Okay, that sounds good."

Juan Kevin drove off, and Plum walked over to her golf cart. She put the key in the ignition, clicked on the lights, and something to her right caught her eye. In the patchy shadows, a golf cart was idling across the street. She swerved her head for a closer look. Just as she did, the golf cart took off, plowing straight ahead full speed before making a sharp left down the street and disappearing around the curve. Something didn't feel right. The driver of the cart had been watching her. Who was he? What was he waiting for? Plum felt a chill down the back of her neck. She shuddered.

She turned to the policeman "guarding" Casa Mango. He was now talking on his cell phone. Plum asked, "Did you see that?"

"*Que?*" he asked.

"The man there. Did you see who was watching?"

But the security guard didn't understand. He shook his head and continued his call.

"Useless!" said Plum, before taking off in her cart. There was no question that Plum would need to learn Spanish as soon as possible if she wanted to survive on this island.

CHAPTER

8

AN HOUR GAVE PLUM JUST enough time to whiz home and freshen up. She darted into her villa and quickly showered. Although she was unnerved by the idling cart outside Casa Mango, she told herself she was paranoid and pushed thoughts of it away. It helped that she had something to look forward to. For reasons she couldn't quite explain to herself, Plum was excited for her evening with Juan Kevin. The snobby part of her that she had taken so many years to cultivate was whining that she was getting all gussied up to convene with a security guard, but the long-dormant soft side of Plum that yearned to be appreciated kept thinking of Juan Kevin's soulful eyes. However, as she dressed, waves of reality dipped in and out of her consciousness, and she reminded herself that this was merely a fact-finding mission and could not be construed as a date. Plus, she was only planning on being on the island for a very short time. Why get involved with anyone?

After several wardrobe changes, Plum settled on a cornflower-blue, Egyptian cotton poplin dress with smocking embroidery. It was from last season's Prada resort collection, but she figured Juan Kevin didn't keep up with high fashion collections and wouldn't notice. She thought it possible that it was inappropriate attire seeing as they were merely interviewing bartenders, but then was there really a dress code for sleuthing?

Primping in Paraiso was a challenge. Plum's skin was so dewy in this climate that coaxing makeup to stick on her face was an effort, and her hair was an even worse story. She had showered and painstakingly blow-dried her mane, but by the time she was dressed, she looked like Little Orphan Annie. It was the damn humidity. She attempted to brush it out, but her unruly curls battled the bristles, and with irritation, she threw it into a tight bun. Her mother had always looked at Plum with chagrin and said that her curls were her cross to bear. It was indeed true.

The journey back down to the beach reminded Plum that she should lease a car; a golf cart did not work when one was on a mission, particularly at night. The mosquitoes flew straight into her eyes and promptly drowned, and every time she stumbled upon a speed bump, she felt as if a truck had run over her bottom. Plus, a car would be more practical. It would allow her to explore the island beyond the resort and to shop at the larger grocery store in Estrella, the closest town. Her mind wandered, and she imagined taking small road trips around the island with Juan Kevin. They would have picnics on secluded beaches, and her hair would be perfectly coiffed. It wasn't like Plum to have these fantasies, and she wondered if she was becoming a more romantic person. Perhaps it was the warm weather that was generating this passion.

Juan Kevin had beaten her to Coconuts and was chatting in Spanish with a portly, tanned bartender whose name tag identified him as Miguel. For reasons foreign to her, Plum felt shy approaching Juan Kevin but was relieved when he turned and gave her a bright smile.

"Miss Lockhart, you look stunning," he said, eyeing her with appreciation.

As she was not used to receiving compliments, she ignored his words and instead asked, "Any luck?"

"Miguel cannot recall if he was serving the bachelor party," said Juan Kevin.

"I have a picture that can tell a thousand words," replied Plum.

She had asked Deepak to email her a photo of Nick Macpherson, and instead he had sent the link to Nick's Instagram page, where there were plenty of pictures of him partaking in various sporting activities. His profile picture was the most recent one of him that afforded a good facial view. She rifled around her clutch and pulled out her phone, sifting through the pages until she reached Nick's.

She held it up to Miguel. He squinted then took the phone in his hands and studied it for a long time. A surge of hope shot through Plum then deflated when Miguel ultimately shook his head and moved to the end of the bar to help a customer.

"At least he was thorough." She sniffed.

Plum slid onto the barstool next to Juan Kevin and ordered a glass of wine.

"The trouble is a cruise ship was in port that night, so the bar was very crowded," said Juan Kevin. "It may be like looking for a needle in a haystack. But it's worth a shot."

"It's the best picture. There's a more recent post from two days ago, taken at Las Frutas, but he's wearing sunglasses and a hat."

"Let me see," asked Juan Kevin, taking her phone into his hands.

The picture was taken on the craggy coral edge of the La Cereza Golf Course. Nick, Deepak, Jason, and another man stood by the pin of the sixteenth hole, the jagged rocks and dramatic coastline behind them.

"I don't know who that guy is," said Plum, pointing to the fourth man, who appeared to be in his late twenties.

"I do," said Juan Kevin. "That's Tony Spira. He's one of the golf pros."

"Huh," said Plum. "Maybe we should ask him if he noticed any tension between Nick and Jason and Deepak."

"Good idea," said Juan Kevin. "In the meantime, let's try the other waitstaff."

They struck gold with the third server they asked.

"Yes, I remember him," said a skinny, young waiter whose name tag identified him as Pedro. He had big, dark eyes and a hint of a mustache and was waiting for the bartender to prepare his drink order.

"And?" asked Plum.

"He was sitting in that corner. They were having tequila sunrises and shots of tequila. They were a very happy group."

"*They*, who was *they*?" Plum asked eagerly.

"He was with two women. There was much laughter. But then a man came and said something in a loud, angry voice, and the man in the picture started yelling," said Pedro as he refilled the peanut bowls.

"And then what happened?" asked Plum.

"They yelled at each other and then stopped. A woman was yelling also."

"Did you see the women before or since?"

The young man leaned against the bar and cocked his head to the side as if to think. "One maybe, two, yes."

"What does that mean?" asked Plum.

"One, maybe I saw before. She looked familiar, but I cannot be sure. She is also Paraison. The other, yes. She has been here many times. She came in last night."

"Can you describe her?" asked Juan Kevin.

"She is not young, but she looks young. She has blond hair and a very nice figure, but her face is strange."

"What did the man who yelled at him look like?" asked Juan Kevin.

"He was Paraison. He had dark hair...an expensive watch...my age. I don't know him."

Miguel had approached and heard the tail end of the conversation. He started to nod. "Yes, I saw that man."

"Oh, now you remember." Plum snorted. She took a sip of her wine.

Juan Kevin gave her a look and asked Miguel, "Do you have any idea who either of the women were?"

"Yes." Miguel nodded slowly. So slowly that Plum wanted to reach over and shake him. "One was Carmen Rijo."

"Carmen Rijo?" Juan Kevin said with surprise.

"Who's Carmen Rijo?" asked Plum.

"She was talking with him," continued Miguel slowly. "They were drinking together with her friend."

"Do you know the man who was making a scene?"

"*Sí.*" Miguel nodded.

"Well, who?" snapped Plum. Could this Miguel not understand urgency?

"It was Martin Rijo," Miguel said slowly.

"Martin Rijo?" repeated Juan Kevin, somewhat alarmed.

"*Sí.*"

"Who are these Rijos?" asked Plum.

"Let's go sit down at the restaurant and have a bite to eat, and I will explain," said Juan Kevin.

"I'm not very hungry. I'll just get another glass of wine."

Juan Kevin shook his head. "I've seen that play out before. This time, you eat when you drink."

The restaurant was attached to the bar. It was a large, airy, whitewashed room divided by equidistant pillars and canopied by a double-height ceiling. The floors and wooden tables were bleached white. In the daytime, it afforded sweeping views of the Caribbean, but as it was now dark outside, they had to make do with the sound of the waves lapping the shore. There were hurricane lamps dotting the tables and a large basket of overhead lanterns hanging from the rafters. The dim lighting, caressing breeze, and the rhythmic music gave it a sexy vibe.

They were seated in a corner booth and had placed their

orders—seared, marinated red snapper with creole seasoning for Plum and grilled octopus with Romesco sauce for Juan Kevin, who also ordered a bottle of white wine. A busboy instantly placed a basket of herbed flatbreads with piquillo butter and a dish of marinated olives on the table. Juan Kevin pushed the dish towards her, and she was about to refuse but decided to sample one. The Kalamata olives were plump and flecked with rosemary and quite delicious. She immediately popped another one in her mouth.

"Try the bread. It's excellent."

She was about to say she generally eschewed carbs, but then she shrugged. Why not? One bite and she was hooked. "Delicious."

"Paraiso has the best bread."

"You're not biased, are you?"

"Absolutely not," he said with a smile. "But I do believe my island to be the most special place in the world and generally have the best of everything."

"Everything except the ability to do things on time."

"Yes, we have our own pace. But trust me, you will get used to it."

"I doubt it," said Plum. "But it's a nice switch for now."

"Do you miss your family?" he asked. He took a sip of water and wiped his mouth with the cloth napkin.

Plum shook her head. "I don't have any family."

Juan Kevin's face became sad. "Oh, I'm sorry."

"I have parents, but we are…estranged. I'm an only child. It makes life easier. I can travel anywhere on a moment's notice without a bother. I have no one to check in with or look after. No Thanksgiving dinners with an aunt in Westchester. I am completely self-sufficient and nimble with no one tying me down."

It was a pat response that usually elicited envy in her high-pressured New York world, but Juan Kevin gave her a sympathetic look.

"That sounds lonely."

She paused. It was not the expected reaction. In fact, no one had ever even had a follow-up comment when she responded that way before. But Plum was unwilling to expose more of herself to this stranger, so she brushed him off. "It's not, it's lovely. Now tell me about these Rijos."

Juan Kevin sat back in his seat. "Carmen Rijo is the widow of Emilio Rijo."

"Am I supposed to know who that is?"

"You are not supposed to know, but you *should* know."

"Who is he?"

"Who *was* he," Juan Kevin corrected. "Emilio Rijo was the founder of Las Frutas, but more importantly his family members are sugar barons and control the sugar and molasses industry. Las Frutas was his family's estate, and he was responsible for transforming it into this luxury paradise."

"He did a good job."

"Yes. He was a wonderful man. Brilliant. A visionary. We were very close; he was like a father figure to me."

"And Carmen is a mother figure?"

Juan Kevin chuckled. "Not exactly. She is much younger than me. You see, Emilio had been married for thirty-five years to Alexandra, a former beauty queen, who is still very beautiful by the way. But Emilio had his head turned by Carmen. Although Emilio had strayed before, Carmen captivated him, and he left Alexandra and married Carmen. Within a year, he was dead."

"Wow."

"It was a terrible situation. Emilio and Alexandra have two grown sons—Martin and Julian—and they're convinced that Carmen killed their father or at least had something to do with his death. Now there's a battle for the estate. Martin is leading the fight. Although Alexandra and the sons were well taken care of in the will, Emilio left his new wife Carmen a beautiful villa and half of the resort. There is strife at Las Frutas and beyond. Much of the island is taking sides."

"Which side are you on?"

Juan Kevin hesitated. "I prefer to stay neutral."

"I don't blame the sons for being mad. The new wife is there for five minutes and gets millions?"

"Emilio had a very volatile relationship with his sons. They disappointed him. He knew the boys would make Carmen's life difficult, and he wanted her to be protected. It's no surprise that Martin showed up and caused a scene. He is vengeful."

"I'm sensing you're not a fan of the sons."

Juan Kevin chose his words carefully. "We are not close."

"But do you think Carmen offed her husband?" asked Plum. "Sure sounds like she had motive."

"I do not." Juan Kevin bristled. "It was widely known that Emilio had a heart condition."

"Maybe she did something to expedite his demise."

"I do not see her as that sort of person. I've known her since she was young."

"She's the sort of person who would steal someone's husband."

Juan Kevin was about to protest but conceded. "Yes, that's true, unfortunately. That came as a surprise to me. She was so sweet, *is* so sweet, I would never have believed it."

"It's always the sweet ones who have the killer instincts."

He smiled. "You know from experience?"

"Daily. The publishing business in New York is ruthless."

"I understand now why you left. That is why you quit, right?"

"It was time to move on. Have a new adventure."

Plum was worried Juan Kevin would ask her more about her departure from the magazine world and she would have to reveal her termination, but fortunately, the waiter arrived at the table with their bottle. The white wine was crisp and fruity.

"Why do Emilio's sons think Carmen killed their father? Do they have any proof?" Plum asked when the waiter had left.

"They believe they do, but it is hard to prove."

"What is it?"

He took a sip of his wine before speaking. "Have you heard of Paraison obeah?"

"No."

"It is a kind of sorcery practiced here by a small number of the population, especially in the village from which Carmen hails. What you might call 'black magic'. Martin and Julian Rijo know Carmen is superstitious, and they claim that she mixed a potion to first enchant and then kill their father."

"Do you think that?"

He shook his head. "No. I don't think Carmen needs potions to enchant someone. She is…breathtaking… Well, you will meet her and see for yourself."

Plum did not like Juan Kevin's response. It seemed he had a soft spot for Mrs. Rijo.

"But if Carmen is such a grieving widow, why was she at the bar doing shots with Nicholas Macpherson?" asked Plum.

"Emilio has been dead for a year; I cannot blame her for going out."

"But having drinks with a bachelor party?"

"I am sure the men sought her out. She is very attractive."

"Yeah, you said that," snapped Plum. Jealousy was welling up inside her and that irritated her to no end. Juan Kevin was handsome, but he was a hotel employee clearly in love with his former boss's wife. Plum could do better. "I think it's bad form for a lady to be out boozing alone and cruising for men."

He gave her a wry smile. "Didn't I find you at the bar boozing alone?"

"That was entirely different," she barked, angry that he had brought it up again. "I was getting a lay of the land."

"No judgment from me."

"I didn't expect any."

"And I would ask you to withhold judgment of Carmen until you meet her."

"Sure," lied Plum. She had already made up her mind.

The mood shifted, and after the food came, they stuck mostly to the topic of Nick Macpherson's death, analyzing the information they had learned from Jason and Deepak and trying to avoid mention of the Rijo family. The rest of the night felt flat to Plum, and she was disappointed. It certainly wasn't the romantic event she had imagined. Suddenly it wasn't that fun spending time with Juan Kevin, who undoubtedly had a mad crush on Carmen. That realization made Plum gloomy, whereas Juan Kevin seemed aloof. They both seemed relieved when the dinner was over, and they quickly left the restaurant as soon as they had eaten.

CHAPTER

9

PLUM WOKE TO A BANGING on her door. She was momentarily befuddled and wondered why she was waking up in a sun-filled room rather than her dark New York City apartment, but then reality came rushing back. The banging continued, and she shot out of bed and rummaged around for a bathrobe. She shrugged into it and tied it tightly around her waist before stumbling to the door, bleary-eyed.

Captain Diaz and a tanned young officer with a pencil mustache stood on the threshold.

"Did I wake you?" Captain Diaz asked with a crocodile smile.

"No. I was just doing my sit-ups," she lied.

"I apologize if it's early, but I thought you would be excited to know the coroner has returned with his conclusion, and he has stated in his findings that Nicholas Macpherson was indeed murdered."

Plum was flooded with a variety of emotions. "I'm not *excited* that he was murdered, but I am gratified that my hunch proved to be true," she corrected. "What does this mean?"

"It means that there will be an investigation," stated Captain Diaz. "The friends will have to remain on the island until further notice. They are suspects. And you will have to come with us and tell us everything you remember about the man who came to your office claiming to be Nicholas Macpherson as well as give us a list of anyone who had access to the villa."

"Okay, let me get dressed."

"It will be a very long day for you," said Captain Diaz, almost tauntingly. "In fact, a very long week."

"I get it," she snarled.

Captain Diaz was not wrong. It was a very long day. The police headquarters was a squat, grayish stucco building located between Las Frutas and the town of Estrella. It was centered on a half-acre, dusty, terracotta plot shrouded by untamed bushes and stumpy trees. The doors and windows were framed by bars, and there were two white plastic chairs on the porch, which appeared inharmonious with the rest of the staid enterprise. There were plenty of people in attendance, but it was unclear what their jobs were, and there was a languorous air in the building.

The scarred desk at which Plum sat fielding questions was in a stifling back corner where the heavy air was ripe with sweat. Captain Diaz was primarily interviewing her, although other unidentified officers came and went to either listen to her or ask a random question. Every now and then, Captain Diaz rose and congregated with his colleagues in a cluster in the middle of the room, presumably discussing the case. There seemed to be no sense of urgency, and Plum's irritation was increasing with her impatience. She found herself answering the same questions over and over again and was annoyed by the passivity her responses elicited. She wasn't sure if it was penance for her insistence that they look into this case or if it was the pace at which things were done in Paraiso, which was definitely slower than the pace of life in New York City. She figured it was a bit of both.

"Why is there no air-conditioning in here? I'm roasting."

She realized that her designer cap-sleeve dress in textured silk with stilettos might have been the wrong choice to wear to the police station. Or anywhere in Paraiso, for that matter. She had wanted to appear in control and professional, but she realized she might need to rethink her wardrobe choices.

Captain Diaz leaned towards her. "Sweating under pressure?"

Plum wanted to roll her eyes, but as this was "law enforcement," she knew it would be a bad move. "Of course not. I'm just not used to this climate."

"Many cannot take the heat."

"Right."

"*Señorita*, can you please tell me why you immediately thought this was murder?"

She sighed, aggravated. "Like I told you, anyone could tell that his face exhibited bruising consistent with a vicious attack. It didn't look like a fall."

Captain Diaz nodded slowly, staring at her with his wolflike eyes. "Do you have experience with murder?"

"No."

"Did you have a relationship with the victim?"

"A relationship?" Plum repeated skeptically. "Absolutely not."

"Aha! Why did you repeat 'a relationship'?"

"Because I thought it was an absurd question."

He rubbed chubby fingers on his stubbled chin. "Very interesting."

"Why is that interesting?" asked Plum.

Plum could not believe that this was the line of questioning. Was this man serious? Captain Diaz scribbled something down in a notebook. Plum wished that she could read upside down. And she really wished she could read Spanish upside down.

"Do you have a criminal past?" asked Captain Diaz.

"No."

"Have you ever been accused of a crime?"

She thought back to when she was accused of throwing the

gum in Brad Cooke's hair on the school bus and was about to say she had been falsely accused, but clearly Captain Diaz had no sense of humor, and it would only delay the interview.

"Never," she said with certainty.

"I see," he said, slowly. Then he wrote something down.

After another half hour of mundane questions, some of the same ones over and over again, Plum was finally breaking. The clock struck noon.

"Can I go now?" she demanded truculently. "I cannot tolerate this inefficiency any longer, and I have told you all I know."

"Soon."

"You should be talking to Jason Manger and Deepak Gupta. I think they know more than they have said."

Captain Diaz didn't respond but instead went to the center of the station again to consult with his colleagues. They appeared to have given him the green light, because when he returned, he told her she could go.

"But remember, you are a person of interest. Don't leave the island."

"I wasn't planning on it."

He scoffed. "Of course."

"What's that supposed to mean?"

"You tourists don't listen to our rules. You do whatever you want. You come to our beautiful island and play by your own rules and then return home."

"This is my home. I'm not a tourist."

He smiled, baring all his teeth. "We will see how long you last."

She was about to protest but had to acknowledge that it was true; she was actively trying to move back home. She thought of staying just to prove Captain Diaz wrong, but it wasn't worth it.

When Plum mounted the steps to Golf Villa 24, she heard raised voices emanating from Jonathan's office through the open window. She paused and moved closer in order to hear better.

"Jonathan, this will destroy the company. We have worked so hard. You must get rid of the American."

Plum's ears pricked. It was Damián. That little scoundrel.

"I will get rid of her, but not until after we get the article in the *Market Street Journal*," said Jonathan smoothly.

"Is it really worth it? She will ruin us before then."

"I don't think so. I can contain this."

"I have already heard a competitor mention they heard of the murder."

"Tell them Jonathan Mayhew Caribbean Escapes has nothing to do with Casa Mango or anything that happened at all. Plum was acting as an independent contractor—she is not on staff, and we have no official agreement with her. That contract self-implodes in three months. I will terminate her after she gets us that good press."

"This is risky."

Plum heard Jonathan sigh. "I know you didn't want me to hire her…"

"And I was right!"

"Yes, you were right. But let's use the old girl for all she's worth and then send her packing back to New York!"

Plum waited in the bushes until she was sure that Damián had left Jonathan's office and she could properly compose herself. She was humiliated and felt more sorry than angry, which was not her usual reaction. When had Plum become vulnerable to criticism? What was happening to her thick skin? Was the blazing sunshine melting it away?

She had no choice but to act as if she hadn't been eavesdropping, so she sauntered into the office as if she hadn't a care in the world. When she entered, Damián was staring at his computer, and Lucia was on the telephone. Plum moved toward her desk where there was a woven basket stuffed with fruit.

"What's this?" she asked.

"I brought it for you," said Damián.

"That was very nice of you. It's not my birthday, you know," she said, eyeing him suspiciously.

"I know that, of course," said Damián. "I believe you said you had your fortieth birthday in June."

"My birthday is in June, but I am not forty. Not even close," Plum scoffed.

"Oh, I'm sorry. I simply want to say you look good for your age."

"We are almost the same age."

"I think not," sneered Damián. "But no matter. It is not a birthday gift. I am presenting you this basket with my deepest condolences."

"Condolences? What do you mean?"

He didn't wait for her to finish. "Plum, I heard the police confirmed that your bachelor party client was murdered in Casa Mango. The client that you promised a safe vacation in paradise ended up dead. He is no more. Under suspicious circumstances. And I have brought you this fruit basket to extend my deepest condolences for him and your future."

Plum was seething. The nerve of this man! She looked down at the fruit basket—full of rock-hard mangos and green bananas and snatched it off her desk and slammed it on his.

"Thank you for your gift of unripe fruit…"

"As the tragic death happened at Villa Mango, I thought it appropriate…"

"You are too cunning for your own good."

Damián gave her a faux sympathetic look. "I am sure it will take a long, long time to recover from this terrible situation. Especially when there is the inevitable lawsuit. Therefore, I present you with fruit to remind you that you will never go hungry with friends like me."

"I am not worried about going hungry, Damián."

"Yes, I know you have extra flesh on your bones, but I worry about the future."

"Unreal."

"It is just a friendly gesture."

"Okay, that's it, Damián," said Plum. "Don't you have to be somewhere else? Isn't one of your girlfriends waiting for you?"

"My date this evening is a young, beautiful woman who is back from modeling in Europe."

"Where there are many diseases," Plum pointed out. "All of which I hope you get!"

"What's this?" asked Jonathan, who was standing by the door, his face decidedly grim.

Plum quickly sat down at her desk and picked up her phone. "I'm about to get on a call with the *Journal*. Let's chat about it later."

Jonathan's face brightened. "Of course. And do tell them about the new pickleball courts."

"Absolutely. I think that's a game changer," fibbed Plum, doing everything in her power not to roll her eyes.

🦋

Plum was eager to evacuate the office and found that she was famished after forgetting to eat breakfast, so she decided to call over to Casa Mango to see if Jason and Deepak wanted to join her for lunch. She felt it was the least she could do, and it could be an opportunity to milk them for more information. Lourdes answered and said Jason and Deepak had signed up for an excursion and taken off on the catamaran to Carolina Island for the day. Plum thought it was a curious move and wondered if Captain Diaz would be annoyed.

Plum decided to set off on her own for lunch, and instead of heading to the beach, she ventured to the marina, a fifteen-minute drive from her office. While still technically part of the resort, the marina was designed to be reminiscent of a Mediterranean fishing village and was where the Caribbean Sea met the La Cereza River. Dozens of fancy yachts docked at its port, and there were several restaurants and high-end fashion boutiques full of skimpy designer clothing and sunglasses. It was also the location of the overpriced grocery store Plum had been frequenting, and she was becoming increasingly aware that their inflated prices were making a huge dent in her bank account.

Plum had been told the marina usually came alive at night—and late at night. There were families there at seven for an early, child-filled dinner, but it was around nine when the younger crowds thronged the palazzo and the festivities began. Loud music would waft out of the invisible speakers. During the day it was pretty much dead and very easy to find a table at which to dine. All of the restaurants were clustered in a square, and their seating was indistinguishable from one another. The palazzo boasted two Italian restaurants, a Japanese sushi bar, a gelato place, and a Paraison restaurant, the latter of which Plum selected.

In general, Plum was not a foodie. She had adored the long restaurant lunches that were de rigueur in publishing, but more for the gossip than for the cuisine. Left to her own devices, she often skipped meals and merely ate to fortify herself. But the dinner at Coconuts had been delicious, as had the traditional dishes that Lucia brought to work and coaxed her to try, and she was interested in sampling local food and eager to peruse the offerings.

She scanned the lengthy menu and found that many of the items seemed incongruous with the tropical weather. There were hot bean soups and a seven-meat stew that sounded delicious but a meal that Plum would tuck into on a cold snowy night, not in the blazing heat. She opted for something called a *catibia*, which was a cheese and chicken empanada made of yuca flour, as well as an order of *salpicón*, which promised to be chunks of boiled seafood with chopped vegetables marinated in a vinaigrette. Eating like a local would perhaps make her feel more like a local. She ordered a glass of white wine.

There was a nice breeze coming off the water and a salty brine in the air. As she sat watching the sailboats bobble in the crested wavelets, Plum felt content. If only this murder hadn't happened and everything was okay, her life in Paraiso just might work out. Of course she couldn't be dining at restaurants and living like a tourist all the time, but she allowed herself some leeway to integrate into her new existence. Feeling optimistic, she completed a Spanish lesson on her phone as she dined. She lingered as long as she could before realizing the afternoon was slipping by and she should return to the office.

On her way out of the marina, Plum saw a beautiful, white, eyelet dress on a mannequin in the window of a store. It wasn't her normal style—she generally favored strictly tailored, dark clothing, and this was undoubtedly feminine and flirty, but it felt appropriate. She left the store with the dress as well as a floral maxi skirt, a white, puffy-sleeved top, a pair of strappy, blue sandals, and a lime-green strapless dress in her shopping bag.

It was rush hour at Las Frutas. Sandy resort guests were flooding back from the beach to their villas to siesta, shower, and head out to dinner. A Jeep full of teenagers passed Plum, the radio blasting music so loudly that it left a trail in its wake. A man driving a golf cart in the opposite direction drove by, and Plum gave him a sideways look. Then, suddenly, her stomach dropped. That was the man who said he was Nicholas Macpherson! She was almost certain of it!

Plum wanted to make a U-turn and follow, but she had to wait for the deluge of cars to go by before she could safely do so. She silently cursed them all for taking so long and then swerved around in front of a pokey bicyclist. She especially loathed bikers in general—they were always a menace in traffic. She floored her cart and tried to follow "Nicholas Macpherson's" cart, which was now several yards in front of her, two vehicles between them. She quickly passed a cart driven by a very old woman and aggressively pushed ahead.

She continued her pursuit of "Nicholas" and saw that he took a sharp right turn onto a path that cut through the beachfront properties. Was he aware that she was following him? Had he seen her? Plum turned as well, so quickly that her left wheels almost went up in the air. She readjusted her cart and pressed the pedal to the metal. She saw his cart up ahead and tried to gain on him by furiously pumping the accelerator, but unfortunately her golf cart tapped out at twenty miles an hour. There was a Range Rover at the end of a driveway about to pull out, but Plum went around it and pushed ahead. The driver sat on his horn and yelled obscenities. This caused "Nicholas" to turn around. He saw her, she was sure of it. She fumbled with one hand to extract her phone and take a picture but found herself veering off the road and replaced both hands on the wheel. If only he would slow down so she could snap a photo. Suddenly, his cart started accelerating faster, and he was swiftly moving ahead and increasing the distance between them. Damn, he must have one of those fancy new golf carts!

He took a sharp left around a corner and was temporarily out of sight. Plum swerved around the curve recklessly and onto a very narrow road. Coming straight at her was a golf cart driven by a young child on his father's lap. Plum was speeding too fast to avoid them. She couldn't hit them head-on, so she jerked the wheel of her cart, swung off the road, bumped up the curb, and crashed straight into a hibiscus bush. She came to a lurching and unglamorous stop. The cart was damaged, and there was no way she would catch up with "Nicholas" today.

"Are you okay?" asked the man.

Plum jumped out of her cart and brushed herself off.

"What is it with parents thinking resorts are a good place to teach children how to drive? Are you daft?"

CHAPTER

10

PLUM QUICKLY LEARNED THAT HAVING a fit or creating a scene was not a successful approach to getting things done in Paraiso. An event like a crashed golf cart drew an enormous amount of resort personnel to stand and evaluate the scene and discuss endlessly what should be done before no one did anything. Things happened when they happened. And when Plum tried to hasten their reactions, she was met with the requisite *"tranquilo."*

Lucia picked her up and drove her back to the office. She arranged for Plum's golf cart to be towed away and advised that she had better rent a cart from the resort while it was being repaired, which could take days or even weeks. The resort garage said they would bring one right over, but after a couple of hours, there was still no sign of them. She telephoned Casa Mango, but there was no answer.

When Lucia left, Plum decided to do a deep internet dive into Juan Kevin. There was very little except an image of him standing next to a blond woman at a party that was on the Las Frutas website. Reluctantly, Plum conceded that she was attractive, if one likes that type. Much to Plum's chagrin, it didn't identify her. Must be his girlfriend. Or that Carmen Rijo he was undoubtedly in love with. She clicked off the computer.

Plum realized she had a throbbing pain in her heel and slid off her stilettos to reveal a giant, pus-filled blister. Her feet had expanded in the Paraison heat, and her shoes were like manacles. She wasn't sure she could walk. The day was quickly ending on a bitter note. To salvage it, Plum called her contact at the *Market Street Journal* again, hoping to finally catch her this time.

"Mimi Wasserman is no longer working here," a nasally voice told her when she asked for her friend.

"Where did she go?" asked Plum.

"Not sure. I think she's like, freelancing now."

"She was laid off?"

"I'm not at liberty to say," answered the smug little brat.

Plum was initially filled with a surge of glee. She had never really liked Mimi, who had beaten her out for a position at *Beauty Bop Magazine* years ago. Plus, it was nice to not be the only one put out to pasture. But that was quickly replaced with frustration when she grasped that she had no legitimate contact at the *Market Street Journal*. If she wanted to keep her job, she needed to get an article in there as soon as possible.

"What about Bert Jonas, is he there?"

"Nope."

"Frankie Danes?"

"Who?"

"Well, who is working there? Are you the only one running the show? I highly doubt that."

"I'm sorry, who is this again?" sneered the voice on the other end of the phone.

"It's Plum Lockhart, Editor-in-Chief of *Travel and Respite Magazine*."

"I thought that magazine folded."

"Just recently. Doesn't matter. I have a very hot story for your paper…"

"Please hold," interrupted the snarky voice.

There was silence on the phone for what seemed like an eternity. Then a familiar voice purred out her name.

"Plum Lockhart, you're alive."

Plum's stomach dropped. "Gerald? Is that you?"

"Yes, it is."

"Visiting the *Market* offices, are you?"

Gerald Hand emitted that obnoxious cackle that she wished she would never hear again for the rest of her life. "I'm the new creative director, sweetie."

She wanted to take her phone, bang it against her desk, and scream, but instead she cooed, "How wonderful! Congratulations!"

"It's a huge deal. They really wanted me, and of course I wasn't sure if I wanted to go work at a newspaper magazine as opposed to a monthly, but as you said when I saw you in your pajamas at the drug store, 'they made me an offer I couldn't refuse.'"

"Exciting!" said Plum, her face contorted into a grimace. "Well, I have some fabulous news for you! I am going to treat you to an all-expenses paid jaunt down here to Las Frutas."

"You are?"

"Yes! I hear it's still snowing and frigid in New York. You need to come down to the sunshine; I'll wine you and dine you."

"No strings attached?"

"Of course not!" she said. "I mean, of course, I need you to do a feature, but really, it's worth it…"

He cut her off. "Sorry, sweetie. Las Frutas is old news. The Caribbean is so passé. I'm heading off to Mongolia soon…"

"Mongolia?"

"Yes. Oh, right, remember the horseback riding trip you were going to do? I called them up when I landed this gig and told them, since you were fired and downtrodden, I would take the trip."

"You little…" She stopped herself. Sadly, she needed Gerald. "How industrious of you. Well done. I hope you have the best time.

But you will want to work on your base tan before you head off into the wild. No better place to catch some rays than Las Frutas."

"Why don't you send me a proper pitch letter, and I'll think about it."

She sighed. "We have pickleball now!"

"Pickleball? Am I eighty? What the hell would I do with a pickleball? That's a fake activity for people at retirement homes who don't want to move."

"It's a rapidly growing sport."

"It can grow without me."

"There are lots of new restaurants..."

"I have to run. But so much fun how the tables have turned! Have a good life, Plum!"

He clicked off, and Plum pounded her fists on the desk. Her phone rang again, and she answered it in her rudest voice.

"Hello?" she barked.

There was a pause, then Juan Kevin Muñoz spoke. "Plum? Are you okay?"

"I'm fine."

He paused again. "In that case, there's a benefit party tonight for the Paraiso Children's Foundation. It's hosted by Carmen Rijo and at her villa. I'm attending and would like to invite you to accompany me. Now that we know for sure that she spent Nicholas's last evening with him at the bar, perhaps this is a subtle way we can learn some more information."

She was about to refuse. The day had been crappy, why not quit before it got even worse? And could she bear meeting this glamorous goddess who had Juan Kevin panting like a schoolboy? But then she saw the man delivering her rented golf cart out the window, and things started to look up. Besides, she hadn't been to a party in so long. She would just have to remove any latent romantic thoughts about Juan Kevin and treat him like a colleague. "Okay."

"Pick you up at seven."

Plum's hair was not cooperating, despite how rigorously she ironed it. The humidity was her enemy. She sprayed a copious amount of hairspray on her head, enough to set the hair of any 1960s astronaut's wife, but as soon as she walked into her bedroom, the ends were already starting to curl up. She had done a keratin treatment only a week before she left, but she may as well have thrown the money out the window. Frustrated, Plum pinned the top back in a clip and focused on what to wear. At first she thought she would go with one of her designer dresses from New York, but then she thought as long as she was attending a local event, she may as well wear her new green strapless dress. She covered her shoulders in a gauzy, white pashmina, in case there was a breeze by the water.

"You look very nice," said Juan Kevin, who was wearing a white dinner jacket and a pale-pink tie. His hair was slicked back, his face handsome as ever.

"Thank you. I wasn't sure what the attire was, as I didn't see the invitation."

"You are perfect."

Plum felt a frisson of uncertainty. If it had been a date, it wouldn't be so disconcerting, but the fact that this was a work expedition made her insecure. In the publishing world in New York, she never worked with men who were romantically available. They were either gay or married, so there was no sexual tension. And now here she was with Juan Kevin, who looked like he stepped out of a men's fashion magazine, and she didn't know how to act casual.

They made their way in his dark sedan. The air was redolent with the smell of coconuts, and she couldn't tell if it emitted from the trees or some cologne Juan Kevin wore. In any case, it was pleasant.

She decided to forget the awkward ending to the dinner they

had shared the night before and instead filled him in on her visit to the police station and her possible sighting of the man who claimed to be Nicholas Macpherson.

"Why didn't you call someone to help you follow him?" Juan Kevin asked.

"I didn't have time."

"It's worrisome. As director of security, I need to find out how this man penetrated the resort. And why."

"I think Jason and Deepak know who he is."

"You do?"

"They gave each other a look when I asked them."

"Why wouldn't they tell us?"

"Good question. Maybe they hired a hit man to kill their friend."

"What's the motive?"

"I'm not sure. We'll have to find out."

Juan Kevin turned the car into a gated driveway flanked by two guards with machine guns.

"I thought we were safe inside the resort?" asked Plum.

"*We* are," said Juan Kevin, leaning into the gatehouse and exchanging remarks with the guards on duty. "But Carmen is not."

The Rijo mansion was a Mediterranean behemoth with a barrel-tiled roof that teetered on the edge of a giant limestone cliff. It was at the westernmost end of the small peninsula that jutted out into the Caribbean and possessed its own private strip of sugar-white beach below that was accessible by a treacherous-looking wooden staircase. The landscaping was immaculate, with nary a blade of grass overgrown. Plum instantly wondered what it would rent for. If only she could get her hands on a property like this and not that dingy crime scene of Casa Mango.

After the valet took the car, Juan Kevin and Plum each picked up a mojito from a uniformed caterer in the capacious entrance before making their way to the courtyard, where clutches of guests had assembled. There was a live band led by a dark-haired female singer in a fire-engine-red dress crooning in Spanish. Two performers were playing guitars, one was playing a bongo, and another was playing an odd metal instrument that looked to Plum like a cheese grater.

"What's that?" she asked, pointing to it.

"It's a *guira*. They are performing bachata, our local music."

Plum found herself enjoying the song and became enraptured, even going so far as to sway her hips to the beat, something she never did in public and probably should have kept that way. Her lack of rhythm was appalling, she knew, but the music was so mesmerizing that it didn't matter. She was lost in reverie and was only pulled out of it when a woman materialized in front of them.

"Juan Kevin."

"Carmen," he responded, giving his hostess a double kiss. "Allow me to introduce you to Plum Lockhart. She's new to the island."

Plum scrutinized the woman in front of her. She was wearing one of those tight, shimmering dresses that accentuated her ample cleavage and very round booty. Her thick, wavy hair cascaded down her back in glossy ringlets, her plump lips were painted a rosy red, and she had heavily lashed dark eyes. A strong, spicy perfume emanated from her. There was no question as to why a man as powerful and wealthy as Emilio Rijo would be attracted to Carmen. *Or any man for that matter*, she thought as she glanced at Juan Kevin, who was staring at the hostess. She was a femme fatale in every sense of the word. Plum thought instantly of the sexy women in the calendar above Damián's desk and decided Carmen would not be out of place as Miss November.

"It is wonderful to meet you," said Carmen Rijo warmly. She took both of Plum's hands in hers and squeezed. "Juan Kevin has told me of you. I am so happy to have what I hope will be a new friend here at the resort."

"Thank you," said Plum. She hadn't expected an affable greeting. "You have a beautiful house."

"It *is* beautiful," agreed Carmen. "And I hope it will be my house forever. But there are many evil spirits attacking me."

"Evil spirits?" asked Plum, hoping she had misheard.

"I am sure no one wishes you harm," said Juan Kevin quickly.

Carmen's eyes widened in amazement. "You know that's not true. You were here when I found that poisonous snake by the pool."

"Poisonous snake?" exclaimed Plum with alarm. She glanced around the lawn as if one was currently lurking in the grass. "They have snakes on the island? I'm terrified of snakes."

Plum wondered how quickly she could bolt out of the party.

"We do not have snakes," said Juan Kevin quickly. "Just small garden snakes, nothing big or lethal."

"But there was one on my patio," insisted Carmen.

"An aberration," said Juan Kevin.

Carmen ignored him and gave Plum a worried look. "That is how I know that there is a *bacá* trying to harm me."

"What's a *bacá*?" asked Plum.

"It is a spirit that causes sickness to the unsuspecting. My stepson Martin believes this property to be his, and he is using his magic to chase me away. I have no doubt he left the snake to kill me. But it didn't work. It was fortunate that Juan Kevin stopped by and removed it. He saved my life."

Plum gave Juan Kevin a sidelong glance. "How very valiant of you."

"To protect and to serve, that's my motto," he said with a smile.

"Unfortunately, Juan Kevin is a busy man and cannot always protect me," whispered Carmen with urgency. "And Martin will not be stopped."

"You don't know that," reprimanded Juan Kevin. "There is no proof."

"He threatens me. He says he will destroy me. He blames me for the death of my beloved Emilio. I am prepared for him to send a *brujo* to kill me."

"What's a *brujo*?" asked Plum, who felt clueless for the second time in a minute. It was a feeling she did not appreciate.

"Carmen believes in *fukú*," explained Juan Kevin. "Bad omens. A *brujo* is a male sorcerer, and she thinks one will come and make her sick."

"Or worse!" insisted Carmen. She turned to Plum. "It is true I believe in *fukú*," confirmed Carmen, quickly making the sign of the cross and whispering, "*Zafa*." At normal volume, she said, "And I will be prepared."

"But if this is true, can't you go to the police or something?" asked Plum with a twinge of impatience.

"The police will not help me. They are loyal to Emilio and his first wife, Alexandra."

"They seem pretty useless anyway. There's that horrible man, Captain Diaz. Clearly a woman hater," said Plum with certainty.

"You've met him already?" asked Carmen.

"Yes. Odious man."

"Miss Lockhart does not hold back her feelings," said Juan Kevin.

"Why should I?"

"Captain Diaz does not like the visitors to the island. He feels that they disrespect him," said Carmen.

"That's no excuse for condescension," said Plum.

At that moment the party was disrupted by a noisy group that had arrived and was ordering the waiter to bring them drinks. The manner in which they spoke revealed that they had already imbibed several cocktails, and indeed, one of the scantily clad women was leaning against a man as if she would fall down without his support.

"Oh no," Carmen moaned, her face awash in horror. "He's not allowed here."

"It's a charity event. He may have bought a ticket," said Juan Kevin.

"He will cause a scene."

"Let me guess…is that your stepson?" asked Plum.

"Yes, he's the one in the blue shirt," said Carmen.

Plum followed Carmen's gaze to the man who stood in the center of the group. He was a muscular, hard-faced young man with pugnacious eyes that were staring at Carmen with venom. A thick, gold chain hung around his neck, and his shiny silk shirt was unbuttoned to reveal a nest of chest hair. The women around him stared at him adoringly.

"He's coming over here," said Carmen with fear in her voice.

"Don't worry," said Juan Kevin.

As she watched Martin stride toward them in his super tight pants flanked by his crew, Plum felt as if she were witnessing the precursor to a rumble. She wouldn't be surprised if everyone started snapping their fingers and broke into song like in *West Side Story*. But as he moved closer, the hatred on Martin's face became more visible, and Carmen's genuine fear was palpable. *No wonder she believes in evil spirits*, Plum thought. This guy looked like the devil himself.

"Hello, Martin, how are you?" asked Juan Kevin cheerfully.

Martin responded in Spanish—no doubt something offensive, judging by the astonished looks on Carmen and Juan Kevin's faces.

"This is Miss Plum Lockhart," said Juan Kevin in English, as if everything were normal. "She has just moved to the island to work for Jonathan Mayhew."

"Nice to meet you," said Plum.

Martin sized her up, and then his nostrils flared. "Word of advice. Don't hang around this piece of trash if you want to be successful here," he said, motioning toward Carmen.

"Stop that at once, Martin," scolded Juan Kevin. "There is no reason to be impolite to your hostess."

"My hostess?" snorted Martin. "You mean the whore that seduced my father and stole my inheritance. My dad is barely in the ground and she's out at bars trying to pick up guys."

"That's not true," Carmen insisted. Her large eyes widened and were flooded with tears.

"Oh yeah? You and that face-lift were out sweeping for rich men at the bar the other night."

"I was having drinks with a friend," Carmen said softly.

Martin chortled, a long, slow, evil cackle that reminded Plum of the sounds emitted by a villain in a cartoon.

"Martin, we are here for a good cause. Your attitude towards Carmen is noted. Now please be gracious. Let's not cause a scene," advised Juan Kevin.

"She's the one who caused the scene," roared Martin.

Other guests turned and stared. Plum took a step back, eager to be away from the volatile Martin. Juan Kevin moved closely to Martin and stood so their bodies were an inch apart. The director of security was about a foot taller than the trust-fund kid and glared down at him intimidatingly.

"We are here for the children. Do not be disrespectful. I will ask you and your friends to leave at once."

Martin looked like he was about to challenge him but instead just shook his head and spat at the ground.

"I want to get away from that whore anyway!" he said.

He motioned to his crew and said something in Spanish. They all made a rowdy departure, but not before Martin kicked over a small table that held a tray of drinks on his way out.

"Lovely guy," murmured Plum.

Carmen burst into tears and ran into the house.

CHAPTER

11

IT TOOK ABOUT A QUARTER of an hour, but Plum and Juan Kevin were finally able to console Carmen. Initially she had sobbed into Juan Kevin's arms, and he patted her back as she did so, raising Plum's suspicions that there was something more to their relationship than Juan Kevin had revealed. Then they sat with Carmen in what had been her late husband's study and settled her into a chocolate-brown leather sofa. A maid had brought her water, and Carmen clutched a lace handkerchief that she used to blot the tears running down her cheeks.

The walls of the room were covered with dozens of photographs of Emilio Rijo greeting various dignitaries who had visited the island, as well as other snaps of him around the world. He was with Queen Elizabeth, shaking her gloved hand at the grand entrance of the hotel at Las Frutas. There was one of him and Harrison Ford at a black-tie gala. Several pictures were of Emilio and former Presidents Clinton and George W. Bush on the golf course. Emilio had been attractive, with movie-star looks, and had that polished debonair glow. Nothing like his hard-faced, belligerent son Martin, who looked like a battered boxer who took too many blows to the face. Plum stood studying the pictures, noting the recent ones that featured the bombshell Carmen, while Juan Kevin tended to the widow.

"I should be used to it now, but Martin is able to cause me great pain," said Carmen in a feeble voice.

"He should not have come," said Juan Kevin. He placed a soothing hand on Carmen's shoulder, a move that did not go unnoticed by Plum. "But it's typical Martin. I'll make sure it doesn't happen again."

"I should probably get back to my guests," said Carmen.

"A good idea," said Juan Kevin.

Plum gave Juan Kevin a quizzical look before turning to Carmen. "Well, hang on a second, Carmen, because we actually have some questions for you."

"You do?"

"Yes, we want to know about two nights ago, actually, the night that Martin was referring to…"

"This is probably not the best time," interrupted Juan Kevin. He shook his head at Plum.

"Why not?"

"Because Carmen is hosting a party. She has to return to her guests."

"But isn't it why we came?"

"We came to be supportive."

"This will only take a minute," insisted Plum.

"She's just recovered from an upset…" Juan Kevin pressed.

"Great! She's recovered," said Plum, turning her attention to Carmen. "Listen, we need to know what happened that night at the bar. Because the man you were with, Nick Macpherson, is now dead, and we need to find out who killed him."

"Yes, I heard that," said Carmen. "It's shocking. My interaction with him was brief. I was with my friend Leslie, and we were having drinks. Unlike what Martin implies, I do not go out often. In fact, Leslie pleaded with me to come out."

"Who is Leslie?" interrupted Plum.

"Leslie Abernathy. She's from Texas but spends winters here."

"Do you know her?" Plum asked Juan Kevin.

"The name is familiar, but I do not know her."

"And is she married?" Plum asked Carmen.

"No longer," said Carmen. "She has had several husbands and enjoys the company of men. It was Leslie who met Nick at the bar and invited him to sit with us. He was very charming, but he had obviously had some drinks and told us his friends were annoyed with him."

"Which friends?" asked Plum eagerly.

"He didn't say."

"He didn't make a pass at you?"

"No."

"What did you talk about?"

Carmen looked at the ceiling as if the answers were written there. "He said he was here for a bachelor party. He mentioned that he did not approve of his friend's impending marriage and wanted to put a stop to it."

"Really?" asked Plum.

"Yes, he said they were wrong for each other, his friend could do better. And Nick was very…open. He said he was always making trouble with his friends and thought it was funny, and in fact, at that moment he was pulling a prank on his friend. It might result in the friend ending his engagement."

"Jason," Plum said to Juan Kevin. Before he could respond, she turned back to Carmen. "Did he say what kind of prank?"

"We were interrupted. Martin came and yelled. Nick and I tried to talk more, but it proved impossible. Martin will not leave me alone. I'm afraid he misinterpreted that I was trying to romance this Nick. It's not true." She turned to Juan Kevin, tears filling her eyes again. "It's not fair! I made his father happy. He shouldn't hate me."

"He behaves badly," Juan Kevin said soothingly.

"He won't stop harassing me. He follows me! And he spreads bad rumors about me. He has no reason to do that. I have been very nice to him!"

Juan Kevin nodded. Plum couldn't help but snort. She didn't realize she had made a noise out loud until they turned and stared at her.

"Why do you laugh?" asked Carmen.

"I'm not laughing, I just...well, you can't blame him," said Plum. "You did break up his parents' marriage."

"Who told you that?" she asked.

Plum looked at Juan Kevin, whose face was slowly becoming consumed with fury. "I mean, isn't it true? Doesn't everyone know?"

"Do people talk badly about me, Juan Kevin? Do you?" asked Carmen.

Plum was astonished that this woman could be so clueless. What did she expect? You run off with the billionaire who practically owns the entire island, and no one will gab about it?

"No one talks badly about you, Carmen," said Juan Kevin sternly. He glared at Plum. "I wouldn't stand for it. You don't have to worry."

"Thank you," said Carmen sadly. Then she suddenly transformed, pulled herself together, and said in a brisk tone. "It's time for us to go back to the party."

They rose, and as they were on their way out, Plum stopped.

"One more question, are you by chance missing a turquoise earring?"

"No," said Carmen quickly.

"Are you sure?"

"Yes, why?"

"No reason. We just want to return it to its rightful owner," said Plum.

"Let's go now," said Juan Kevin.

The sun had dunked under the horizon, and by the time they emerged from Carmen's house the night was pitch black with a large expanse of stars scattered across the sky. Plum was excited when she entered Juan Kevin's car. It had been because of *her* journalistic expertise that they had inveigled all the information out of Carmen. And now they were closer to a motive. She was hoping Juan Kevin would acknowledge her efforts.

"You shouldn't have done that," he reprimanded once they had driven out of the gate.

"What are you talking about?" she asked, stupefied. She glanced at Juan Kevin's profile and found him glaring straight ahead, his knuckles white from gripping the steering wheel so tightly.

"Pressed Carmen like that. She's very fragile. It was not polite."

"Polite? You're joking, right?"

"Perhaps it's okay in your country to be so…pushy, but there are ways we do things here in Paraiso."

Plum did not like to be referred to as pushy, and any such accusation unleashed her attack mode.

"Yes, I know all about your ways here in Paraiso. It's always *tranquilo!*"

"We do things differently…"

"You do things at a snail's pace! There's a lot of discussion but no action. If I had not pressed your beloved Carmen, then we wouldn't know that Jason and Deepak were mad at Nick! We wouldn't know he was planning to sabotage Jason's marriage. That's motive."

"She is not my beloved Carmen."

"Oh, puh-leeze!" sneered Plum. "You were practically throwing yourself at the merry widow. And if you ask me, she totally plays up being the damsel in distress. Sitting there in her trillion-dollar house with the lace hankie, sobbing about the mean stepson! Cry me a river!"

Juan Kevin's temper flared. "That's not true! She is not like that!"

"Oh, yes, she is. I know the type oh so well. She shoves her big breasts into some married guy's face, and next thing you know, he dumps his wife or girlfriend and is walking her down the aisle!"

"Enough!" said Juan Kevin, slamming the steering wheel. "She is my friend. Do not say anything more."

"Fine."

They rode in hostile silence to Plum's town house. When Juan Kevin put the car in park, he turned to her.

"In the short time I have spent with you, I have learned that you have no tolerance for the shortcomings of others, and you rigorously point out the flaws and deficiencies of people you cross paths with as well as the imperfections of my beloved island. I realize criticism is a sporting game from where you come from and harshness is a way of life, but I don't appreciate cruelty of any sort. And to hear it coming out of the mouth of a beautiful and successful woman makes it all the more repugnant. If we continue to investigate this murder together, I would ask you to refrain from the negative commentary."

Plum was incensed. How dare this security guard talk to her like that? "I would not dream of working with you again! I'm trying to solve this murder, and you are worried about being polite!"

She slammed the car door on her way out.

After huffing and puffing around her house, Plum pulled a bottle of chardonnay out of the fridge and settled down with a large bag of plantain chips. They were a recent discovery at the grocery store and would prove transformative to her waistline. But now was not time to think about that.

Plum had been so exhilarated only to have Juan Kevin demolish her excitement. His ruthless criticism of her stung. Not to mention that it was clear he was in love with Carmen, which also made Plum irate. Carmen had clearly achieved success by marriage and a wealthy husband and not through hard work, unlike Plum, who had done everything for herself. *Well, let her have him,* she thought. Nothing was ever going to happen between Plum and Juan Kevin. He was a nobody who worked at a resort, sneered Plum, completely ignoring that she also worked at the same resort.

As she drifted to sleep later that night, she promised herself that she would do everything in her power to get back to New York. There was nothing for her on Paraiso.

Plum woke early to her phone ringing. She squinted at the screen, her eyes still bleary with sleep. She bolted up and swung her legs around the edge of the bed. It was Juan Kevin. She debated whether or not to answer it but then decided it was best to get it over with, as he was undoubtedly calling to apologize for his insolence.

"Hello?"

"You need to come at once."

"I think an apology is in order before you summon me," she replied briskly.

"There's been a break-in at Casa Mango. The police need you to identify if anything is missing."

He clicked off without waiting for her response, stoking her irritation.

When Plum arrived, the air was already heavy with heat. Today would be a scorcher. She peeled off the cardigan that matched her sheath dress and knotted it around her neck. In her haste she had forgotten to lather herself with sunblock and worried her pale skin would crisp. That was one addition to her morning routine that she had to remember. She was used to giant skyscrapers acting as sunblock, but now she required the real thing.

A sour-looking young policeman tried to wave her away from Casa Mango's entrance, but she snapped at him, and after seeming momentarily confused, he waved her through. She had learned early in her career that making it appear as if you belonged, whether you did or not, always worked like a charm. And today she did not have time for explanations.

She found Jason and Deepak looking sulky, seated on the sofa in the living room when she entered. Voices were coming from down the hall, and two policemen stood and stared at the front window and discussed something without urgency.

"What happened?" asked Plum.

"I was sleeping and heard a strange sound, and when I woke up, there was a guy in my room," Jason explained. "He was dressed in all black and wore a mask. I yelled and then threw a pillow at him, and he ran off."

"What did he look like?" asked Plum.

Jason gave her an angry look. "Like I said, he had a mask on."

"Right, right, but was he tall? Short? Fat? Thin?"

"Average, I guess. I was half-asleep; the shades were drawn. It was hard to tell."

"What do you think he was after?" asked Plum.

"What do *you* think he was after?" asked Jason.

"I don't know."

"Well, I don't either."

Deepak tried to be more diplomatic. "The point is, Plum, that we don't feel safe here anymore. Last night they told us Nick was murdered, and then hours later, someone breaks into our house. We need to return home."

"We are sitting ducks here. Someone wants us dead!" Jason wagged a finger in her face. "You better get us out or find us another place to stay. Our contract states that you would guarantee our safety. We have a deal."

She couldn't argue with him. "The hotel and villas are fully booked, but I will see what I can do. And I will find out where that useless police officer was when this man was breaking into the villa!"

Plum stormed down the hallway toward Jason's bedroom and

found Juan Kevin in conversation with Captain Diaz. She couldn't decide whom she was less enthused to see, and she was particularly piqued that Juan Kevin looked handsome in a baseball cap he had placed on top of his tousled hair.

They both ceased their dialogue and gave her imperturbable looks.

"What's going on?" asked Plum.

"Someone was in the house, in this bedroom. We don't know what he was after," said Juan Kevin.

"That's unacceptable," said Plum. "My guests are in danger. Where was the police officer that was supposedly guarding the house?"

"He was on a break," said Captain Diaz defensively.

"This is amateur hour. You will have more blood on your hands if you don't protect them," said Plum.

Captain Diaz's V-shaped eyebrows rose to his scalp. "You must move them to a different residence."

"I'm working on it," said Plum. She turned to Juan Kevin and said in her harshest tone, "And what about hotel security? I thought you were in charge of a crackerjack team, and yet there are murders and break-ins."

Juan Kevin took a deep breath and looked about to explode at her, but after a pause he said evenly, "You are right. We have failed."

Surprised by his easy acceptance of responsibility, she returned her attention to Captain Diaz. "When can my guests go home?" she asked accusatorily (conveniently ignoring that they had been originally detained at her urging).

"It is still unclear," announced Captain Diaz.

Plum glanced around the bedroom. "Do we know if the intruder took anything?"

"Jason and Deepak said everything of theirs is still here," said Juan Kevin. "But we need you to look through the villa and make sure all of the furnishings are here."

"Fine."

Plum did a sweep of the house and found everything intact. If the intruder wasn't stealing anything, maybe he really was there to murder Jason and Deepak? And yet, if he was, why didn't he? Jason's only defense had been a pillow. If the intruder had a gun, Jason would be toast by now.

Plum reported back to Juan Kevin and Captain Diaz that nothing was amiss. She then called Lucia on her cell and demanded she move hell and high water to find new accommodations for the bachelor party. Lucia said she would work on it.

Jason and Deepak were still slumped in their seats where she had found them earlier. Plum sat across from them.

"Okay, here's the deal. I'm going to find you another place to stay until you're clear to go."

Jason groaned.

"Listen, it's the best I can do," she snapped, thinking of how ungrateful they were. At the very least, they should be thankful for her efforts. It wasn't like it was her responsibility, she thought, forgetting that it was her responsibility. "But you need to tell me what's going on. I got the impression you may know who claimed to be Nicholas Macpherson and took the key."

Juan Kevin approached. "It would be very helpful if you were candid," he coaxed.

Both men shifted, and finally Deepak spoke. "We thought maybe it was a prank. You know, Nick was always playing tricks on someone, he had schemes, and he told us the night he died that he had some big prank up his sleeve."

"But why would this be a funny prank? To have some impersonator get the keys?" asked Plum.

Jason crossed his arms like a pouting child while Deepak sighed deeply, letting out a stream of air.

"Nick…look, we loved him, but he was the sort of guy who would do bad things to get out of responsibilities," said Deepak.

"Like, he would go to a fancy restaurant and order the most expensive meal then slip a dead cockroach in the last course so he wouldn't have to pay. Once, he put a used condom under the bed of his hotel in Miami and told them that housekeeping didn't clean before he checked in, so they would comp the room. He did stuff like that."

"Very immature."

"In retrospect, but when were young, it was funny."

"You think he may have sent in some fake guy to pretend to be him as part of some sort of devious plan to evade payment?" demanded Plum.

"It seems elaborate, but it was the sort of thing Nick did," admitted Jason.

"And do you think this is the same person who was in your bedroom?" Juan Kevin asked the men.

"That I can't say," said Jason.

"No idea," confirmed Deepak. "But why would he come here?"

Juan Kevin shook his head. "Who do you think killed your friend?"

"Everyone keeps asking, and we don't know," whined Deepak.

"We talked to a woman who was at the bar with Nick. A very attractive woman," Plum said pointedly, giving Juan Kevin a snarky look. He purposely didn't return her gaze. "She said you were both angry at Nick. And that Nick said he didn't like your fiancée and was pulling a prank to break you up."

The vein in Jason's temple pulsed. "That's not true at all."

"Maybe it was a prank?"

"I don't buy it. I don't buy it at all. Nick could be a jerk, but he wouldn't destroy my relationship with Kirstie."

"What if he did? Would you be angry enough to kill him?" she asked.

"What is this?" asked Jason, standing up. "If you are going to accuse me, I want my lawyer. This is outrageous!"

Jason stomped off. Deepak remained. Plum turned to him and said in a gentler voice, "Did Nick like Kirstie?"

He paused. "No one likes Kirstie. She's high-maintenance."

Plum immediately became defensive. "That doesn't mean she's not a wonderful person. What is it with you men? A strong woman is high-maintenance?"

Deepak put his hands up as if to surrender. "Do you even know her?"

"No. But I don't like that description. It is so derogatory. No one says it about a man."

Juan Kevin intervened before Plum pursued this line of conversation. "Why would Nick tell these women at the bar that he wanted to break up Jason and his fiancée?"

"I don't know; I'm not sure I buy it. But like I said, we weren't hanging out with him at the bar. We were with our friends."

"Your friends?" asked Plum. And then she remembered that Deepak had mentioned they had run into friends at the bar. "Oh, right, can you give me their names again? I'd like to talk to them."

12

JUAN KEVIN CAUGHT UP WITH Plum as she stood at the end of the driveway.

"Where are you going?" he asked.

"Why do you care?"

"Plum, let's put our differences aside. We need to work together to fix this situation. I'm director of security, as you know, and you have a job to protect. We need to make sure the guests are safe and this is all taken care of. No use quarreling."

"I don't think I'm quarreling."

"I'm sorry we had words last night. Let's forget it and work together."

"What about my negative commentary? My harsh and critical ways?"

He sighed, clearly making an effort to control his temper. "Our styles are very different. I will try and respect your way of doing things if you are sensitive to the traditions and ways of business in Paraiso."

"I don't know if I am capable of changing," said Plum, folding her arms defiantly.

"That's probably true. But I ask that you try so we can find out who murdered Nicholas Macpherson and who broke into Casa Mango last night. I think together we could figure it out."

Plum was about to say, "What would Carmen think about that?" but bit her tongue. It was strange that, for someone who wasn't really the jealous type, she was certainly having twinges of it in regard to Juan Kevin. What was it about him?

"Okay, fine. I'm leaving this godforsaken place soon, anyway."

"I hope it's not because of what I said."

She snorted. "No. Because I have better opportunities on the horizon."

"I see."

"But for now, we can have peace," she said, holding out her pale hand. Juan Kevin shook it.

"Peace."

"I'm going to try and find Lila Donovan and AJ Thompson, the friends Jason and Deepak were drinking with. Maybe they can tell us what was really going on between the guys."

"I thought as much. Let me give you a ride."

"I have my cart."

Juan Kevin gave it a sidelong glance. "It will take you an hour to get to the hotel. In my car, it's five minutes."

She was dismayed that her loaner was even worse than her original cart and didn't exceed fifteen miles an hour. "Fine," she finally conceded.

Before they set off, a blue sports car came tearing down the road and flung itself into the neighboring driveway. Through the bushes they saw a young woman with perfectly coiffed, long blond hair slam her car door and walk toward her house. She wore very tight pants and high heels. The woman disappeared into her villa.

"The neighbor's back. Let's go talk to her," said Juan Kevin. "Maybe she knows something."

Plum hesitated, not sure she wanted all this time together with

Juan Kevin, but then acquiesced. She would be completely formal and professional from now on. In the past, she could have won a gold medal at keeping colleagues at arm's length. Why should that change now? "Okay," she capitulated.

They walked down the driveway of Casa Mango then up the neighboring footpath, winding through a manicured grove of hibiscus and coconut trees. Like Casa Mango, the house was white stucco with a red, Spanish-style tiled roof, ornate archways, and a massive mahogany front door. Clusters of flowers thronged the villa, and the lawn was a vivid shade of green. There was a small sign that identified the house as Casa Avocado. They rang the doorbell, and a low gong sounded.

The woman opened the door, and Plum almost recoiled in shock. From a distance, the woman had appeared young—especially with the long blond hair and skimpy outfit. But they found themselves staring into the visage of someone in her sixties who had undoubtedly indulged in extensive face work. The skin on her forehead was peeled back so tightly and filled with so much collagen and Botox that her expression appeared to permanently be one of alarm or surprise. Plum had no problem with people who wanted to look younger, but it was jarring when she expected youth and was met with something else entirely.

"Yes?" said the woman in a Southern accent. She had on a purple shirt that had small, lavender tassels hanging off the edges and elaborate embroidered stitching along the neckline.

"I am sorry to disturb you, Miss, but I am Juan Kevin Muñoz, the director of security, and this is Miss Plum Lockhart, who manages Casa Mango."

"Well, hello there. I'm Leslie Abernathy."

Plum and Juan Kevin exchanged surprised looks.

"You're Leslie? Carmen Rijo's friend?" asked an astonished Plum.

"Why, yes, she's a doll."

What were the chances that Leslie, who spent time with Nicholas Macpherson at the bar, lived next door to him? Neither Plum and Juan Kevin could believe it was a coincidence.

"How do you know her?" asked Plum.

"I met her through her late husband, Emilio. My former husband played polo with him."

"Small world," said Plum.

"Las Frutas is a very small world," confirmed Leslie.

"We were wondering if we could have a word with you about the recent…activities next door," said Juan Kevin.

"I already talked to the police, but why don't y'all come on in, and I can fill you in on anything I know."

"That would be great," Plum said.

They followed her through a vaulted-ceiling living room that was a cacophony of colors and textiles then outside to the pool area. Their hostess evidently took great pride in her garden, which was redolent with every variety of flower and bush possible and tended with assiduous care. Patches of soil were colonized with a profusion of rich purple and pink blossoms. There were urns and clay pots bursting with gigantic-leafed greenery. A small stone fountain was spitting water out of the carved lion's head.

"Beautiful house," said Plum. "How long have you lived here?"

"Why, about ten years. I'm from Dallas but spend half my time here. Hard to beat the weather, and I just love the sun. I'll follow it anywhere. 'Course, I know it's bad for you and all, but nothing better than a gal with a tan. I don't care about wrinkles; I'll worry about them when I'm dead!"

Plum's eyes inadvertently slid down Leslie's sun-damaged body that was the color of leather. She thought the crypt was not far away for poor Leslie.

"Can I get y'all something to drink? Maybe some sweet tea or a lemonade?"

"That's okay, thank you, Mrs. Abernathy," said Juan Kevin.

"We don't want to inconvenience you," said Plum.

"It's no trouble at all. Why don't y'all sit down?"

She motioned to the chairs and table under a heavily vined, trellised area. An unfinished game of solitaire was left abandoned next to an ashtray filled with lipstick-smeared cigarette butts on the glass table. Despite their refusal of refreshments, Leslie rang a little bell, and a maid appeared. Leslie introduced her as Nina and gave her a drink order.

"Mrs. Abernathy," began Juan Kevin.

"Please, call me Leslie. I was Leslie longer than I was Mrs. Abernathy."

"Leslie. Obviously, you have been informed that Nicholas Macpherson has…died. Possible murder."

"*Probable* murder," corrected Plum.

"Yes, I know," said Leslie. "The police confirmed it when they came by, but I heard that morning from Nina, who is friends with Lourdes, the gal that works over there. When Lourdes found the body, she came running over here for help. I woke up a few hours later. Nina assumed I'd heard her friend's screams, but I sleep with a white noise machine, and not even fireworks could wake me. There's a damn woodpecker going to town on the tree by my window that likes to work at all hours."

Plum thought the woman might have winked at her, but with the frozen face, it was difficult to tell.

"Yes, we do have our share of woodpeckers," said Juan Kevin. "Interesting fact: on Paraiso they only attack the south side of the trees. I'm not sure why."

"Really? How fascinating," said Leslie.

"How did you end up meeting Nick?" asked Plum.

"I was at the beach bar with Carmen. I wanted her to have a fun evening because she has not been treated very nicely by the gang on the island."

"I agree," said Juan Kevin quickly, and Plum glowered.

"She is too young and too gorgeous to stay at home all the time, so this week I said I would not take no for an answer! I have a group of lady friends down here, and we try to get together on Friday nights. We search for drinks and men. Piñas and Penises, we call it. Good old-fashioned fun. Sometimes not old-fashioned, and that's even more fun! Sorry, I think I made you blush!"

"No..." protested Juan Kevin.

"I'm allowed. I'm divorced. Three times. I always say I married well but divorced better!" She turned to Juan Kevin. "Are you married?"

"Divorced," he said.

"Interesting, we probably have a lot to talk about."

Leslie gave him a flirtatious look—at least that's what Plum thought it was, but since Leslie's face muscles were paralyzed, it was hard for Plum to decode.

Juan Kevin squirmed. "Possibly."

"Let's swap war stories. I'm here until next month."

"Okay..."

Fortunately, Nina arrived with the drinks and placed them on the table. She also included a platter of fruit and coconut cookies. The pineapple looked so tantalizing that Plum speared a piece. It melted in her mouth. She realized she hadn't had breakfast.

"Thanks so much, Nina," said Leslie.

"And what happened with Nick?" asked Plum.

"We were all having a drink and a giggle. That Nick was a load of fun, a real flirt," said Leslie. "Then Martin shows up and yells that Carmen is a disgrace and accuses her and Nick of sleeping together—they had only just met, I mean, *really*! And besides, his daddy's been dead for a year now, so what if she was? She deserves a little hoot. But Martin doesn't want her to have any fun. He sat at the bar and stared daggers at us. Finally, we decided to leave."

"Did you all leave together?" asked Juan Kevin.

"We walked out together, but then I scurried home. A gal needs her beauty sleep, don't you agree, Juan Kevin?"

He shifted in his seat. "It appears you have had plenty of sleep then, if that is true."

"You flirt!" she said, placing her veined hand on top of his. "Heck, the funny part is that I didn't even realize that Nick was staying next door! I'd only met the other fella when he was checking in."

Plum quickly gulped down a cookie. "Which fella? Nick or Jason?"

"I'm not sure."

Plum leaned toward her. Had Leslie also met the impostor? "What did he look like?"

"I don't know; it was through the bushes. I was unloading the groceries, and he was going in the villa. I said howdy. Honestly, I thought he might offer to help, seeing as I was carrying all these large bags, but he just sort of mumbled and went inside."

"When was this?" asked Plum.

"It was Thursday around lunch."

Plum whipped out her cell phone and pulled up Nick's Instagram page. "Was it either of these guys?" she asked pointing to Deepak and Jason.

"He definitely wasn't Indian. I don't know about the other guy; I don't think so because this guy was not very buff. It was hard to tell because he was wearing those wraparound sunglasses."

Plum turned to Juan Kevin and gave him a knowing look. "Must have been the guy who came to see me."

Juan Kevin nodded then turned back to Leslie. "What happened to Carmen when you left the beach bar?"

"I'm not sure about Carmen. When I left, she was talking to Nick. But I doubt they stayed there much longer; Martin was still lurking around giving them the hairy eyeball."

"Is it possible they came back to Nick's villa together?" asked Plum.

"I've no idea. I stay out of other people's hanky-panky. I have my own to worry about!" She laughed then turned and gave what was possibly a seductive look (again, hard to tell with the surgery) to Juan Kevin.

"One more question," asked Plum. "Do you own a pair of turquoise earrings?"

"Well, I'm not sure, but probably, I'd have to say."

"Is it possible you were wearing one and lost it the other night?"

"No, all my baubles are accounted for."

LILA DONOVAN AND AJ THOMPSON, the couple Deepak and Jason had run into at the bar, were staying in one of the rooms at the hotel—a three-story structure set back from the beach, nestled between two golf courses. The limestone building was long and shaded by deep verandas and balconies on each floor. Juan Kevin had one of his security associates track them down, and they agreed to meet up at Las Casitas, the tapas restaurant on the first floor.

Plum had only done a quick walk-through of the hotel the day after she arrived and was surprised to see there was so much activity. Dozens of sunbathers were relaxing on lounge chairs by the pool, which featured a giant, thatched-roof bar in the center that people had to swim to in order to access. Children in floaties were splashing about and jumping off the ledge. Techno music was thumping from the speakers along the wall, and waiters were carrying trays of blended fruit cocktails.

"Lots of people here," said Plum as they strode past the pool toward the restaurant. "I'm surprised guests aren't at the beach. What's the point of coming all the way to the Caribbean and sitting by a pool? May as well be in Florida."

"Many with young children prefer the pool, as it is easier to access, but it is also a favorite amongst the British clientele."

"British? Why's that?"

"I've no idea. But I've found through the years that visitors from various cultures generally operate the same way. The Americans and the Russians are the first to the beach—very early in the morning. The Americans generally put on large amounts of sunblock and sit under umbrellas. The fathers and sons toss footballs or baseballs over the crowds. They stay until early afternoon, when they then retire to play tennis or golf or do fitness. The Russians leave around lunchtime."

"Fascinating. What about the Spanish or Italians?"

"They generally arrive later to the beach. They have long lunches, then stay late, party late, and sleep late. They can be quite loud on the beach."

"I think I've heard them."

Las Casitas was buzzing. The open-walled restaurant was completely white from the tables and chairs to the umbrellas. Whitewashed rattan pendants hung from the cavernous ceilings. Sunlight poured in from every angle. It was situated on a balcony overlooking the pool area, and the pulsing music crept its way up.

"That must be them," said Juan Kevin.

They walked towards a couple sitting at a table in the corner, their backs against the wall. The man gave a half wave. He was in his early thirties and had a rectilinear face, cropped sandy hair, and the stocky, muscular, broad-shouldered body of a college athlete. The word *jock* instantly sprang to Plum's mind. He wore a polo shirt and khaki shorts straight out of a Lands' End catalog. He rose to greet them and thrust out his hand.

"I'm AJ Thompson; this is Lila Donovan," he said, motioning toward his girlfriend.

Lila was wearing a diaphanous white caftan and a wide-brimmed sun hat. She had a dainty nose, small blue eyes, and pale blond hair. Trendy bracelets that looked like Chiclets dangled on her bony wrists, and stylish beaded earrings hung from her tiny ears. She was clearly someone who cultivated undernourishment, the sort that Plum had run into often at parties in New York. Her expression was set in that disappointed-and-bored mode that clung to twentysomethings. Dealing with these types was in Plum's wheelhouse.

After a few brief moments of polite conversation about the weather and the resort, they segued into the name game, where both Plum and Lila brought up people they might know in common. It became a frantic contest of one-upmanship as they rattled off names in the publishing, fashion, and society world. AJ and Juan Kevin's heads kept swerving back and forth between them as they fired questions at one another.

"Mimi Wasserman?" asked Plum.

"Yes, she was just fired from the *Market Street Journal*," Lila replied. "She totally ruined it."

"I agree," said Plum. "It was unbearable."

"Very boring."

"Gerald Hand?" asked Plum.

"Never heard of him."

"Right. He worked for me. He's at the *Market Street Journal*." Lila shrugged. "Not in my social world."

"What do you do?" asked Plum.

"I'm an influencer," said Lila, brightening for the first time. "You can check out my Instagram @SomethingVeryWhite. I have over two million followers. There are links to where I buy all my super cute clothing and accessories."

"Oh, really?" asked Plum. A bitter taste entered her mouth. It was as if Lila had said she was a mass murderer. Plum hated influencers. Influencers were the reason she was out of a job. They did none of the hard work like research or writing and only posted pictures of themselves in chic locations, and now no one read magazines—they just turned to social media. "That's nice," said Plum dismissively.

Juan Kevin could sense it was time to interject and finally broached the topic of Nick's murder.

"Can you walk us through your evening, if you don't mind?" he asked AJ.

"Sure," said AJ, running a hand through his hair. Plum noticed it barely moved, just swayed a bit like blades of grass in a gentle breeze. "Lila and I came down to Las Frutas on Thursday for the week. We were having dinner at the beach, and we saw Jason, Deepak, and Nick. We had no idea they were down here."

"How do you know them?" asked Plum.

"Let's see, I guess we met them a few years ago. We all had share houses in the Hamptons for the summer. I mean, they were in one, and Lila and I were in another. We'd take turns having parties, and we'd see each other at the beach."

"Which Hampton?" asked Plum. This was her area of expertise.

"West," said AJ.

"Oh," said Plum, losing interest. It was the least fancy. Really shouldn't even have *Hampton* attached to the name.

"Ever sense any friction between the men back then?" asked Juan Kevin.

"No," said AJ. "But then, I'm not sure I would. I was usually around other people when they were there. It wasn't like we spent any quality time together."

"What about you?" Plum asked Lila.

"I never saw or heard anything like that," she answered in a bored voice.

"What about the night of Nick's death?" asked Juan Kevin.

"Right," said AJ. "We told them we would meet up with them after we finished our dinner. We found Jason and Deepak sitting at the bar, you know, on the barstools. Nick was bouncing around the restaurant; he was already pretty loaded and chasing after anything in a skirt. That's the kind of guy he was."

"AJ, you make Nick sound like a real jerk," said Lila. "He's *dead*. You can't talk about the dead that way."

AJ gave her a look indicating he didn't agree. "He was fine."

She cocked her head to the side and said in a disapproving voice, "Come on."

"What?" he asked.

Lila turned toward Juan Kevin and Plum. "I don't want you to get the wrong impression. Nick was a nice guy."

"A nice guy who had a revolving door of women," said AJ.

"You can be a nice guy and like the ladies," said Juan Kevin diplomatically.

"Yes," agreed Lila.

Plum wanted to analyze Juan Kevin's statement (was *he* a nice guy who liked the ladies?) but instead posed a question to AJ. "We know Jason was irritated at Nick that night for hitting on women. Did he tell you that?"

"He was annoyed because he didn't want Nick to pull him into it. Jason said his fiancée is really possessive and thinks Nick is—was—a bad influence."

"Do you know anything about a prank Nick was going to play on Jason?" asked Plum.

"What do you mean?" asked AJ.

"We heard he was going to play a prank on his friend who was going to get married."

AJ shook his head. "I know nothing about that. Honestly, I didn't really hang out with Nick that night. I was with Jason, Deepak, and Lila."

"What about you?" Plum asked Lila.

"I talked to Nick for a bit," she said, taking a sip of her iced tea. "Just about what we've been up to, catching up on people in common. But we didn't talk about any prank."

"Did he say anything to either of you about feeling fearful or in danger?" asked Juan Kevin.

"Nope," said AJ.

"No," said Lila.

"Are you sure?" asked Plum.

They nodded. "Hey, does this mean we should be frightened? Are our lives in danger?" asked AJ, as if the thought just occurred to him.

"Of course not," said Juan Kevin. "We have no reason to believe anyone is in danger."

"It's kind of sketchy that this happened," said AJ. "Do you know if they have any suspects?"

"I'm sure the police have someone in mind," assured Juan Kevin.

"I wish they had burglar alarms for the room. I'm not sure I feel safe," said Lila.

"You got me, babe," said AJ, placing his beefy hand on top of her pale, slender one.

"Before I drive you back to the office, do you want to grab a quick bite from the taco truck? I'm starving," said Juan Kevin.

Plum's instinct was to decline. The less social time spent with a man who found her critical and harsh, the better. But she was also ravenous, and hunger was trumping dignity. "Fine," she said.

They stood eating their lunch—chili-rubbed grilled chicken with refried beans and avocado cream for Juan Kevin and Baja-style fish taco with shredded cabbage and chipotle mayo for Plum—under the shade of the papaya trees.

"Well, that meeting with AJ and Lila was fruitless," said Plum. "Doesn't seem like they know anything."

"Perhaps, but maybe we jogged their memories. Often, people

know more or pick up more than they realize, and it comes to them later, like a delayed reaction."

"You know, something they said did remind me of something, but I can't think of it."

What was it they said that reminded Plum of something? Ugh, if only she could remember. Juan Kevin noticed her grimacing and smiled.

"It'll come back to you."

"How can you be so sure people are not in danger?"

"My security team is all over the resort. We increased surveillance."

"It didn't help last night."

"True," admitted Juan Kevin. "I've added even more men today. And, to be honest, maybe it's just instinct, but I don't think someone is on a killing spree. I think there was a particular reason that Nick Macpherson was killed. He enraged the wrong person."

"Well, as you enjoyed telling me last night, I've enraged a lot of people. I was never murdered."

"You've enraged people?" repeated Juan Kevin sarcastically. "No, I can't imagine that."

"Very funny."

"Listen, I'm sorry I was so blunt," he began.

Plum interrupted. "Let's not talk about it again. Let's restrict our conversations to the case or the mundane. No reason to exchange personal commentary."

"Very well."

Plum bit into her taco. She usually avoided mayonnaise, but it really added flavor. She would love to order a glass of crisp white wine to accompany it, but she had to get back to the office.

"If it's not too personal, may I ask if you like it?" asked Juan Kevin.

"It's delicious," said Plum.

He gave her a strange look. "You know, you look really red. Are you wearing sunblock?"

"Sunblock? I put it on every day."

"Maybe it's not strong enough."

She remembered that after Juan Kevin had called and awoken her, she had made a hasty exit.

"I forgot this morning. I need to get inside. My skin doesn't do well in the sun; I look like a tomato."

"You must be careful. I'll take you back."

"Thanks."

Juan Kevin said, "I have a staff meeting for the rest of the afternoon and won't be available, but I'll call Tony the golf pro and see if we can chat with him later, say, five o'clock?"

"If you think you can bear being with me again."

Plum was unwilling to let Juan Kevin completely forget his critique of her. But as someone who didn't enjoy conflict, he was willing to make amends so she could preserve her pride.

"I can."

14

DAMIÁN AND LUCIA WERE BOTH at their desks when she arrived. Plum was about to make a preemptive snarky comment to Damián, but he gave her a satisfied cat-that-ate-the-canary look, and she was immediately suspicious.

"You are wanted in Jonathan's office," said Lucia with a worried expression.

"Okay," said Plum breezily.

"I was able to pull some strings and use up some favors and secured accommodation for Jason and Deepak. I booked them in the hotel, and their rooms will be ready at five today."

"Thank you," said Plum.

As she walked toward Jonathan's door, Damián swiveled in his chair to look at her. "Are you okay? You are as red as the devil."

"Just a little sunburned." Plum sniffed..

"I was going to recommend a little color for your ghost skin, but you overdid it."

Plum didn't even bother with a response. But he was right; her skin was starting to sizzle, and she knew she would definitely pay for forgetting the sunblock. That was the damn problem with her pale complexion!

When she entered, she found a pensive Jonathan with his hands folded tensely. Captain Diaz seated across from him. The latter swerved around in his chair with a malicious look.

"Plum, Captain Diaz would like a word with you," said Jonathan.

"Okay."

"Yes, *señorita*. I have some follow-up questions."

They all looked at each other before Jonathan understood he was being displaced from his office, as the interview would transpire there.

"Very well, then, I'll be off. Please let me know if I can be of further assistance," said Jonathan cordially. But his face was less than friendly.

"You already have been a tremendous help," said Captain Diaz.

Plum sat down in Jonathan's recently vacated seat and stared at her interrogator. He opened up a notebook and glanced down at his scribbles.

"Señorita Lockhart, it has come to my attention that you were very eager to rent Casa Mango to this particular party. In fact, you defied your boss's direct orders that you not rent to them."

Plum shifted in her seat. No doubt Damián was behind this new line of questioning. The little turd.

"It's true. But it's because I couldn't find anyone else to rent it, and there was a bit of a ticking clock."

"But there is a wait list this weekend," said Captain Diaz. "It is very hard to find anything to rent. Are you sure no one else inquired about renting Casa Mango but you were set on this bachelor party?"

"Absolutely not. They were the only interested people. I don't know why," said Plum. She agreed it was strange. Why had no one else tried to rent it if there was such demand for lodging on the island?

"I see," he said, smiling his reptilian smile and writing something down.

"I can show you my emails," offered Plum, irritated that he didn't believe her.

"Later." He stared at her as if studying every pore on her face. "Are you sure you did not know this Nicholas Macpherson?"

"No. I never met him."

"That is interesting, because we discovered that you lived on the same street in New York City."

Captain Diaz pulled a Google map printout from his notebook and slid it across the table toward Plum. She glanced down at it. Her apartment building was circled, as was Nicholas Macpherson's. She squinted and then started to laugh.

"Are you serious?"

"I am very serious."

"Okay, yes, it looks like Nicholas and I lived on the same street. Third Avenue. But you clearly haven't been to New York. My apartment building was near East Eighty-Eighth Street. Nicholas lived near Ninth Street. That's four miles, but in New York, it may as well be four hundred miles. Totally different neighborhoods in a city of eight million people. We probably never crossed paths."

If Captain Diaz was disappointed in this revelation, his face didn't show it. In fact, he appeared almost defiant. "It is of note."

"Honestly, it isn't. I didn't know the guy."

He gave her a look of disbelief. Plum had to keep her irritation in check. She glanced out the window at the golfers putting on the green and took a deep breath. If those people could appear laissez-faire trying to place a tiny ball in a tiny hole, then there was no reason she couldn't relax. It was important to maintain calm at times like this.

"I want to warn you, *señorita*, that we are looking at you very carefully. We know you insisted on overseeing all of the renovation of Casa Mango yourself. That is very suspicious."

"Suspicious? It's called being thorough. I wanted the house to be done and in top shape before we rented it. I suppose in Paraiso it's suspicious because you all like to have things done *mañana*!"

He acted as if he didn't hear her. "Witnesses have you monitoring the plantings, the pool finishing, the painting. You have wired the house extensively with alarms. You added furniture..."

Something sparked in Plum's mind. She shot upright. "What did you say?"

He stared at her. "Is this a game? You heard what I said."

"No, I mean about wiring the house extensively with alarms."

"Yes, the alarms."

"Which alarms?"

"The fire alarms."

"I didn't add any alarms. They were there."

He looked confused. "Yes, I know."

"Then why do you say I wired the house extensively?" she asked, exasperated.

"It is not I who said that, it is witnesses."

"Right," answered Plum. "Who?"

He glanced at his notebook. "Witnesses."

It was useless to engage with Captain Diaz, but Plum was reminded of something that had been nagging at the back of her mind, something Lila reminded her of today. Alarms. Juan Kevin had said there were two fire alarms in each room, but when Plum did a last look at Casa Mango before the bachelor party arrived, there was only one alarm in each room. Had Juan Kevin been wrong? Or had someone put something in the bedrooms?

"Okay, Captain Diaz, I get it. You think my actions are suspicious. So, what next? Are you going to charge me with something? Or can I get back to work?"

He appeared surprised that she was not more intimidated by him. "I have a few more questions."

He fired a few more inane queries in her direction, which she answered flatly.

"When will you wrap this up?" she asked.

"When we are finished," said Captain Diaz. "Hopefully *mañana*."

Once he said she was free to go, she scurried out of Jonathan's office. Damián was not there, but Jonathan stood holding a cup of tea, talking in a hushed tone to Lucia.

"I have to run," Plum said.

"Wait a minute, we need to talk," said Jonathan crossly.

"It is urgent, Jonathan. I'll be back later."

"What about the article? Where are we on that?"

"That's why I'm running out!" fibbed Plum. "Lucia, can I borrow your car? I left my cart at Casa Mango. I'll be back soon."

She left without awaiting an answer.

Plum tucked herself into Lucia's car and was pleasantly reminded of how comfortable it was to drive a real automobile. She decided she needed to lease a similar four-door sedan for herself. Having a proper car was the first step to restoring her dignity.

She glanced at her face in the rearview mirror and was alarmed at how sunburnt she was. She would have to smear some aloe on as soon as possible or else she would continue frying through the night. But she didn't have time to worry about that now.

The trip to Casa Mango was made slower by the fact that she was caught behind a caravan of senior citizens in golf carts unhurriedly proceeding as if they were in a funeral procession and knew the guest of honor would still be dead when they made it to the cemetery. It took all of Plum's restraint not to honk her horn. Instead she switched on the radio and was amazed when rap music came on. Was this what Lucia listened to? *Just goes to show you that you never know people's predilections*, Plum thought.

Lourdes the maid answered the door of Casa Mango and

informed Plum that Jason and Deepak were by the pool. *Perfect*, thought Plum. She was not ready to talk to them. She moved down the hall and entered Jason's room. Her eyes scanned the walls and ceiling. Juan Kevin was right: there were two fire alarms. Plum was certain there had been only one when she signed off on the house. In fact, Plum had spent a lot of time in this bedroom with the painter and handyman, coordinating a plan to fix the plaster and the fixtures. Her limited knowledge of Spanish and their limited knowledge of English had protracted the discussion, but the outcome was that she was quite familiar with how the room was arranged. The original fire alarm was in the corner by the window. But the second one was fixed above the bed.

Plum stepped up onto Jason's bed, her feet smashing down the comforter. The ceiling was low enough and she was tall enough that once she was up there, she had to slouch and crane her neck in an effort to examine the second alarm. Sometimes it was a real pain being so tall. On closer inspection, Plum deciphered that it was not an alarm at all. She peeled it off the ceiling and lowered herself off the bed to get a closer look.

It looked like a recording device. A spy camera like the ones in banner advertisements on social media. Who put it there? The impostor? She turned it around in her hands but gathered it was streaming somewhere. Someone was probably watching her right now. It gave her chills.

Plum went into Nick's room and glanced around. There was still only one fire alarm. Ditto with Deepak's room, although when she put the flashlight on her phone and scanned the ceiling, she could make out a faint mark above the bed where a device could possibly have been placed and then removed. She performed a quick survey of the house but didn't find any more devices. However, Juan Kevin had said she had two fire alarms per room. She tried to call him from her cell, but there was no answer. She recalled that he said he would be in a staff meeting for the rest of the day. She walked outside and found Jason and Deepak sitting gloomily on chaises. They looked up at her eagerly.

"Any update?" asked Jason. "Did you find us a place to stay? We want to get out of here; this place gives us the creeps."

"Yes," said Plum. "We booked you two rooms at the hotel. Ready by five. Here is the information."

"Finally," said Jason, snatching the piece of paper.

Plum thought he could show a little more gratitude.

"Let me ask you, do either of you know what this is?"

They both glanced at the device and shook their heads. "No, why?" asked Deepak.

"I found it above your bed, Jason."

"My bed? Let me see it."

She handed it to him. He examined it. "This is a camera. Do you mean someone was recording me?"

"It looks like it."

"Who?" exploded Jason.

"I've no idea," said Plum. She turned to Deepak. "Did you see one in your room?"

He shook his head. "No."

"Deepak, do you think the person who was in Jason's room the other night had been in your room first? Could you have possibly slept through someone coming into your room?"

Deepak sighed. "Honestly, it's possible. I probably passed out. I had a lot to drink."

"I don't feel safe anymore. I'm packing up and going to those hotel rooms now," Jason roared. He shot out of the chaise and stormed into the house. Deepak rose as well.

"We're losing it," he said.

"I'm sorry," Plum responded.

On her way out, Plum stopped by the kitchen to have a word with Lourdes. She had not asked the maid what she knew about the bachelors and also wanted information on the lady of the house next door. Often staff members knew the most secrets, at least according to British mysteries, and it was a matter of carefully siphoning the salacious tidbits out of them.

Lourdes was extremely short, with a cherubic face and dark hair that she wore pulled back in a bun. She worked diligently and quietly and had worked for the Swiss owner of Casa Mango for years. She came highly recommended. Plum found her in the kitchen wiping down the stovetop. She had removed all the burners and was cleaning invisible grease spots with a rag.

"Lourdes, can I take a few minutes of your time?" asked Plum gently.

"*Sí*, is everything okay?"

"It is. Why don't you and I sit down for a minute?"

Lourdes looked worried and quickly sat across from Plum. She folded her hands neatly in her lap and stared at Plum with nervous apprehension. Plum addressed her in a low voice in case Jason and Deepak finished packing early and wandered into the kitchen.

"Don't worry, you're not in trouble. I just wanted to find out if there was anything you could tell me about the men who were staying here. Did you hear them fighting at all?"

"No," said Lourdes, shaking her head.

"Are you sure? No one seemed angry or anything?"

"No," said Lourdes. "I try not to listen. I want to do my work and not bother them. I know they are on vacation."

"Right, well, yes," said Plum. It was the correct answer, but she was disappointed. How she yearned for Lourdes to tell her she saw either Jason or Deepak bash Nick's head in. And if not them then whoever did it. "Tell me about Leslie Abernathy. Your friend Nina works for her?"

"*Sí*," said Lourdes.

"For how long?"

"I think maybe six years? I'm not sure. She's worked there for a long time."

"And what does she think about Leslie Abernathy?"

"Señora Abernathy? She's very nice. Nina likes working there very much."

"But did she ever see anything…I don't know, untoward happening there?"

"I'm sorry?" asked Lourdes, confused.

"I mean, did Nina say that maybe Leslie Abernathy becomes enraged or jealous and, I don't know, she thinks Leslie will kill someone?"

Lourdes shook her head. "No, she never said that."

"Does Leslie have fits of anger?"

"No," said Lourdes.

Plum was impressed with Lourdes and Nina's discretion but also irked at the same time. She needed a scheming and disgruntled employee in order to advance her investigation. Lourdes and Nina didn't appear to be that.

"Is there anything you can think of that might be useful?" asked Plum.

Lourdes stared at her blankly but then spoke. "I'm sorry. You are hoping to find out something about the man who was murdered?"

"Yes," said Plum.

"I can tell you only this. Nina said that when she told Señora Abernathy that the man was dead, she said she…it was not happy, the word. But that he…that he deserves to die because he did not like her."

Plum's eyebrows shot up in surprise. "What do you mean, 'like her'?"

"I think she meant, you know, he did not choose her for romance."

"I see."

Lourdes became even more anxious. "I probably should not have said that. It is not…professional. I'm sorry."

"No, please don't be sorry. This is a murder investigation, and we need to know everyone we are dealing with. Everyone is a suspect."

"You think Señora Abernathy killed the man? I do not think she would."

"I hope not. But you never know."

Lourdes made the sign of the cross.

15

PLUM DROVE BACK TO THE office to pick up Lucia, then they both returned to Casa Mango so Plum could retrieve her loaner golf cart from the driveway and Lucia could bring the men to their hotel rooms. At the office, Lucia had nicely proffered her a bottle of aloe. Plum had heard Jonathan in his office and did not want to interact with him, so she quickly absconded to the bathroom to smear aloe all over. It felt soothing, although now when she looked in a mirror, she was tinted green.

On the ride over to the villa, Plum told Lucia about finding the camera devices. Lucia thought she should immediately report the information to the police, but Plum thought that would be ineffectual.

"Captain Diaz is a moron," said Plum dismissively.

"But he is the law," Lucia said firmly.

"I'll ask Juan Kevin, see what he thinks."

"You need to be careful. If that man broke in to get the device, he may do it again. He is probably watching the villa."

"True," agreed Plum.

"That reminds me of something…"

"What?"

Lucia paused, her mind casting around for a memory. "Maybe it was nothing, but the other night when I left work, there was a man across the street. He was staring at our office but quickly looked away when I came out. I thought he was waiting for someone, but maybe he was watching us. When I drove off, I saw him in my rearview mirror, and he had crossed the street and was closer to our office."

"That's odd."

"Yes. I don't know, he could have been going to meet Jonathan, but now that I think about the spy devices, maybe he was involved?"

"We need to find this guy."

The idea that this impostor/voyeur was around didn't unnerve Plum until she stood in the driveway after Lucia had driven away with Jason and Deepak. Jason had practically slammed his car door in her face without even a thank-you. The police officer that was "standing guard" left as well, presumably escorting them to the hotel. When everyone had departed, she felt the deathly silence from the absence of people at the villa, and it scared her.

Was the intruder lying in wait in the bushes? She scanned the front yard and neighboring villas for signs of life. The faintest of breezes ruffled the palm trees. A lizard skittered down the pebbled path. Children were shrieking and splashing in a pool across the road. Everything appeared normal. But Plum's heart was beating strongly, as if it sensed something. Peril was lying in wait.

❦

Las Frutas boasted two golf courses that spread their green tentacles across the resort. One was a more modest links course, which was not inspiring enough to have a name and was merely referred to as the links. La Cereza was the crown jewel and was considered one of the premiere golf courses in the Caribbean. It had been carved from the jagged earth along the pristine, azure sea. Eight holes hugged the sea and afforded spectacular views, dramatic slopes, and undulating greens. The front four holes slinked around the La Cereza (Cherry) River, for which the course was named. When Plum was at the helm of *Travel and Respite Magazine*, they named it one of the top twenty courses in the Caribbean.

Both courses shared a thatched-roof golf shop. Plum drove up at five o'clock and found Juan Kevin outside talking to Tony Spira, the golf pro she could identify from Nick's Instagram picture. She had wanted to show Juan Kevin the spy camera but thought it best to wait until after they had chatted with the pro.

Introductions were made, and they decided to convene in the hitting shed, which appeared less busy than the shop area. Golfers were streaming in from their rounds, and caddies were unloading carts and hoisting bags into lockers and cars. They meandered by the driving range, and Plum was surprised to see a small boy who could not have been more than eight years old hit a long drive. Her competitive juices kicked in, and she thought perhaps she could take up golf. How hard could it be if infants played? She had tried it once when she was on a press junket in Scotland, but the weather was so cold and dreary, she had been less than enthusiastic. Golf in a tropical climate was more her speed. Plus, the outfits were chicer.

"Let's talk in here," said Tony.

Tony was a compact man with heavy, horizontal eyebrows and dark hair that he wore under a baseball cap with the resort's logo emblazoned on the front. His skin was tawny from overexposure to the sun. Both his polo shirt and khakis were neatly pressed as if he had just donned them, with nary a sweat mark despite a full day's work in the blazing sun. He exuded the enthusiasm and conciliatory manner that someone who works as a service professional in a fancy hotel needs to possess, thought Plum. She forgot entirely that she also worked as a service professional in a fancy hotel but decidedly did not possess that attitude.

He led them into a deceptively spacious, white cabin. The flooring was covered in fake green turf. A plastic basket of balls was next to a rack of clubs. On the back wall was a giant screen that pictured the ninth hole. There was a golf simulator and all sorts of technical equipment. A desk was in the corner, and next to it, two director's chairs clothed in spearmint fabric. They all sat down.

"What do you do with all this stuff?" Plum asked, motioning toward the golf simulator.

"It's state of the art. We use doppler technology to track and record 3D characteristics of the ball while in motion," said Tony enthusiastically. "It's the best performance-enhancing software because we can monitor granular swing changes and track a player's improvement and skills."

"Oh," said Plum, who felt as if he may as well have been speaking Spanish.

"I take it you're not a player?"

"Not at the moment," she said.

"Well, if you ever want a lesson, we can start you in here. It works for all levels. Beginners use it to form a correct swing, and golfers of every level use it to get feedback on launch angles and ball flight and trajectory. I even have scratch golfers coming in to work on distance and accuracy."

"I see," said Plum, wondering what would make a golfer itch.

"Come by and try it."

"Tony, we won't take up much of your time; we just had a few questions for you," began Juan Kevin, who could clearly tell Plum was wishing she had not asked Tony any golf questions. The director of security then explained the reason for their visit.

Tony nodded. "Yes, I played a few holes with those guys. I don't normally do that, but it was my day off, and I'm friendly with the golf pro at Jason's club back in the Hamptons, and he connected us. I thought they were nice guys."

"Did you sense any tension between them?" asked Plum.

Tony shook his head. "No. But we mostly just talked about golf. I was telling them about the history of the course, they asked me some questions about club usage and lies, and that was pretty much it. We had a beer afterward, but again, it was pretty golf-focused."

Sounds completely boring, thought Plum.

"Did Nick say anything about feeling fearful or in danger?" asked Juan Kevin.

"No, not at all," said Tony. "He seemed in great spirits. They were loving the resort, excited to be here. Such a pity that he died. Very sad."

"What about Jason's fiancée?" asked Plum. "Did anyone mention her? Or the wedding?"

"They were teasing Jason that this was his swan song, that soon he'd have a ball and chain, you know, just ribbing him. Nothing serious."

"How did Jason take that?" Plum asked.

"He didn't get annoyed or anything like that. But you know...if I really analyze it, he didn't seem very excited when they brought it up. I mean, who knows, people react differently, and maybe he's just stressed, but he wasn't like, yeah, this is great."

"Angry?" asked Plum.

"No, more like tense. And you know, maybe he is. It's a big step; it's a big expense, a wedding. Maybe he's worried about that."

"Or maybe something else," said Plum.

Juan Kevin folded his long fingers and sighed. "We're trying to assist the police to make sense of all this. Is there anything at all you can remember that stood out? Any interaction or comment?"

"I'm trying to think," said Tony. "They mentioned they were going to Coconuts for drinks and dinner and asked if I wanted to join them, but I told them it was my fiancée Cindy's birthday, and we had plans. Oh, and Jason did say to Nick, 'You better not try anything.'"

"What does that mean?" asked Plum.

"I took it to mean, you know, it better not be one of those

old-fashioned bachelor parties, with, you know, strippers or something," said Tony.

"Got it."

"But again, it was all innocuous. I'm putting a very carefree conversation under a microscope. There was no way I left them and thought, 'That man will be murdered tonight, possibly by his friends.' No way."

"That was futile," sighed Plum as they walked back toward their carts. They had given instructions for Tony to contact them if he thought of anything else that might be relevant.

"Every conversation is important," said Juan Kevin. "Elimination is helpful. And besides, maybe we'll jog his memory and he'll remember that Jason said he was going to kill Nick."

Plum gave him a look of disbelief, and he gave her a sneaky smile that turned into an intent stare.

"What?" she asked.

"It's just…you look like Christmas," he said.

"What does *that* mean?"

"Your white skin is red but now has a layer of green."

She scowled. "I lathered myself in aloe. My sunburn is painful."

"The sun is cruel," said Juan Kevin. "People forget."

"Well, I doubt I'll forget again."

"There's an old Paraison proverb that says, 'keep the fruit in the sun for a day, and it will ripen, but keep it for a week, and it will become putrid.'"

"I think someone should tell Leslie Abernathy that," said Plum unkindly. "But the sun is not the only reason I'm feeling really uncomfortable," she said.

They reached Plum's car, and she pulled out the spy camera. Juan Kevin's eyes grew larger as she filled him in.

"I can't believe I missed that it was a wireless camcorder. I'm embarrassed. I should have known better," said Juan Kevin.

"Maybe your subconscious knew better, because you at least mentioned it to me."

"I thought it was a fire alarm, though. I was certain you had purchased something American. High tech."

He studied the gadget, turning it around to see all angles. "This is connected through Wi-Fi. The person who put it in probably saw you take it down."

"Oh, don't say that, it freaks me out," she said, taking it from his hands and staring at it. "I wonder if it can be disconnected?"

"Probably when the connection is lost."

"I'm going to hide it in my underwear drawer. Give them an eyeful."

Juan Kevin arched an eyebrow. "I can take it if you like."

"No, I want to hang on to it for now. I was thinking…it must be the fake Nicholas Macpherson who installed it."

"Most likely. The question is: Why? Have you asked Deepak and Jason?"

"No," said Plum. "I don't really trust them. Although maybe if we could get Deepak alone, we could break him. He's the more vulnerable of the two."

Just then Plum's phone buzzed, and she answered it. She quickly rang off.

"Well, speak of the devil. That was Jason."

"What did he want?"

"He wants me to meet him in his hotel room. His fiancée, Kirstie, has just arrived, and she would like a word with me."

"I hope you don't mind if I accompany you."

Plum was distinctly impressed by the hotel accommodations, which had clearly been renovated in recent years. The stylish room had towering cathedral ceilings and grand, louvered windows that folded back to expose a view of the turquoise sea. The floors were covered in cool-white stone and striped blue-and-white throw rugs. There was a king-size, four-poster mahogany bed with crisp white sheets and blue accents that matched the color of the sky, as well as a generous seating area with striped, upholstered furniture and a writing desk.

Plum marveled at the aesthetically pleasing environment and instantly decided it was imperative that she redecorate her town house. Why live in a space that looked like the set of a bad sitcom? She began fantasizing about her renovations. She'd replace her own bed with one similar to this but cover the canopy in gauzy, white fabric that would flutter in the soft breeze. But then she remembered that she wasn't going to be here that long.

"Plum, this is Kirstie Adler, my fiancée," said Jason.

The slender brunette in front of her was pretty. Her upturned nose looked like it was fashioned in a doctor's office as opposed to in utero, and her lips were unnaturally puffy, but the enhancements worked to her advantage. It was evident she put in a lot of time at spin class and Pilates or perhaps had removed a rib or two in order to attain a certain level of tininess. She wore a tight, fuchsia tank top and skinny jeans. The expression on her face was decidedly unfriendly.

"I would like to know why my fiancé and his friend are being held hostage on this godforsaken island!" Kirstie demanded. "I will sue you if you don't get us out of here."

"Now, Kirst," said Jason. "Let's not…"

She put up her manicured talon, and Jason was silenced. Plum had a vague memory that she used to do that herself in staff meetings when she wanted the team to quiet down. She hoped she didn't come off as badly as Kirstie did. A little niggling thought told her that she had.

"That's quite a trick, how you've trained your fiancé. I'm sure you will have a lovely marriage," said Plum.

"Miss Adler," said Juan Kevin quickly, in a mollifying tone. "It is not up to us. The local government is investigating the cause of death of your friend Nicholas Macpherson…"

"Oh, he was no friend of mine!" said Kirstie. "His death is a blessing, or it will be when we get out of this horrible place. We need to leave now."

"I understand," said Juan Kevin. "But regardless, there are procedures and protocols. The police are working as quickly as possible to ascertain who killed him, and as soon as there's a conclusion, Jason and Deepak can leave."

She folded her arms like a spoiled child. "Well, we will see about that. My father's lawyer is making calls, and no doubt Jason will be on the next plane. My father is a very, very powerful man and does not like this one bit. Not one bit."

Plum was thinking that she didn't like this Kirstie one bit, not one bit, but she decided to remain diplomatic.

"It might expedite things if we sat down and chatted for a minute," said Plum. "Maybe you have some information that could be helpful."

"Fine. If it can get us out of this hellhole," Kirstie snapped.

"Let's talk on the balcony," said Plum hastily, before she said anything that she would regret. "Where's Deepak?"

"He went for a walk," said Jason.

They situated themselves in the comfortable recliners that overlooked the pool area. In the distance they could see the shoreline and mountains to the left. *It is heavenly*, thought Plum. What was this entitled New York City brat thinking calling it a hellhole?

"You want to know what I think?" asked Kirstie, unprompted. "Nick pissed off some guy because he was pulling one of his stunts."

"What are his stunts?" asked Juan Kevin.

She looked vexed. "Here is what Nick does: he cheats, he scams, he uses, and he lies. Or did—thank God, he's no more."

"Kirstie, that's not fair," protested Jason.

He was again silenced by the manicured finger. Plum was shocked. Jason was a bully when his little lady wasn't around, but all she needed to do was raise a finger and he was putty? Kirstie must have some very special skills. Probably in the bedroom, mused Plum.

"I never understood why someone as good-looking as Jason would hang out with Nick. Jason is a catch. Nick was a liability. He was the guy who would drag people down. Make them cheat. Stiff people at the bar. I bet he stiffed Jason for this trip!" said Kirstie.

"He definitely ended up stiff," murmured Plum under her breath.

Juan Kevin shot her a look, but fortunately Kirstie and Jason didn't hear her.

"Jason told me there was a really angry guy at the bar. Nick was hitting on his mother or wife or something?"

"Martin Rijo," said Juan Kevin, leaning closer. "It is his step-mother. Carmen Rijo."

"Right. There's your guy," said Kirstie.

"Why do think that?" asked Juan Kevin.

"Jason told me how furious he was at Nick and then he ended up following Nick and the wife out of the bar all the way home…"

"What?" both Juan Kevin and Plum said simultaneously.

Their heads swiveled from Kirstie to Jason. He shot his betrothed a peeved look then rolled his neck back with exasperation.

"What?" said Kirstie. "Was I not supposed to say that? Jason, I don't know why you're holding back. You need to give them all the information so we can get the hell off the island. My wedding is in two weeks, and I have a lot of prep to do. And so do you. That detox cleanse is not going to do itself. I am NOT walking down the aisle to some flabby finance guy."

"Can you tell us about this, Jason?" asked Juan Kevin gently.

"And why you didn't tell us this before?" asked Plum less gently.

"I told the police," said Jason, defensively.

"They're useless," said Plum.

"Exactly what I said," confirmed Kirstie.

Plum stared at her and suddenly felt protective of Captain Diaz and his crew. How dare this girl criticize them?

"Please just tell us what you know," asked Juan Kevin.

Jason sighed. "Nick was talking to that woman Carmen. And Martin showed up with his goons. He saw Carmen, and he went over and said something to her—I don't know what, it was in Spanish—and she got upset. And Nick can't let sleeping dogs lie…"

"Always had to be a wise ass," interjected Kirstie.

"Unfortunately. He mouthed off to Martin, then Martin got in his face, and they had words. Then the freaky-looking lady with them left, but Nick and Carmen remained talking. Nick decided it would be hilarious to send a Flaming Asshole to Martin—that's a Fireball drink—and Martin got pissed off. Then more words. Nick and Carmen decided to leave. They were going to drink at our house. She had a separate car, so Nick went with her, and Deepak and I took the golf cart. We got there first, and I was about to call it a night, but we heard shouting in the driveway, so we went out and saw that Martin and his goons had followed Nick and Carmen and were making a scene. Nick told them to get lost, but they wouldn't. I was pissed. I didn't want trouble…"

"You *promised* me there would be no trouble," interjected Kirstie.

"Right. I suggested Nick go back to the bar and get security to do something. He then took off again with Carmen. I thought they either went back to the bar or to her house."

"And that was the last time you saw him or Carmen?" asked Juan Kevin.

"Yes. I went to bed."

Kirstie looked smug. "I suggest you go and arrest this Martin person as soon as possible. My father is great, great friends with the President of the United States, and I'll have him tweet a strong warning to the government of Paraiso. I will decimate your tourist industry."

"I'll see what I can do," said Juan Kevin, rising.

CHAPTER

16

"LOOKS LIKE YOUR FRIEND CARMEN lied," said Plum gleefully.

It had taken all of her self-control to wait until they were in the lobby to rub it in Juan Kevin's face. What would he say now about his precious Carmen?

He looked as if he was about to defend her but conceded, "She was less than forthcoming."

"Why do you think she lied?"

"She did not lie," he said. "She just didn't tell us everything."

"That's lying," trilled Plum.

"It appears that no one is telling us the whole story. Jason never mentioned that Nick had brought Carmen back to his villa."

"Yes, everyone is a liar. And now everyone has a motive, and they are all suspects."

Juan Kevin didn't reply but continued walking towards his car, his jaw set firmly. Plum suddenly felt guilty. It wasn't kind to taunt Juan Kevin about Carmen. Maybe he really was in love with her and his heart was broken. She decided to drop it.

"Well, that Kirstie certainly keeps Jason on a short leash," she said, attempting to steer the subject away from Carmen.

"Yes. I wonder if he has given her reason to be so controlling."

"Maybe. I honestly question what he sees in her. Why would he marry her?" said Plum. "I once had a boyfriend who used to say there are more attractive single women in New York than grains of sand on the beach here. He could find one blindfolded."

"Perhaps her 'very important father' is attractive to him."

"Good point. She sounds wealthy."

They continued in silence. Plum's sunburn was feeling itchy and uncomfortable, and she was ready to take a cool bath and lather more aloe on her skin. But she really felt as if they were on to something and wasn't sure they could afford to call it quits for the night. Although Juan Kevin was probably eager to get rid of her and drown his sorrows over his beloved Carmen.

"If this father is very powerful, then we don't have much time," said Juan Kevin. "We need more answers before Jason leaves the island. I think we need to return to Coconuts and reinterview everyone there."

"Agreed," said Plum.

"I'll pick you up at eight. No need to drive your loaner."

"Thank you. I'll do anything to avoid that jalopy."

Coconuts was busy, and Plum and Juan Kevin had to wade their way through throngs of people at the bar to order a drink. Plum was jostled by a beer-bellied man in a tank top who almost sent her white wine flying.

"Watch it," she snapped at him.

"Ease up, sweetie," said the tattooed woman standing with him. She had a brittle, hard face and wore the kind of short denim overalls that one might find on a cast member of a reality show about teen grandmothers.

Juan Kevin led Plum to a table in the back corner that had a RESERVED FOR MANAGEMENT sign on it and motioned for her to sit down.

"The perks of working at the resort," said Juan Kevin.

"Very nice," said Plum, settling into her seat. "It looks like the circus is in town. What the heck is going on?"

"Twice a week a cruise ship docks in Estrella and we allow the guests to purchase day passes to Las Frutas. This affords them the opportunity to play golf or tennis, lounge on the beach, and frequent the restaurants. For the most part, it works very well, especially since they pay premiums for the golf. But the crowd that makes it to the bar is usually very animated and has spent the better part of the day drinking."

"I'll say."

"I've arranged for the server Pedro to take a break and join us. He was the one who alerted us that Carmen was at the bar with Nick, and perhaps he remembers more than he realizes. I also ordered some food in advance to make sure we don't drink on an empty stomach."

Plum rolled her eyes. "That only happened one time."

Juan Kevin smiled. "Just a precaution."

A waiter came and placed a platter of tostadas on the table. There was tuna, shrimp, poblano pepper, and chicken. Additionally, there were garnishes such as refried beans, guacamole, pico de gallo, and chipotle mayonnaise.

"These look delicious," said Plum.

"Enjoy."

Plum shrugged off her white shawl so it wouldn't end up in the salsa. Although it was a hot evening, her body temperature was oscillating between boiling and freezing due to her sunburn. She'd wanted to stick to a more businesslike outfit and maintain formality with Juan Kevin, but she had to wear the bare minimum (a spaghetti-strapped floral dress) so all the aloe didn't stick to her clothes.

"How's the sunburn?" asked Juan Kevin, noticing her itching.

"Torture. The things you don't think about when you decide to move to a tropical island."

"What did you think about?"

"I didn't," Plum said, quickly downing a tuna tostada. "It was impulsive."

"I don't know you very well, but that doesn't seem in character."

"It wasn't." She abruptly stopped talking. She didn't want to confide in Juan Kevin and open herself up to ridicule. She took a bite of her shrimp tostada to end the conversation, and thankfully, at that moment Pedro appeared at their table. Standing next to him was another young Paraison who wore a white chef's jacket and a bandanna on his head. He was a handsome and muscular man with green eyes.

Pedro nodded hello and then said, "I thought you should also talk to Joby. After we talked last time, I told him, and he said he remembered them."

Introductions were made, and Joby and Pedro were encouraged to sit down.

Pedro spoke first. "I wanted to tell you that Martin Rijo came here last night with his friends. I heard him saying that he wanted to kill that…" Pedro's voice trailed off. He had been addressing Juan Kevin, but then he glanced at Plum and back at Juan Kevin.

"Go on," prompted Juan Kevin.

Pedro said a word in Spanish that Plum didn't know but was sure was not very nice. She was struck that he didn't want to say the word in front of her, because she was a lady. Rather than feel riled, as she might have in the past, she thought it nice that he was considerate.

"And then?" asked Juan Kevin.

"He was bragging to his friends. He said, 'I can make things happen. I can have people killed. I have had people killed,'" said Pedro.

"Are you sure he was not just boasting?" asked Juan Kevin.

"I do not know. But that is what I heard," said Pedro.

"Thank you for telling us," said Juan Kevin before turning to Joby. "What was it you thought we should know?"

"Pedro told me you asked about that man who died, Nick, and I remembered Nick because I had gone outside to have my cigarette break and saw him arguing with another man. They were both very mad."

"Who was the other man?" asked Juan Kevin.

"Was it Martin Rijo?" asked Plum.

"No," said Joby, shaking his head. "I believe it was his friend by the way they were talking. I couldn't see clearly because they were behind a tree, but Nick told the friend that there was no way the marriage will take place. And the man said to him that he was just jealous, that he wanted the girl for himself. They started poking each other in the chest but didn't fight. Nick walked away, and the other man then kicked the garbage can. Then he also walked back to the bar."

"Wow," said Plum.

"That's very helpful," said Juan Kevin.

"I didn't think much of it until Pedro mentioned you were asking. And I remembered that the guy was named Nick because his friend said his name."

"Well done," said Juan Kevin.

"I only have five minutes; I need to get back to the kitchen," said Joby.

"Oh, did you make these?" asked Plum. Her mouth was again full of a tostada. She couldn't resist them.

"Yes."

"They're delicious."

When they had left, Plum turned to Juan Kevin. "What do you think of that? Maybe Jason Manger did kill his best man after all. And maybe Kirstie suspects it and that's why she wants him to hightail it out of here."

"Could be."

They were interrupted by the scent of strong cologne, the type that made Plum want to gag. She glanced up at the possessor of the stench and found her nemesis, Damián, leering down at her. His arm was looped around a young woman with long hair and dewy skin.

"It's my killer colleague!" exclaimed Damián. He then turned to his lady friend and made introductions. "Stefania, this is Juan Kevin, the director of security at Las Frutas, and this is Plum Lockhart, my new associate."

"I'm not your associate," snapped Plum.

"Do you prefer *killer colleague*?" he said.

"You have some nerve." Plum seethed.

"It's nice to meet you, Stefania," Juan Kevin said loudly, hoping to break up the bickering.

"You too," said Stefania. "Security? Are you arresting Plum?"

"What?" asked Plum.

"No, of course not. We are having dinner," said Juan Kevin smoothly.

"Oh, because Damián told me that there was never a murder here until Plum showed up," said Stefania.

"Maybe Damián killed my client because he was jealous that I was able to rent out Casa Mango and he wasn't!" barked Plum.

"I wouldn't waste my time," said Damián. "I do not consider you competition."

"Nor do I consider you competition," said Plum.

"We're going to get back to our dinner," said Juan Kevin. "Nice to see you."

Damián gave Plum an unctuous grin before swaggering away.

"He is such a bastard," raged Plum. She then went on a five-minute tangent about how much she hated Damián while Juan Kevin listened with an amused look on his face.

"He's under your skin," said Juan Kevin.

"I wish he were under the ground."

"You have very strong and passionate feelings about him."

"All negative."

"Are they?" mused Juan Kevin.

"What's that supposed to mean?"

"I'm only asking. In my experience, this fervor you express is usually reserved for cases when there are romantically interested parties."

"Well, that's not the case here," snapped Plum.

Juan Kevin nodded but said nothing. He continued to give her a penetrating look. Was it disbelief? She wasn't sure. Plum forced herself to look away and saw that AJ Thompson and Lila Donovan were dining at a high-top table by the bar. Lila, once again clad in all white, was tapping on her phone, completely oblivious to her surroundings. AJ caught Plum's eye and gave her a wave.

"We should go say hi," Plum said.

"Sure. I'll pay, you go ahead," he said.

"But you paid last time," she protested.

"I never let a lady pay. Call it chivalry, and you may subject me to rants about how I'm sexist, but this is how I was brought up, and I refuse to change in this regard."

She was about to protest, talk about women's rights, that she shouldn't be undermined or something like that, but she stopped herself. Juan Kevin wasn't paying to belittle her. He was paying because he was a gentleman.

"Thank you," she said.

Lila barely gave her a glance and returned to texting when Plum approached, but AJ looked grateful to have someone talk to him. There was a platter of half-eaten seafood and chorizo paella in front of them, but judging by the clean plate in front of Lila, it appeared that only AJ was dining.

"Any update?" he asked.

"Not really," said Plum. "Have you seen Jason and Deepak?"

"Yes, I saw them today. They both are pretty devastated. At least Jason's fiancée flew in. I think Deepak is struggling alone."

"I should go talk to him tomorrow."

"Do you think they're going to let them go home?" asked AJ.

"I hope so," said Plum.

"Tell her what you remembered," prompted Lila, not looking up from her phone. From this angle, Plum had a very good view of Lila's roots, which looked like they might need a touch-up soon.

"I don't want to say anything that could get anyone in trouble," began AJ.

"If it's important to the investigation, you need to tell me," urged Plum.

He sighed and then took a large swig of his beer and wiped his mouth with a paper napkin. "It's probably nothing, but when we met the other day, I was really focused on what Jason had said that night because he was annoyed with Nick. But actually, there was one point, and it was a throwaway comment, but Deepak said this would be the last time Nick pulled his crap."

"What crap?" asked Plum.

"He was sick of Nick cheating on his girlfriend and hitting on other people's girlfriends. Nick would also specifically hit on women he knew his friends liked. It was a jerky move. Deepak said it was enough."

Juan Kevin had approached in time to hear AJ's last remarks. "What was his demeanor when he said that?" he asked.

"It was, well, I've always thought of Deepak as sort of a mild type. But this was a flash of anger. It was a side of him I hadn't seen before," said AJ.

"That's not true," said Lila, in between texting.

"What do you mean?" asked Plum.

Finally, Lila glanced up. Her small, blue eyes blinked like a cat's just roused from a nap. "There was this one time back when we were in the Hamptons when Deepak lost his mind. He was hitting on some girl, and then Nick came up behind him and pulled Deepak's swimsuit down, so he was fully exposed. And it was cold that day. If you catch my drift. Deepak was mortified. Everyone was laughing at him, so he turned around and slugged Nick, who ended up falling into the pool."

"That's right," said AJ. "I remember that. I mean, again we're talking about things that don't stand out at the time, but now I recall that look on Deepak's face when that happened. He was furious. And then Nick ended up dating that girl. Nick was really cruel like that, stealing chicks out from under people."

"Sounds like it," said Plum. "But why was anyone friends with him?"

"Don't get me wrong," said AJ, putting up his hand in protest. "The guy could be a lot of fun. He was hilarious, in fact. Just thought I should tell you about the dark side."

"Thanks for letting us know," said Juan Kevin.

"You won't quote us on this, right?" asked AJ. "It's all discreet?"

"Of course," said Plum confidently. "I hope you enjoy the rest of your stay."

"Thanks. A couple more days then back to the grind," said AJ. He took a bite of his paella.

"Yes, back to work," sighed Lila. "My travelogue here is *finito*. I've posted everything there is to know about Las Frutas. My followers are really psyched."

"Did you write up a story?" asked Plum.

"No, my followers don't have time for that. I just post pics of me with cute backdrops. Take a few snaps of the food," said Lila, motioning towards her empty plate.

"Did you go to journalism school?"

"No."

"Photography school?"

"No. But I'm like, educated. I went to college. Being an influencer is a skill. Lots of people try to do it and bomb. You really need to tap into your fans' psyches," said Lila patronizingly.

Plum felt her anger rise. This fake journalism was destroying the entire publishing industry.

"And are you getting likes on your Las Frutas posts?"

"Yes, I took a picture of AJ's paella ten minutes ago and already have four thousand likes. And everyone is asking where I got this cute dress I'm wearing."

"I see," was all Plum could say.

Lila's eyes slid up Plum's body, and she added, "I really think you should check out my site. I believe you could really benefit from my advice and clothing sources. We carry some extra-large clothes as well."

"I'll definitely check it out," said Plum. It took all of her self-control not to throw her drink in Lila's face.

CHAPTER

17

PLUM AND JUAN KEVIN LEFT the bar and were en route to the parking lot when she realized she had left her shawl at the table. Juan Kevin said he would bring the car around while she retrieved it. She returned to her table and saw it squashed under the quaggy thighs of a middle-aged woman with stringy, jet-black hair and unbecoming makeup who had taken her seat. After negotiating its recovery with the inebriated woman, Plum made a note to ask Lucia for a good dry-cleaning service.

The stars were out and the moon a white sliver in the sky, but apart from the glittering skylights, it was quite dark. Plum was walking down the stone path toward the parking lot when a figure stepped out from the shadows and blocked her way. She found herself staring into Martin Rijo's belligerent face. She could smell the alcohol fumes his body was emitting and took a small step backward.

"You're not going to survive here if you keep doing what you're doing," he warned, jabbing a stubby finger in her face.

"I'll keep that in mind," she said, adopting a light tone that belied her fear. She scanned behind him to see if per chance Juan Kevin had not yet reached the car, but there was only darkness.

"There are rules in Paraiso. And rulers. I'm a ruler, and I make the rules. You should remember that. I'm a true-blooded Rijo," he said, before leaning over and spitting on the ground.

"Got it," said Plum. Her heart was racing, but she dared to be brazen. "Lots of people think you killed Nick."

"Who thinks that?" he demanded.

"People. His friends. You were seen in a fight with Nick because he was with Carmen."

He cackled. "I'll have to talk to his friends about that. They shouldn't be slandering me. They don't know what they're dealing with."

"Maybe you shouldn't be harassing your stepmother."

"She's no mother of mine. Carmen is bad news. Everyone in her camp, bad news. You probably think our director of security, Mr. Big Man, is a good guy. That's a joke."

"Juan Kevin?" she asked with surprise.

Martin came very close to her again. She could feel his breath. "You think I'm dangerous? Juan Kevin puts me to shame. Word of advice, stay away from him. He's not what you think."

"I'll keep that in mind," said Plum.

"You don't know about the ex-wife, do you?"

Plum hated to admit ignorance. "Of course, I know all about her," she lied.

"Then you know what kind of man he is."

Martin snorted before giving her a last look with his narrowed eyelids and heading toward the bar. Plum exhaled.

"It took you some time. Did you find it?" asked Juan Kevin when she entered his car.

"Find what?" she asked.

"Your shawl," he said and put the car into drive.

"Yes. It was submerged."

Juan Kevin began analyzing the latest information they had learned that evening. Plum didn't want to reveal her interaction with Martin and had to admit he had gotten under her skin. She sat as far away from Juan Kevin as possible and snuck small glances at him. What had Martin meant by saying Juan Kevin was dangerous? What exactly happened with his ex-wife? She realized she had put complete trust in this person she barely knew. And she had been foolish enough to put herself in the vulnerable position of being alone in a car with him. (She forgot that she often was alone in cars with men when she took Ubers in New York.) She couldn't let on about what Martin had told her. Maybe *Juan Kevin* had murdered Nick and was keeping her close to find out everything she knew?

"You're very quiet," he said after a few minutes.

"Just tired. Sunburnt. You know, ready for bed," she rambled.

"Yes, it's been a long day."

"Very."

She could not have fled his car faster. She thanked him for dinner then rushed into the town house, locking the door behind her. She went to her bedroom, tore off her dress, lathered herself up with more aloe, and put on a nightgown. When she was finally in bed and the initial shock had elapsed, she laughed at herself. Why should she believe Martin? He was the scary one. Plum was being ridiculous. She quickly fell asleep.

❧

The noise was so subtle that Plum might not have roused if she hadn't been having a nightmare about Martin. He had been beckoning her to follow him down a blackened road, telling her to trust him. He led her to a door and slowly turned the knob. Inside the murky room, she discovered Juan Kevin and Carmen in an intimate embrace. Martin cackled wickedly and kept repeating, "I told you so." Juan Kevin motioned for Plum to leave. She tried to, but she couldn't open the door. She woke up in a cold sweat.

Plum glanced about, disoriented. Her heart was pounding, and she was breathing heavily. It took a minute to sink in that it was only a bad dream. (Although, oddly, her rage at Juan Kevin for dismissing her felt very real.) She sat up in bed, her eyes darting around her darkened bedroom, trying to compose herself and calm down. *It was just a nightmare*, she repeated. But then, just as she began to relax, a strong surge of fear enveloped her. Something—no, someone—had woken her up.

Her eyes focused on her bedroom door. She was certain she had left it open when she went to bed. But now it was completely closed. She stared at the knob, her eyes narrowing. It was slowly turning. Someone was either leaving and quietly closing it or... trying to enter! Plum leapt out of bed and scanned the room for something to use as a weapon. She didn't have time to unplug the table lamp, and it would be too clunky to maneuver anyway. Think! She had thrown her stilettos in the back of the closet when they strangled her feet and didn't have time to rummage around for them in order to stab him in the eye with the heel. There must be a potential weapon in her room. If only she had mace or a stun gun, she could spray it at her intruder. Hair spray would do the trick!

Plum slunk into the bathroom and grabbed the can off her vanity. She peeked through the crack in the door and could see her bedroom door open. Someone was coming in. What was the best move? To hide in the bathroom and wait and see if the intruder came in? At this point she figured he could hear her heart beating or the adrenaline coursing through her body. She gripped the can tightly and kept her eyeballs glued to the gap in the door, waiting for the perpetrator to emerge from behind the half-open door. The air felt heavy with anticipation. Plum was choking in fear. Was someone about to jump out and kill her? She waited. It felt endless. Nothing happened.

Why? Plum wondered. Was he lying in wait? Did he see she

wasn't in bed and that made him stop? Plum strained her ear and thought she could discern faint footsteps. Was the intruder calling in reinforcements? Or retreating? Unfortunately, she was charging her phone in the kitchen and was unable to ring for help. And who would she call, Juan Kevin? Could she trust him? She had no idea if she even had neighbors, so to yell out the window for assistance could be futile. Did 911 exist in Paraiso? Plum couldn't live in this suspended terror; she would drop dead of a heart attack before the killer reached her.

Plum slowly crept into her bedroom. She had once been sent to a New Age retreat to do a story on the benefits of yoga and meditation, which she quite honestly dismissed as a waste of time and had only attended because she wanted to visit Nepal, but now she tried to channel the breathing exercises. In and out, she told herself, trying to calm her nerves. She exited her bedroom, her grip on the hair spray can so tight that she thought it might slip out of her sweaty hands. She cocked her head into the living room. The intruder was there. Dressed in all black, in a ski mask, looking like a ninja from a very scary slasher film. Going through her handbag. She didn't think he saw her.

Plum pivoted back to the little hallway off her bedroom and took a deep breath. In and out. The leader of the sanctuary had been a stinky, dreadlocked white guy with body odor and dirty toenails, and she had been convinced that he was a scam. Now she desperately wished she had paid attention to his lecture on channeling warrior energy to overcome predators. She never thought she would need it before, but now she did.

She heard the intruder moving through her living room, opening drawers. What was he looking for? Wouldn't he hit the fancier houses? She was basically living in the most low-income zip code in the resort. Then it hit her: he was after the spy camera. There could be no doubt. The camera that was currently nestled safely under her brassieres, which were stacked according to color and level of fanciness. Needless to say, the less fancy ones got the most rotation.

Plum decided to be brave. And proactive. She couldn't wait for the intruder to come for her. Taking a deep breath, which that sham guru would be proud of, Plum let out a wail that was something between a primal moan and the sound a chicken makes when its neck is broken. Then she rushed into the living room at full force.

The intruder turned around and put his hands up. Plum charged at him and squirted the hair spray into his masked face. The intruder yelped and put his fingers to his eyes. She was about to smash the can on his head when he fell to his knees and spoke.

"Please! Stop! I'm not here to hurt you," he begged before adding, "ah, my eyes!"

"Who are you, and what do you want?" roared Plum in a warrior voice that would make the guru proud.

"Please, help, it's burning. Can you get me water for my eyes?"

"Who are you?"

Plum held the hair spray high, prepared to spritz him again.

"Robert Glover. I'm a private detective. You can check my wallet. It's in my pocket."

"I'm warning you, don't try anything funny. I have a gun," she lied.

"I won't. Please, my eyes are burning."

Bravely, Plum ripped his mask off his head.

"It's you," she said. The man who had come to her office claiming to be Nicholas Macpherson. "What do you want?"

"I was hired to do surveillance on Jason Manger."

"Did you kill Nick Macpherson?"

"No."

"Do you know who did?"

"No."

"How do I know you're telling the truth?"

"Look at my ID. I'm a private detective. I can give you references."

"Who hired you?"

He sighed. "Please have mercy and get me water for my eyes. Then I will tell you everything."

"Fine."

Plum went to the kitchen and got him some water and a dish towel. She also grabbed her cell phone and the largest knife in her butcher's block.

"Once again I want to remind you that I am armed and dangerous," she said, handing him the water and dish towel.

He immediately poured the water in his eyes and dabbed them. "Thank you."

"Now start talking."

"Jonas Adler hired me. His daughter, Kirstie, is Jason Manger's fiancée. Mr. Adler doesn't think very highly of Jason and wanted to make sure he didn't get up to any funny business this weekend. Or if he did, Mr. Adler wanted to make sure that he knew about it so he could call off the engagement. He gave me the names of the groomsmen, and since I don't look like a Deepak Gupta, I pretended to be Nicholas Macpherson."

"Why did you think it would be so easy to get the keys from me?"

"Well, wasn't it? I mean, I didn't even have to say my name. You asked me if I was Nicholas Macpherson, and I said yes."

Plum wanted to state that it was a lie, but she wasn't sure and that irritated her. "Then you put the spy cams in their rooms?"

"Yes. I figured I could monitor and record any action that took place in the bedroom, and at the same time I could follow Jason around the resort and see if he went off with a woman anywhere else."

"Then you broke in to get them back?"

"Yes," he said. "I went to salvage them and was able to get two out of three, but Jason woke up. It was my lucky day when you came and took it off the ceiling. I tracked you here and entered to retrieve it."

"Broke in, not entered."

"It's still entering."

"But illegally."

"That's a technicality."

The line of questioning had become absurd. "Why bother try and retrieve it?"

"It's state-of-the-art equipment. Very expensive."

"But risky. I could have shot you."

"I know. It was a bad idea. But I've just branched out on my own and can't afford to waste any money."

"I see," said Plum. He did sound believable. Definitely inept, but believable.

"Was Jason cheating?"

"No. Didn't even look at another woman."

"So, all for naught."

"Any chance I can get up now? My knees are killing me."

"Let me check your ID first," said Plum. She awkwardly thrust her hand into his pocket, trying to be careful not to touch any part of his anatomy that she would regret, and clasped a wallet. She extracted it and flipped through. There was a driver's license identifying him as Robert Glover as well as a private detective license and some credit cards. He also had business cards with his name and contact information. "You named your company *Poirot Detectives*?" she asked.

"Yeah, catchy, right?"

"I was always a Miss Marple fan," said Plum.

"It was never believable to me that an old woman could solve crimes," said Robert.

"That's sexist! What about Jessica Fletcher and Agatha Raisin?" she snapped.

"Who?"

"Whatever," said Plum. "Why don't you sit on the sofa and tell me everything you saw the night the real Nicholas Macpherson was killed? No detail is too small."

"Do I have a choice?"

"It's either this or I call the police."

18

ALTHOUGH SHE HAD VERY LITTLE sleep after she released her intruder, Plum was wired the next morning when she awoke. Nervous energy was pumping through her veins, along with caffeine from several cups of coffee. She arrived at the office early to work on her publicity pitches so she would be able to continue her investigation later in the day. It remained a conundrum as to how she would coerce Gerald Hand into writing a travel story on Jonathan Mayhew's Caribbean Escapes. She looked up the weather in New York and saw it was in the low thirties with forty-miles-an-hour winds. She decided it would be a good time to impress upon him that a trip to the tropics was a good idea.

"Are you freezing your butt off?" she asked Gerald when he answered the phone.

"Who is this?" he snarled.

"It's Plum. I was thinking about you because I heard it's just awful there today, and it's sunny and gorgeous down here, and I have an amazing villa for you to stay in."

"Desperate."

"Okay, maybe I am. And I want to apologize to you for, you know."

"Elaborate."

"Fine. For firing you. But they made me," she insisted.

"You were gleeful and spiteful."

"True. That was cruel. But I'm a changed person."

"That quickly? I doubt that."

"Let me make it up to you."

"If I come down there and do a big feature on your company, it only benefits you. And I am not feeling particularly charitable right now."

She decided to try a different tactic and remind him that they had once been friends. "Is it that turd Leonard? He was always a loser, jerking you around. It's great to be done with him."

"We're back together."

"How fabulous! Bring Leonard. I'd love to catch up with him."

"You're shameless."

"Determined."

"Goodbye, Plum."

Undaunted, Plum fired off emails to other journalists, updated promotional materials, and reached out to acquaintances she thought might be interested in renting a villa. She had one idea of how to get Gerald to do the story, and although it was a reach, she placed a call that ended hopefully. When she had finished, it was still too early for her colleagues to come rolling in to work, so she sliced up a mango to nibble on and reapplied aloe to her fried skin, which was fortunately showing some improvement. She transferred money from her dwindling bank account to the animal shelter in Long Island and went to their website to look at the pictures of the dogs recently placed in homes. After that, Plum noticed the plant in the corner of the room was drooping, so she gave it a hefty dose of water and snipped off some dead leaves. After draining another cup of coffee, she made a new batch and organized the packs of sugar and stirrers in the basket next to the machine.

It was quite obvious that Plum was at a loss as to what to do with the information Robert Glover had provided. Instinct wanted her to call Juan Kevin and apprise him of the news, but she was conflicted. Firstly, she was very mad at him for embracing Carmen in her dream. It was irrational, but the feelings that dreams elicit *are* rational, and she couldn't deny them. Secondly, Martin's words still rang in her head. What if Juan Kevin was a bad guy? A murderer? And what had happened with his ex-wife? Had he criticized her the way he criticized Plum?

When Lucia entered, Plum was tapping her anxious fingers on the table and appeared jumpy.

"Everything okay?" asked Lucia warily.

"Yes, fine, yes," Plum said quickly.

"Good," said Lucia, turning on her computer. "I brought some *coconetes*, would you like some?"

She held up a box of coconut cookies. Plum took one.

"These are really delicious."

"Have some more," prompted Lucia. "*Coconetes* are our national cookie."

Plum selected another and popped it in her mouth. "I could eat these all day."

"Help yourself."

"I think I'm stress eating."

"Is something wrong?"

"A strange thing happened last night. A man broke into my house. Not just any man, but you know, the man who came here pretending to be Nicholas Macpherson. And it turns out he's a private detective…"

Plum rambled on for a solid minute as Lucia's eyes widened. Finally, she stopped.

"I think you've had a shock," said Lucia calmly. "Maybe you need to see a doctor?"

"No, no, no, I'll be fine. I just, I would call Juan Kevin, but I've been told he's dangerous, and I don't know if I can trust him. Oh, the coffee's ready, would you like some?" Plum said, popping up.

"No, thank you," said Lucia. "Why do you think Juan Kevin is dangerous?"

"Martin told me he was," said Plum, pouring herself a steep cup, adding some condensed milk from the refrigerator and guzzling it down as if she were a junky getting a fix.

"Martin *Rijo*? Why would you ever listen to Martin? He's trouble."

"But why would he say that?"

Lucia sighed, as if debating whether or not to be candid, before deciding to be.

"Because Martin is jealous. Emilio loved Juan Kevin like a son, and Martin saw him as a rival. When Emilio died, Martin tried to have Juan Kevin fired, but Carmen intervened. Even Martin's mother, Alexandra, intervened. Everyone knows Juan Kevin is a good person. He grew up on the island. I've known him since he was a boy."

"What about his ex-wife? Martin implied something sinister happened there."

She wasn't sure if it was her imagination, but she thought a hardness flickered through Lucia's gaze. It quickly dissipated.

"No. Nothing sinister."

"But why did they divorce?"

"I'm not sure," said Lucia. She began to straighten the mail on her desk, intentionally avoiding eye contact.

"Are you not telling me something? You wouldn't keep a secret."

Lucia glanced up. "I would not. I can tell you that the ex-wife was the one who caused trouble and could not be trusted. Juan Kevin behaved in a dignified manner. I would trust him with my life."

"What did the ex-wife do?"

"I really don't like to gossip. But she is not a good person."

"Okay, really? I should call him. Yes, I'll call him," Plum said, taking another sip out of her mug. She was relieved that Juan Kevin's ex-wife was awful.

"You must tell him about the intruder. As director of security, he should know who it was. But one word of advice, if I may?"

"Yes?"

"I don't think you should have any more coffee. I fear it is agitating you."

"You're probably right."

🌿

Plum had arranged to meet Juan Kevin at Casa Mango. When she arrived, she saw he had beaten her there (surprise, surprise, considering her snail-paced cart) and had entered the villa. She put on a wide-brimmed hat to avoid additional sun damage and walked through the now-empty house.

Juan Kevin was standing by the pool. He didn't see her. She paused to study him. He wore his requisite blue blazer and khakis—the sort of effortlessly elegant but simple outfit that was becoming on any man and especially handsome on him. Very handsome. Her emotions confused her. His words had been hurtful and blunt when he accused her of being hurtful and blunt. It was hypocritical and judgmental. And worst of all, he had wounded her pride. It wasn't the first time people had made similar reproaches, and yet his words stung like no one else's had. Why was that? What did she care what a security guard said?

But she did. She had to be honest with herself—she wanted Juan Kevin to regard her with the same affection he reserved for Carmen. Something about him made her want to be a better person. But why? Was it because he was guileless and uncalculating? And nice? Because Lucia seemed to hold him in high esteem? *Whatever, it didn't matter*, she told herself as she looked at him.

Carmen was probably enjoying that body every night, Plum thought. He looked up, as if suddenly aware of her presence, and smiled. She shook herself out of her reverie, put on her most efficient and businesslike air, and approached.

"Your sunburn looks better," said Juan Kevin in a friendly tone. "I like the hat."

"I'm being diligent about my sun protection from now on."

"It was a rookie mistake," he said, smiling.

She wanted to fall into an easy banter but remembered that they were not friends; therefore, it was better to stick to the mission at hand.

"I figured out who the fake Nicholas Macpherson is," she said.

"Who?" asked Juan Kevin eagerly.

Plum filled him in on the private detective Robert Glover, from his breaking into her house to her dramatic apprehension of him and the fact he was working for Kirstie's father. She made sure to dwell on her personal heroics. She doubted Carmen could ever capture an intruder as she did. Juan Kevin listened in astonishment.

"You could have been hurt," he said, his voice awash with concern.

"Yeah, well, I wasn't." She shrugged.

"Still. I'm sorry that you went through that. It's very upsetting."

"I'm fine. I can take care of myself."

"I know you can, but I would have been displeased if something happened to you."

Plum didn't know how to respond, so she immediately fished out Robert Glover's card and gave it to Juan Kevin. He got on his walkie-talkie and asked one of his security men to go to Glover's office and detain him.

"He will be charged with trespassing and criminal mischief. This man cannot operate like this at Las Frutas. I will not allow it."

"Fair enough," she said. "But he did end up being helpful."

"How?"

"Robert said his job was only to watch Jason and make sure he wasn't cheating on his fiancé. After Jason went to bed, Robert then slipped out the back of Casa Mango and saw Nick embracing Leslie Abernathy."

"Definitely Leslie?"

She turned and pointed toward the bushes that bordered Casa Mango and Leslie Abernathy's villa. "Robert Glover said he saw her come through the hedge that bordered the property and watched them kiss right there," she said, pointing to the spot where the grass had been matted on the day they found the deceased.

"And he is sure it was her?" asked Juan Kevin.

"Yes," said Plum with conviction. "He said it was the blond neighbor."

"I need to figure out how to proceed. It's a very big accusation, and Leslie is a homeowner here at Las Frutas. We have specific protocols as to how we engage with them. They have certain privacy rights."

"I understand, but if she was kissing Nick and didn't tell us, that's a big deal. She probably killed him."

"I can't imagine what her motive would be," said Juan Kevin.

"Jealousy," said Plum. "She fancied him and tried to kiss him. Remember, Lourdes told me Leslie told her maid Nina that he shouldn't have rejected her and that it sent her into a rage. Maybe he humiliated her and dismissed her as being, I don't know, too old, or too tall, or too American."

Juan Kevin raised his eyebrows. "Why would being too American be a negative?"

"Some men think American women are too blunt."

He gave her a curious look. "I see. But we must tread lightly. Allow her to do the talking."

"Fine with me."

"Let's go and see what Mrs. Leslie Abernathy has to say for herself," suggested Juan Kevin.

Casa Avocado's housekeeper, Nina, opened the front door and asked them to wait in the living room while she fetched the lady of the villa. She returned a moment later and said Mrs. Abernathy was finishing up a workout with her trainer via Skype, and if they wouldn't mind terribly waiting for ten minutes, she would complete her exercises. They agreed. Nina offered them a beverage, which they refused. Juan Kevin sat down on the oversize yellow sofa and took a phone call from his employee who had evidently found a reluctant Robert Glover and was bringing him in for questioning. At least that was what Plum could glean from hearing only one side of the conversation.

Plum sat down across from Juan Kevin. There were several large books on decor and gardening stacked on the table in front of her, as well as a scrapbook with a picture of Leslie in a bunny suit on the cover. *If it is displayed in public, it must be fair game,* thought Plum, picking it up and leafing through it. With every page she turned, her astonishment grew.

The scrapbook was a collection of news clippings about Leslie, starting from when she was in her teens on the pageant circuit and known as Leslie Shrum. The once-attractive Leslie had pretty, natural facial features and had sported the layered blond hairdo favored by Farrah Fawcett. According to the press, she had been crowned Miss Little Town Rodeo Lady; Miss Wankleman's Grocery Store Gal; Miss Texas Southern County; and Miss Clover Park. There were ample bikini shots and lots of waving. It appeared she had attempted to do more on the state level, but that abruptly ended with a marriage to one Billy Ray Godspeed, a broad-faced young man with sparse hair and wide hips. Despite the fact it appeared that he only possessed one outfit—jeans, denim shirt, and a cowboy hat—his family owned a large cattle ranch in a town Plum had never heard of but was clearly held in local esteem. The wedding had been covered extensively in the hometown newspapers.

But here was where it got curious to Plum: Leslie had included much more bad press in her scrapbook than good press. There were articles on her vicious divorces—from Billy Ray then someone named Ronald Glock and then finally Carl Abernathy, who owned a Chevrolet franchise. The men accused her of infidelity, fraud, blackmail, and embezzlement. There were also articles on her much-publicized relationship with an octogenarian named Syrus Whittlehead, a financial investor, who had apparently died while they were being intimate. His family tried to have Leslie arrested, but it didn't happen. In fact, even in the face of all the accusations, it appeared that Leslie had escaped any sort of prosecution. There was also a gossip column item about Leslie apparently dating a homicidal gangster named Diller the Crook. (*If they were going to the trouble of making a nickname for him,* Plum mused, *why didn't they call him Diller the Killer?*) It seemed that Leslie spent some time in the dark Southern Texas underworld, according to a puff piece in a supermarket weekly, where she gleefully declared that she liked bad boys and kept a gun under her bed. It was confounding to Plum that she had kept all the articles.

When Juan Kevin finished his call, Plum handed him the scrapbook without commentary, and he flicked through it. He gave her a look of amazement and started to speak when Leslie appeared, interrupting them. She was wearing a purple sweat suit and had a white bandanna across her forehead that she could have stolen from Olivia Newton John during her "Physical" days. In one hand was a thermos she was taking dainty sips out of, and in the other hand was a small towel she dabbed on her chest to soak up the beads of sweat.

"Sorry to keep y'all waiting, but I cannot skip my workouts if I want to keep a youthful behind," she said, swatting her own bottom.

"We didn't mean to come over without an appointment…" began Plum.

Juan Kevin quickly put the scrapbook down, which didn't go unnoticed by Leslie.

"Oh, I see you found my vanity book," said Leslie.

"Yes, I am sorry. It was intrusive of me to read it," said Juan Kevin.

"Don't be silly, that's why I leave it out there. Isn't it a hoot? I am proud to say I have lived a very exciting life," she boasted.

"Yes, it appears that way," said Juan Kevin.

"They should make a television miniseries out of my life. It would break all the records."

"But…why do you save the negative press?" asked Plum.

"I don't believe in negative press," said Leslie. She put down her towel and thermos on the coffee table and began doing jumping jacks.

"That's probably a healthy way to look at it," said Juan Kevin.

"It's all in the eyes of the beholder," said Leslie.

"What is?" asked Juan Kevin.

"If something is good or bad," said Leslie.

"Not exactly," said Plum.

"Are any of the things they accuse you of true?" asked Juan Kevin.

"Nothing has been proven," Leslie bragged. She bent down and touched her toes, affording Juan Kevin a close view of her rear.

"Listen, Mrs. Abernathy…"

"Leslie," she said, wagging a finger at him. "After a look at all the duds I married, you can see now why I like to go by my first name. Like Cher. Or Rihanna. It would have been easier if I had a unique name. I was going by Diamond briefly, but that was too pedestrian."

"Leslie," he continued. "We need to ask you a question. It is perhaps indelicate."

"Fire away," she said, picking up her leg and putting it on the back of the chair so she could stretch.

"It seems there is an eyewitness who said you returned with Nick Macpherson to Casa Mango on the night of his murder and were engaged in an embrace with him."

"I wish!" she roared. "But no, that hot stuff only had eyes for Carmen when we were there. I skedaddled home hoping they would end in a biblical situation. Although Carmen said nothing happened. Pity."

Juan Kevin and Plum exchanged quizzical glances. Plum decided to press Leslie.

"Maybe you had been drinking and don't remember?" suggested Plum.

"Nope. I only had two cocks that night. That's my limit on Piñas and Penises night. It gets messy otherwise."

"I can assure you of our discretion," said Juan Kevin, "if perhaps there is a reason you don't want to admit you visited with Mr. Macpherson."

"Honey, if that were the case, it would be all over town. I know I look very young, but I'm not so young anymore, so if I get some nookie—especially from a youngster—the world will know about it. I'm sorry to shock you, but I am not a virgin, and I have no problem with a lady having a fun time. I can tell you with all my Texas truthfulness that I did not go back to Casa Mango with that strapping young man; I did not kiss him; and I never saw him after I left the bar."

CHAPTER

19

"WHAT DO YOU MAKE OF that?" asked Plum when they had left Leslie Abernathy's villa.

"She seems very convincing," said Juan Kevin.

"How can we really tell? The woman doesn't move her face."

"We only have the private detective's word that she was there. He had incentive to lie."

"He wasn't lying."

"He should be at my office shortly; I will interview him myself."

"All right. In the meantime, I must head to the hotel and check in on Jason and Deepak. I just received a text from them demanding my presence."

Suddenly Juan Kevin's phone beeped. He glanced at it. "It appears Jason and Deepak are causing a scene in the lobby of the hotel. I will need to accompany you to intervene."

"I'll meet you there."

The journey to the hotel from Casa Mango was endless in Plum's wimpy little cart. By the time she arrived, Juan Kevin was in place and attempting to control the situation. From what Plum could gather, Kirstie's daddy had come through and had a plane waiting to whisk Jason and Deepak off the island to the safety of his privileged arms. But somehow Captain Diaz had caught wind of the plan and had arrived with his languid deputies to prevent the bachelor party from departing until the case had been solved. Kirstie had apparently thrown a tantrum in the middle of the lobby, and security had been called in. She was still irate when she saw Plum.

"You had better deal with this," she said, pouncing on Plum and wagging a finger in her face.

Kirstie had her long, dark-brown hair tied back in a ponytail and was wearing a crop top and culottes. For such a tiny and super-stylish person, she had a menacing presence. She reluctantly reminded Plum of a younger version of herself.

"How can I help?" asked Plum.

Captain Diaz had been huddled with Juan Kevin and broke away to speak to Plum.

"By order of the Paraison courts, I have forbidden Jason Manger and Deepak Gupta from leaving the island until we have charged someone with the crime of murdering Nicholas Macpherson," said Captain Diaz smugly.

"And I have told this policeman that I am an American, and his orders don't work for me," yelled Kirstie.

Jason came up behind his fiancée. "Hon, let's just calm down."

Jason's "hon" turned around and glared at him. "Don't ever tell me to calm down," she snapped.

"Captain Diaz," said Plum. "Is there any progress on the investigation? Are you about to arrest a killer?"

"A very interesting question," said Captain Diaz.

Everyone paused for him to continue. He did not.

"Perhaps, Captain, you can provide these men with some sort of timeline," offered Juan Kevin. "If you told them how much longer they would be here, it might alleviate some stress."

"They don't have to be here," said Kirstie.

"Yeah, it would be great if you could either arrest us or free us, because we are living in limbo," said Deepak. "I need to return to work."

"We are making inquiries," said Captain Diaz.

"Inquiries?" Kirstie seethed.

"Can't you do better than that?" demanded Jason.

"We are gathering evidence," said Captain Diaz.

Kirstie turned and unleashed her venom on Plum. "These people are idiots. Everything is *mañana* or *tranquilo*. You're an American. You need to get this case solved and get us off the island, or else I will destroy you and your career."

She snapped her fingers, and Jason followed her out to the pool area. Juan Kevin took Captain Diaz aside to talk to him, and Plum was left with Deepak. Hearing Kirstie complain the same way Plum had been complaining left a bitter taste in her mouth. Did she come off that way?

"She's a real piece of work," said Plum.

"Yes. She can't tolerate anything she perceives as laziness or a character flaw," agreed Deepak.

Juan Kevin had accused Plum of having no tolerance for the shortcomings and deficiencies of others—wasn't that the same thing? Plum shuddered to think she resembled Kirstie. Had she behaved that badly?

"Deepak," said Plum. "I've been meaning to talk to you. Let's sit down."

They settled into the wicker armchairs in a quiet corner on the veranda. It was cool in the shade, and there was a light breeze that riffled the potted ferns.

"This is so messed up," said Deepak.

"I know. I have to ask you, why did Nick plan this whole weekend if he didn't want Jason to marry Kirstie?"

"That's not true."

"I've heard from multiple sources that he was planning on sabotaging this wedding."

"I don't know. Maybe it's because Nick didn't believe in marriage or monogamy, but he figured Jason would do well until he divorced her."

"Are you sure Nick wasn't in love with Kirstie? Wanted her to himself?"

"Absolutely not. You've met her, right?"

"Good point. But why would people say that?"

"I have no idea."

"I've always thought you were withholding something from me."

"Like what?" he asked, but she could see something behind his eyes.

"You tell me."

He paused, about to contradict her, but then his shoulders slumped. "We just had a feeling that maybe Kirstie would show up, or her dad. That's why when you asked me if I knew who had broken into our villa, I was kind of weird."

"You're not wrong," said Plum. "He did hire a private detective. That's who impersonated Nick and was snooping around to make sure Jason didn't cheat."

Deepak shook his head. "That's ridiculous, but it doesn't surprise me."

"Is Kirstie capable of murder?"

He looked askance. "Have you seen her? Nick was a big guy. No way. Plus, she wasn't even on the island."

Plum remembered how AJ Thompson and Lila Donovan spoke of Deepak's anger. She had to broach that topic delicately. "Were you upset with Nick?"

"He drove me crazy, but I'm a pretty laid-back guy. And I wouldn't kill my friend, if that's what you're implying."

"Who would you kill?"

He gave her an astonished look. "No one. I'm not a killer."

She had no choice but to confront Deepak. "I have been told

that you were angry at Nick for going after a girl you were hitting on at the bar the night he died."

"First you accuse Nick of being in love with Kirstie and now of chasing someone I liked? You're grasping."

"Is it true?"

"Absolutely not," he attested. Then his eyes narrowed as if considering something, but he only said, "You're barking up the wrong tree."

"Whose tree shall I bark up?"

"You're the amateur detective. You tell me."

He refused to engage any further and immediately left. Plum and Juan Kevin reconvened in the parking lot.

"Every time I think we make a step forward, we move back," said Plum.

"We should probably talk to Carmen again."

"Would you prefer to go alone?" asked Plum.

"No," he said.

"Are you sure?"

"Let's go. Leave your car here."

Plum promised herself she would allow Juan Kevin to do the talking and try not to be controversial.

Carmen's mansion was even more impressive in the daylight, Plum thought as they walked through the house to the backyard. Sunlight streamed into every room in the house, and in the public areas—which were mostly open-walled rooms— the aquamarine sky was the backdrop. Carmen was seated on a lime-green cushioned chaise by her pool, flipping through a glossy fashion magazine. She wore a leopard-print string bikini that barely covered her impressive bosom. A gold necklace with a shiny jet stone dangled between her breasts. When she rose to greet them, she didn't bother to tie a wraparound over her spectacular body, which somewhat riled Plum. She wished she could fetch a hazmat suit for Carmen. Her wish became fervent when Carmen double kissed Juan Kevin hello and clasped his hands tightly.

"It is very nice of you to stop by and say hello," said Carmen.

She offered them lemonade and then returned to lie on her chaise while Plum and Juan Kevin sat next to each other on the chaise next to her.

"Carmen, I have a delicate question," began Juan Kevin.

"You may ask me anything, Juan Kevin."

Perhaps Plum was imagining it, but she thought Carmen was undressing Juan Kevin with her eyes. That said, Carmen was wearing tinted sunglasses, so it was difficult to tell.

"We have been told you returned to the Casa Mango with Nicholas Macpherson and Martin made a scene. Why didn't you tell us that?"

"I didn't?"

"No," said Juan Kevin.

"It was very terrifying, so I think I wanted to forget it. Yes, we went back to have a nightcap, and then Martin came—Juan Kevin, he is ruining my life. He follows me. He taunts me…"

Her voice became choked with tears. Juan Kevin handed her a handkerchief, and she slid off her sunglasses to dab the yet-to-be-manifested tears. Plum couldn't decide if she was more startled by the fact that Juan Kevin carried a real handkerchief (who does that?) or by the fact Carmen was again turning on the waterworks to garner sympathy.

"I know he does," said Juan Kevin. "I'm sorry."

"Thank you," she said. "He deprives me of any joy. Not that I would be joyful with my beloved Emilio no longer in this world, but I strive for small happinesses. But it was not to be. Martin appeared, yelled, and made a scene, and Nick drove me back to my car. I am cursed…"

"You can't think that," said Juan Kevin.

Plum glanced around the expensive compound that could

house an entire village and wanted to refute this lady's claim of being cursed. But she kept her mouth shut.

"Long ago I met a woman who read my coffee grinds. She told me there would be very big highs and very big threats to me. She said to beware of the evil eye. I wear this *resguardo* to ward them away, but it doesn't help," she said, lifting the stone part of her necklace.

"I am sorry you feel under threat," said Juan Kevin.

Plum wanted to roll her eyes.

"Thank you so much for your tenderness, your caring," she said sweetly. "I only hope one day that Martin will leave me in peace and I can dream of happiness and a future."

A young, uniformed maid with a pleasant, round face came and placed a tray of cookies on the side table. Plum excitedly noted they were *coconetes* like the ones Lucia made. Carmen glanced down at them, and all at once her face morphed from sweet victim to angry devil. She began berating the maid in Spanish and picked up the tray and threw it at her. The cookies all went scattering. The maid started crying and bent down to gather the cookies as quickly as possible. It all happened in Spanish and so fast that Plum had no idea what had ensued.

"What's going on?" asked Plum. "Are you on a diet?"

Juan Kevin was speaking rapidly in Spanish, trying to calm Carmen down and console the maid. Finally, some sort of truce was brokered, and the maid slipped away with the discarded cookies, and Carmen sat down, steaming.

"What was that all about?" asked Plum.

"She tried to kill me," said Carmen. "No doubt she works for Martin."

"Kill you with carbs?" asked Plum.

Carmen's face became vicious. "I am very allergic to coconut. I touch it, I die. My staff has been given strict instructions, and this new maid brings me this?"

"Carmen, she didn't know. She said it was her first day, and she was so proud to bring you cookies that her mother made as thanks for the employment," said Juan Kevin.

Carmen appeared unmoved. "Her employment will be terminated."

There was an awkward silence, and Plum knew that Juan Kevin would use it as an excuse to leave even though there were still more questions to ask of Carmen. But he surprised her.

"Carmen, what did you think of Nick's friends when you met them at the bar? Did he speak of any tension?" asked Juan Kevin.

Carmen shook her head. "No. But I didn't particularly care for the Indian one."

"Deepak?" asked Plum.

"I don't know his name. He was very disapproving of me, I could tell. His aura was condescending."

"How so?" asked Juan Kevin.

"It just was. It is very hard for me. Everyone wants something or judges me. I have a very difficult time. Life is hard for me."

A look of bitter amusement came across Juan Kevin's face. "Carmen, you cannot be serious. I've known you since you were little, and life was much harder for you then. Come on."

Carmen turned and slid off her sunglasses to glare at Juan Kevin. "I need to rest now. This has been a big scare. Please show yourselves out."

He paused before acquiescing. "Of course."

Carmen returned to her magazines.

Plum was amazed that Juan Kevin had confronted Carmen, albeit in his low-key Juan Kevin way. Maybe he could finally see the cracks? The temptation to criticize Carmen was low-hanging fruit, and Plum decided she would not initiate the conversation unless Juan Kevin did. When they were securely in his car and had left the gated estate, Juan Kevin finally spoke.

"That was a side of Carmen that has not been revealed to me

before," he said. Although he was addressing her, he kept his gaze firmly ahead.

Several catty responses flooded Plum's head, but she bit her tongue. She didn't want to be the one to point out Carmen's shortcomings. "Oh, really?" she asked with feigned casualness.

"Yes," he said. "I never knew her to be…cruel like that. I did not like the way she addressed her maid."

Plum sighed and shifted in her seat. "I felt bad for the girl. Not to mention, those cookies are actually delicious."

"Carmen seems to have forgotten who she was and from where she comes."

"Most people try to do that," said Plum, thinking of her depressing childhood and her indifferent parents. For some people, forgetting where they came from was the only way they could survive.

"It's acceptable if they do it as a way to improve themselves. But not if they do it to demean others."

He didn't continue, and Plum decided not to press him. But she did feel a tiny bit vindicated.

A quick call to Lucia revealed that nothing was happening in the office, so Plum was in no rush to return. Plum and Juan Kevin had agreed to interview Robert Glover, and they made their way to Juan Kevin's office. It was a small, cream building with a Spanish-tiled roof situated on an impeccably landscaped plot between the hotel and the entrance to the resort. There were clusters of *coralillo* bushes lining the entrance, with their showy, reddish-orange flowers in bloom.

Inside, the atmosphere was clean but sterile. There was the requisite damp smell that imbued even the most corporate of workplaces in the tropics. Modern, white desks were arranged neatly with matching chairs and sleek laptop computers. Juan Kevin had a separate office visible through a glass picture window. The ceiling was stucco, like cottage cheese that someone had stabbed. Framed aerial photographs of Las Frutas adorned one wall, and opposite it hung a large resort map pockmarked with pushpins.

"Air-conditioning?" exclaimed Plum when she entered. "You are too fancy."

"Never let them see you sweat," he joked.

The office was empty except for an attractive young woman with large, brown eyes and an agreeable face who sat at the first desk. She wore a tailored blue suit, and her dark hair was tucked behind a headband. Delicate gold hoops dangled from her ears.

"Patricia Martinez, Plum Lockhart from Jonathan Mayhew's office," said Juan Kevin.

After pleasantries were exchanged, Juan Kevin asked her where Robert Glover was.

"He went with Captain Diaz," she responded.

"Captain Diaz?" asked Juan Kevin. "But we were to interview him."

A worried look flashed across her face. "The police charged him with trespassing."

"No one was supposed to call the police until I spoke with him," said Juan Kevin sternly.

"A misunderstanding," said Patricia. "I'm sorry."

"What do we do now?" asked Plum.

Juan Kevin shook his head. "Not sure. I don't want to go to the police station now. Captain Diaz won't allow me to speak with him until he's been processed, which could take hours."

"I'm sure," agreed Plum.

"I'll go on my way home from work."

"You don't live at the resort?" asked Plum with surprise.

"No," he said. "I live in Estrella."

"Interesting."

"Why is that interesting?" he asked.

"I don't know. I guess it's not. I just assumed."

"Paraiso is a big island. Despite its vastness, Las Frutas can feel very small if you both work *and* live here. I prefer to have my independence and a life away from the resort."

Plum wanted to press further about what that meant, but Patricia was waiting expectantly at her desk, so Plum decided to drop it for now.

"All right, well, if you don't mind dropping me back at my loaner cart at the hotel, I'll head back to the office."

"I can take you," said Patricia. "I'm heading to the post office."

"Thank you," said Plum. "Juan Kevin, let me know if anything comes up. *And* what happens when you interview Robert Glover."

On the ride with Patricia, Plum tried to casually elicit information about Juan Kevin. She secretly hoped Patricia would tell her how he had been talking about a new American redheaded beauty who had moved to Paraiso. Or at least that she'd reveal something about his ex-wife. But unfortunately, Patricia was very professional and offered little information other than to extol his praises and say that he was a very efficient and fair boss. Plum was slowly gleaning that Paraisons were discreet by nature, which was currently irritating.

CHAPTER

20

THE FOLLOWING MORNING, PLUM WOKE early. She had forgotten to close the blinds, and the sun was streaming through the window and puddling on her bed. It promised to be another glorious day. She made coffee and toast with guava jam and breakfasted on her balcony as she watched the sun ascend in the sky. The air was clear and fresh, and Plum couldn't help but compare it to the polluted sludge she had inhaled for years living in New York. Surely this was a more wholesome and salubrious lifestyle.

After applying plenty of sunblock, Plum donned a floral dress with a cinched waist and slipped on wedged sandals. She had been waging a battle with her fake eyelashes, which were desperate to melt off in this climate, so she decided to pull them off for now. She blinked and thought her eyes didn't look so bad. Her hair was still a problem, and after a half-hearted attempt with the straightening iron, she surrendered and let it go free. A spin in the mirror met with her approval. It was strange. She had always hated her curly hair. But now it didn't really bother her. It actually looked okay.

Plum drove her slow cart down to work. It was early enough that very few people were venturing to the beach. It was mostly joggers, bikers, and landscape workers dotting the scenery. On impulse, she decided to take the scenic route and wander around lanes that were not on her direct route. She still hadn't mastered the network of roads and neighborhoods within the resort and felt compelled to familiarize herself with them.

She glided by villas in all shapes and sizes and wondered if she would ever live in one. That is, if she decided to stay at Paraiso. They were expensive, but perhaps if she wrangled more business for the firm, she would do well enough with her commissions. Although she remembered what Juan Kevin said about not making Las Frutas his entire life and thought there might be some merit to that. Most professionals didn't reside in their place of work. There was a separation of church and state for a reason, and it could be something she needed to consider.

Plum began playing a game with herself that she hadn't played in years. As she cruised along the sunny lanes, she pretended she was picking out a villa where she would live with her family. She had done this when she was on the school bus during her miserable childhood. It had helped her ignore the fact that she was sitting alone, friendless, on a journey that would not end in a welcome in either direction. She had watched her classmates leave their cozy homes, embarrassed that their mother had kissed them goodbye or that their father had waved to them, while she had burned with envy. In her irrational mind, she thought that maybe it was the dingy house that had made her family so gloomy. So, she had fantasized.

She came to a stop in front of a two-story, white house. It wasn't the largest or fanciest house in the neighborhood, but Plum was instantly struck by how much she liked it. Every window was framed by light-mint shutters, and the front door was the same color. All the greenery flanking the house accentuated the whiteness of the manor. It was tropical and whimsical and, most of all, happy. That was what Plum wanted. Before, it had been to get to the top of her profession and amass tons of money. But being happy seemed a better goal. Plum sat gazing at the villa, lost in thought, until someone called her name, and she was brought back to the present.

"Vicki Lee Lockhart? Is that you?"

She squinted at the man coming toward her, who had exited the house of her fantasies. He was vaguely familiar but in a generic way, as if he had been her accountant or one of the suits in the Mosaic Publishing corporate office. His light-brown hair was swept neatly to the side in a way one of the Brady Bunch boys might wear (Bobby or Peter—not Greg; pre-hippie years) and he had horn-rimmed glasses framing his eyes. He was plain but not unattractive; the smile on his face definitely improved his appearance.

As he grew closer and leaned into her golf cart, his identity dawned on her with increasing horror.

"Brad Cooke?" she asked.

He laughed. "Yes! Wow, it's been too long! What are you doing here?"

"I live here."

"You do? Last I heard you had some big publishing job in the city."

"I did, but I decided it was time to step off the corporate ladder for a while, take a break. I was offered a job here for a ridiculous amount of money, I just couldn't say no. It would have been foolish."

"That's great!" he said.

A preppy, blond woman in a smock dress came out of the house with a baby in her arms and walked down the path toward Brad and Plum. She had blue eyes, a smattering of freckles on her nose, and her hair held back in a green headband.

"This is my wife, Meredith, and my daughter, Winnie," he said, turning to the woman. "Meredith, this is Vicki Lee Lockhart."

"It's actually Plum Lockhart now. I went back to the name my parents had originally intended for me," lied Plum. She had repeated that story so many times that it felt like a truth to her.

"Oh, right, I guess I heard that," said Brad.

"Nice to meet you," said Meredith. She turned to her husband. "Is this the woman I've been hearing about for all these years?"

"Yes, can you believe it? This is her!"

Plum's stomach instantly dropped, and she wanted to press the accelerator on her cart, mow them down, and flee the scene. She wanted carnage. The only thing stopping her was that the sluggish cart didn't have enough horsepower, and she would probably only sprain Brad's ankle before she was taken into custody. She could not believe that, after all these years, Brad Cooke would still be bad-mouthing her to his perfect wife, no doubt listing Plum's deficiencies and maintaining that it was she who had thrown the gum in his hair.

"I didn't throw the gum in your hair," Plum insisted.

He smiled. "Of course, I know that. It was all a ruse."

Plum sat up straighter. He was mocking her. "I suffered greatly because of those false accusations."

He appeared taken aback. "I'm sorry," he said with warmth.

"It was Mandy Garabino."

His eyebrows shot up. "I know it was. I asked her to tell you I liked you, and she got jealous and framed you."

"What?"

"Yeah, you were the elusive hot girl everyone wanted to date, but you wouldn't talk to anyone," said Brad.

"It's all I heard about when I met Brad and his high school friends: Vicki Lee," said Meredith. "You're a local celebrity up there."

"I am?" squeaked Plum. This couldn't be; it was revisionist history. She was an outcast. She'd been ridiculed and ostracized.

"Yeah, you never gave us the time of day," said Brad. "It's really good to finally talk to you."

"You too," squeaked Plum. This conversation was surreal. Was she dreaming?

"Funny that here we both are in a foreign country."

"And this is your house?"

"Yes, we live in Chicago, but Meredith used to come here as a kid, so we bought a house with her parents. It stands empty most of the time, but we try and come down when we can."

"Well, if you ever want to rent it, I'm in the biz," said Plum.

"Really? That's not a bad idea. We'd have to run it by Meredith's parents—they own it with us—but do you have a card?" said Brad.

"Sure," said Plum, slipping one out of her handbag.

"Thanks," said Brad. "It's really great to see you. We are heading out tomorrow, but next time we're in town, let's have dinner."

"If you'll deign to dine with us," added Meredith warmly.

"Of course. I would love that," said Plum.

When Plum reached her office, she was in a complete daze. How could she not have known that people regarded her with anything other than revulsion? Had she really been so clueless? Oh, how she wished to have a chance to do it all over again and repeat high school with this knowledge. She laughed at herself; that was something she never thought she would wish in a million years. It felt strange to reflect upon her past with a different lens.

Jonathan Mayhew strode through the office after Plum had been sitting at her desk for an hour doing very little, if she were to be honest with herself. He had on his customary white suit, a dapper pink-and-blue shirt underneath.

"Any update?" he asked by way of greeting.

"Working on it," she replied. Did he really have no faith in her? Just having her be part of his agency added status to this Podunk operation. He should be grateful.

"I hope you are," he said in a tone that meant he had lost faith.

"I am. Also, I have a lead on a new property. They may be interested in renting. It's a very nice house near the beach."

"Excellent," said Jonathan.

Damián arrived in time to hear what Plum was saying. "Tell me which house. I'll deal with it."

"No, thanks."

"Your track record is terrible. I think you may want to shadow me so I can show you how it is done."

"I'd rather drop dead."

"I thought that's what you wanted your clients to do?" he asked.

She was interrupted by a phone call. Juan Kevin said that Tony Spira the golf pro had reached out to him, and he was heading to the driving range to catch up with him. It was a perfect excuse for Plum to exit the office and avoid murdering Damián. He might have been right; there hadn't been any homicide at Las Frutas until she had arrived. But at the rate he was going, he just might be the next victim.

When Plum arrived at the pro shop, she was told by the caddy master that Tony and Juan Kevin were in the café that overlooked the golf course. It was a small, dark-paneled room in which the bar featured prominently. She glanced at the variety of beer on tap and the rows of liquor (especially tequila) and ascertained quickly that the food was secondary to the booze. The café had panoramic views of the golf course and hung over the ledge of the eighteenth hole. This setting put enormous pressure on the players, whose last opportunity to sink the ball would be in front of a gallery of spectators—potentially drunk ones, at that.

Plum found the men sitting at a table for four, two sweating iced teas in front of them. They rose when she approached.

"Are you leaving?" asked Plum.

Juan Kevin looked at her askance and pulled out her chair. She was so unused to the gesture that she sat down quietly.

"I hope you don't mind if I eat while we talk; it's my lunch hour. I'm slammed with lessons for the rest of the day," explained Tony.

"No problem, I'm actually hungry as well," said Plum.

"Likewise," said Juan Kevin.

The waitress came, and Plum ordered a Diet Coke and a Greek salad with grilled chicken. Juan Kevin asked for a medium-rare cheeseburger, and Tony Spira opted for a tuna sandwich with a side of french fries and Russian dressing. Plum decided to change her order and asked for a Paraison specialty, the beef with white rice and stewed beans.

"I want to be discreet, but something strange is going on," began Tony as soon as the waitress left.

"What's that?" asked Juan Kevin.

"This morning I was coming to work, and I saw Jason Manger outside the hotel. He was standing with a woman he introduced as his fiancée, Kirstie Adler. He said she had just arrived from New York."

"Yes, we know that," said Plum.

"What's odd is that I could swear I saw the woman—Kirstie—a couple of days ago."

"What do you mean?" asked Juan Kevin.

"After I had played golf with Jason, Deepak, and Nick, they headed to the locker room to change their shoes, shower, have a beer, whatever. As soon as they went inside, I heard someone trying to start a golf cart behind me. It kept stalling, so I could tell the engine was draining. I went over to the cart—it was off to the side under the tree—and I offered to help the woman. I'm pretty used to these carts by now, living here three years, and I know their tricks."

"They're horrible," said Plum.

"Yeah, finicky vehicles. Anyway, she didn't really say anything, but I got the cart started, and she thanked me and left in a hurry. I didn't think anything of it until I met Kirstie with Jason. I'm sure it was her that I helped."

"Are you positive?" asked Juan Kevin.

"Yes, pretty positive. I mean, I was next to her in the car for a solid two minutes. She was wearing a big sun hat and sunglasses, which obviously is not unusual at Las Frutas, and she didn't turn to face me. I thought nothing of it, but now I'm thinking maybe she didn't want me to be able to recognize her."

"What about when Jason introduced you to her?"

"She waved at me sideways and then took off to oversee her luggage or check in. At first, I didn't place her, but if she had stuck around, I would have for sure said, 'Hey, you look familiar,'" Tony replied.

The waitress brought them their food, and Plum tucked into her dish. It was hearty and satisfying, and she was glad that she wasn't spearing a piece of dried-out chicken on a lettuce leaf.

"When you saw Kirstie in the golf cart the first time, did she have golf clubs?" asked Juan Kevin.

"No. I mean, it wasn't one of the carts that we use for the course, those are green. It was one that guests use to go to their rooms and the beach. A white one."

"And did she seem agitated? Or upset?" asked Juan Kevin.

"A little, but I thought it was frustration over the cart stalling."

"Did she have a camera or anything?" asked Plum. She pictured Kirstie with one of those long-lens cameras for spies.

"I didn't see one," said Tony, dipping his sandwich into the Russian dressing. "But then, people use their phones to take pictures these days."

"True," replied Plum.

"Did you get the impression the guys knew she was there?" asked Juan Kevin.

"I don't think so. Not at all."

"And looking back, do you think she was following you around the course?" asked Plum.

"I doubt it. We would have seen the resort cart on the golf

course path. All I can say is that she was there. She didn't arrive from New York a couple of days later. She was somewhere here in the resort, keeping an eye on her man."

After they ate, Tony rushed off for a lesson, and Plum and Juan Kevin remained to have coffee.

"What did Robert Glover say when you stopped by the station?" asked Plum. She poured milk into her mug and swirled it with her spoon.

"You're not going to believe this—well, actually you are going to believe this because I know you think disparagingly about the way we do business here in Paraiso. But there had been some sort of miscommunication, and Robert Glover was moved to a holding cell in Diego, the closest city to the west. It was completely out of my way, and I was almost home. I will check back with him when he is moved to Estrella."

"What a mess," said Plum. "I can't deal with inefficiency."

"I know how you feel about it," he said. "But I will talk to Robert Glover as soon as possible."

"I guess it's not urgent," said Plum. "What do you think about Kirstie?"

"I think we should go to the welcome center and see if they have her on file. As you will recall, they scan the passport and take a photograph of everyone who enters the resort. There is no way she could have come in without documentation."

"Good idea."

CHAPTER

21

THEY WERE DRIVING ALONG THE road that hugged the coastline when Juan Kevin abruptly stopped.

"What's wrong?" asked Plum.

"Turtle crossing," responded Juan Kevin.

"What? I don't see anything."

"You have to know where to look."

They exited the car, and Plum did indeed see a turtle making its way across the street. Juan Kevin quickly lifted the turtle out of the road to safety.

"She must be lost, so I'm sending her back to the beach," said Kevin.

They watched as the turtle made her slow journey through the bushes toward the sea.

"We have four species of turtle on our island," Juan Kevin explained when they returned to their drive. "The loggerhead, the green sea turtle, the hawksbill turtle, and the leatherback turtle. They are all endangered, sadly. All species are recording only thirty female births a year. We are doing everything we can to help them. In Paraiso, we believe in wildlife preservation as much as possible."

"Funny, I never even thought about wildlife in New York," said

Plum. "Except for those summer nights when all the mice and rats are out and scurrying across the subway platforms."

"I doubt the cars stop for them."

"No, they put their pedal to the metal to squash them."

The welcome center was situated in a grove of mahogany trees to the right of the Las Frutas Resort entrance gates, about thirty yards from the security booth. A large portico provided the entrance to the white stone building. Inside there was a sleek marble counter behind which sat three employees in white shirts and blue blazers. They immediately stood up at attention when Juan Kevin walked in and greeted him with deference.

"I need to access the computer. I want to see the pictures of the women who have entered the resort the past week."

"Yes, sir," said a tall, handsome security guard whose name tag said *Antonio*.

They went into a back office equipped with a desk, a computer, and two chairs. Antonio signed in but proved to be a painfully slow typist, so Juan Kevin asked him to cede the chair and took over the computer. Plum pulled the other chair up next to Juan Kevin, and Antonio leaned over his shoulder.

"It's okay, Antonio, I've got this," said Juan Kevin.

"Okay, sir," he said, before reluctantly departing the office.

Juan Kevin moved quickly, clicking through everyone at a brisk pace. Plum was amazed at how many people passed through the resort during a given week.

"Where do they all stay?" she asked.

"Don't forget that many are day-trippers coming off the cruises," he said.

"And you check them all in?"

"Of course, we need to keep track of everyone at the resort. That's why I was so agitated that there had been an intruder. I run a tight ship. I don't want people getting murdered or having their villas broken into. Leave that to the resorts on the other side of the island."

Plum felt as if she were watching an ad for the United Nations. The faces of guests of every race, color, and age zoomed past her. Juan Kevin stopped when he reached a picture of a youngish brunette.

"Is that her?" he asked.

Plum squinted. It looked a little like Kirstie, but the nose was off. "No."

Juan Kevin continued through to the end of the list, which stopped abruptly with a photograph of a heavyset woman with orange hair.

"Could I have missed it?" said Juan Kevin.

"You did go really fast."

He started again from the beginning, this time pausing on each picture before he clicked through. It took fifteen minutes. Once again, they reached the end of the list without success.

"How could this be?" asked Plum.

Juan Kevin looked pensive. "The only thing I can think of is that she arrived by helicopter. We ask the control tower at our heliport to take everyone's pictures, but sometimes they refuse. It's usually just friends of the Rijo family, celebrities, or very important people who arrive that way, and they can intimidate my staff. It's possible that she refused to have her picture taken."

"Maybe her very important daddy arranged it."

"Yes," said Juan Kevin. "And she has just the personality to growl at someone and have them back off."

"Can we go there and ask them?"

"We can, but at this point maybe we're better off going directly to Kirstie and confronting her."

"I don't think she'll fess up. We need something on her."

Juan Kevin paused. "I can cross-reference the names with the hotel bookings and eliminate those guests. I somehow don't think she was staying in the hotel, though, if she were hiding. She was probably renting a villa. And as you know, all renters and villa brokers have to register their guests and clients. I will check those lists and see whose name was registered yet wasn't photographed."

"Good idea," said Plum.

He began typing on the computer, and Plum wandered over to the window while he worked. There were two hummingbirds buzzing around the bush, interacting with one another as if they were in conversation. She wished she could understand what they were conveying to each other.

"Interesting," said Juan Kevin finally.

Plum turned around. "What?"

"You're not going to believe it."

"I believe anything these days."

"There's one person I found who did not check in but rented a villa this week. It's a man, though."

"So not our girl Kirstie."

He smiled. "Not necessarily. The villa was rented to Jonas Adler. Kirstie's father. He paid for it, but she is the one who stayed here, obviously."

"Wow. We need to talk to her."

"There's more," said Juan Kevin.

"What's that?"

"The person who rented her the villa was Damián Rodriguez from Jonathan Mayhew Caribbean Escapes."

"That little slimeball."

They called Jason to find out his whereabouts and caught a lucky break when he grunted that he was in the gym and Kirstie was taking a yoga class. It was fortuitous, as they had wanted to interview Kirstie alone.

"I didn't even know there was a yoga center here," said Plum when they drove out of the welcome center.

"Oh yes, it's a big deal. It's in a palapa at the very end of the beach."

"A what?" she asked.

"Palapa is Spanish for 'petiole of the palm leaf.' It's an open-sided dwelling with a thatched roof made of dried palm leaves."

"Is that conducive to yoga?"

"I think the goal is to inspire the practitioners with nature and the sea."

"I can't relate."

"No?"

"Yoga is too pretentious for me. I hate all those people walking around with rolled-up mats and thermoses full of coconut water."

"What type of exercise do you prefer?"

"None."

He laughed. "Well, you obviously don't need to do a thing to look perfect."

Plum's face flushed, but she didn't say anything.

When they arrived at the beach parking lot, Juan Kevin took a sharp left turn down a sandy road that Plum had not noticed before. It was unmanicured, unlike the rest of the resort, and looked more like it was utilized by service vehicles. But when they reached the end of it and walked down a small path, they saw other carts and cars parked. Plum noted that they were fancier carts and cars.

"In my personal experience, the yoga practitioners who come to Las Frutas are the more aggressive guests," said Juan Kevin before adding, "but no judgment."

The palapa had a thatched roof and a 360-degree view of the Caribbean and mountains. It was at the end of a long, wooden walkway over the sea. As they moved closer, Plum saw that there were about fifteen spandex-clad women with rippling arm muscles clenching their faces tightly and chanting *om*. A pretty, blond teacher with pigtails was leading them in their practice.

"Let's wait until they're done," advised Juan Kevin. "They're at Savasana."

"Sava-what?" asked Plum.

"Savasana. It's the final pose. Otherwise known as the corpse pose."

"How appropriate."

The women played dead for another five minutes before sitting up, bowing to their pigtailed leader and rising. Plum spotted Kirstie in the front. She was wearing a purple tank top and languidly rolling up her yoga mat. They waited until the other women passed by before approaching Kirstie.

"Miss Adler, may we have a word with you?" asked Juan Kevin.

Kirstie glanced up and rolled her eyes when she realized who was addressing her.

"What is it?"

"We have a few questions," said Plum.

Kirstie jutted out her hip and put her arm on it. "What do you want?"

"We would like to know..." began Juan Kevin before he was interrupted by Pigtails.

"Namaste, Juan Kevin!"

"Namaste, Gigi," he said.

The perky yoga teacher looked at him adoringly with her blue eyes. Plum gave her a once over and was disappointed to find that she had nary a wrinkle or hair out of place.

"I'm Plum Lockhart."

"Gigi Cabrese. Are you interested in yoga?"

"Not in the least. We just need to talk to Kirstie."

"All right," Gigi said, not making a move.

"Alone," said Plum.

"Oh, sorry," said Gigi, quickly moving away to pack her things.

"I don't have all day," said Kirstie with impatience.

"Neither do we," countered Plum.

"We want to know why you were staying at the resort this week," said Juan Kevin.

"What are you talking about?" she asked.

"Don't play dumb," said Plum. "We have proof."

Kirstie hesitated, obviously weighing her options. "What proof?"

"Your father rented a villa for the week," said Plum.

"So?" Kirstie asked.

"You were seen here by a member of the resort staff," said Juan Kevin.

"Who?" asked Kirstie.

"It's not important," said Juan Kevin. "We want to know why you were here and why you didn't tell us."

Kirstie stared at them. "I don't have to tell you anything."

"Does Jason know you were here?" asked Plum.

Kirstie wagged her finger at Plum. "It's none of your damn business."

She turned and stormed away.

"Can we stop her?" asked Plum.

"Technically, no. She's right; she doesn't need to tell us anything."

"Let's go talk to Damián," said Plum.

When Plum called Lucia to see if Damián was in the office, she was told he was on site, overseeing the pool repair at Casa Ciruela Pasa, one of the properties that he managed. Juan Kevin knew where it was, so they headed over.

"What does *ciruela pasa* mean?" asked Plum.

"It means prune."

"That's a terrible name for a villa. You might as well name it Casa Diarrhea."

"Prunes get a bad reputation," said Juan Kevin.

"For a reason."

Casa Ciruela Pasa was located on a small lot by the heliport. It was on a quiet street and was the standard, white house with Spanish-tiled roof. This one was charmless. Several trucks and Damián's car were parked in the driveway. They pressed the doorbell, but there was no answer.

"We know he's here," said Plum.

"Let's go around back," said Juan Kevin.

They unlocked the gate to the backyard and walked through to the pool area. Latin music was playing loudly. Two men were cleaning the pool while another washed the deck. Damián was sunbathing in his swimming trunks, doused in oil, lounging on a chaise. He had a soda next to him and was chatting on his cell phone. He quickly finished his call when he saw Juan Kevin and Plum and shot up.

"This is where you go during the workday?" asked Plum contemptuously.

"I'm working," he said, wrapping a towel around his waist. "It should be obvious. I am managing the pool cleaning."

"Yeah, right," said Plum sarcastically. "Doing a great job."

"Better than you are."

"Does Jonathan know this is how you work?"

"Jonathan is very happy with how I work. It is you he is unhappy with."

"Let's not get into this," said Juan Kevin, stretching out his arms to stop the two coworkers from attacking each other. "We are here to get answers."

"To what?"

"Did you rent out a villa to Jonas Adler last week?" Juan Kevin asked.

"Yes," said Damián.

"And did you meet him when he arrived?"

"I—" Damián stopped himself, as if calculating his official story. "I did not see him, but he assured me that he was all taken care of and checked in."

"You little hypocrite!" said Plum. "You criticized me for not checking IDs, and yet you did the same thing—even worse! Allowed someone to check in without even meeting them."

"He paid a lot of money for my discretion," said Damián. "He told me his daughter had just had plastic surgery and she didn't want anyone to see her, so she asked that I send a car to the heliport and allow her to spend the week alone."

"Did you know that she might have come to murder her husband's best man?" asked Plum.

"What?" asked Damián. "Not possible."

"Kirstie Adler is the fiancée of Jason Manger. We don't know her motive for coming to the island," said Juan Kevin.

"To spy on him or to kill Nick," said Plum. "That is a question we are looking hard at. And if she killed him, then you are an accessory."

Juan Kevin gave her a look. "Well, not exactly."

"I had no idea," protested Damián. "You can't blame me. I blame you, Plum. You have destroyed the ethics of Jonathan Mayhew Caribbean Escapes. We did everything correctly until you arrived. You have corrupted us. You have destroyed our reputation and our integrity."

"I'm about to destroy you if you don't shut up," said Plum.

"Let's stop this now," said Juan Kevin.

"Yes, I never fear women, but Plum is so tall and large, she could harm any man," said Damián.

"You little…" But Plum didn't get to finish, because Juan Kevin wisely took her by the arm and dragged her away.

CHAPTER

22

JUAN KEVIN DROVE PLUM BACK to the golf shop so she could retrieve her cart. Along the journey, she listed endless ways she wanted to torture Damián. They agreed to keep in touch and share information if it arose. Plum continued on to her office, which to her relief was empty except for Lucia, who gave her a friendly smile. Plum plopped down in her chair and sighed deeply.

"I thought when I moved here, there would be less stress," she confided. "But instead, I'm up against a killer and a crime I need to solve."

"You don't need to solve it," said Lucia. "Let the police do that."

They both stared at each other before bursting into laughter. "That's a good one," said Plum.

"I'm leaving now, do you need anything?" asked Lucia.

"No, I'm set," said Plum, looking at her desk. She didn't really have any tangible work, but the thought of going home for the rest of the night depressed her. Lucia eyed her curiously.

"My daughter-in-law is picking up my grandson today, and I'm going to the supermarket in Estrella. Would you like to come with me? It's the opposite direction of my house, so I could drop you home after."

"Really?" asked Plum.

"Yes," said Lucia. "You should stop shopping at the resort grocery store. It will bankrupt you."

"I know," agreed Plum. "And they don't even have good produce, which is strange for an island. There's an abundance of holiday snacks—chips, dips, drinks—but it is slim on the basics."

"That's why you have to shop like a local," said Lucia firmly. "Let's go."

When Lucia turned on the car, once again rap music came blasting out. Lucia quickly snapped it off.

"Do you listen to this?" asked Plum.

"It's my guilty pleasure."

"Lucia, you surprise me," said Plum.

"There's lots to me you don't know."

"I'm sure."

When they drove out of the Las Frutas gates, the scenery became less manicured and wilder. The dusty road cut through a large farming region that was growing sugarcane. The eight-foot-high fibrous stalks swayed in the wind.

"The world's largest crop," said Lucia.

"Sugarcane?"

"Yes. Brought to Paraiso by Christopher Columbus."

"That guy got around," said Plum.

"He did," Lucia agreed. "It's provided my country with a complicated history, not to mention economic disparity. It has brought many extreme wealth—like the Rijo family—and others a steady income. But there are people who live in horrible conditions and work themselves to the bone for the bread on their table. Also, we can never forget how the production of sugar was entangled with the slave trade."

Plum nodded.

"When we learn of the sugarcane industry in school, the

teachers have a saying: How can something so sweet be borne of something so bitter?"

"Are the Rijos despised in Paraiso?"

Lucia paused before she answered. "There are those people that revere them. They employ thousands and thousands and are very generous to many charities. They established schools, paved roads, built villages."

"And to others?"

"Others believe they exploited their own people. There was always a story that Eduardo Rijo—that was Emilio's father—made a pact with the devil. And the devil often comes to claim his debt."

"Do you think that's true?"

Lucia shrugged. "I'm not a big believer in that, but I respect the people who do. The Rijos have had their share of tragedy, but so do most people. And the rest of the time, the Rijos are living a lot better than everyone else."

The quaint buildings in downtown Estrella ranged in height from one to four stories. The facades were a mixture of bright colors: teal, turquoise, and coral. Most had striped awnings and large signage advertising the lottery, ATMs, or Coca-Cola. Motorbikes were dotted along the streets in the parking spots. The downtown was abuzz with activity. Music was emanating from an unidentifiable location, but it provided an upbeat backdrop, like the soundtrack to a movie.

Lucia pulled into the lot of a building that looked entirely different from the neighboring structures. It was a boxy, windowless, cinder block construction that identified itself as *La Sirena*. Crowds were leaving with grocery bags bursting with products, abandoning their carts all over the parking lot.

Once inside, Plum was overwhelmed by the options. She had never seen so many varieties of fruit and couldn't wait to stock up. She held up a yellow starfruit.

"What's this?"

"We call it *cinco dedos*, which means five fingers. It's delicious."

Plum wanted to try everything. Under Lucia's tutelage, she filled her basket with the most exotic fruit. There was something called sea grapes, which Lucia said was great to make jelly out of, so Plum put that in her basket in hopes that she might pick up a new hobby. Lucia demonstrated how to crack open the hard shell of *limoncillo* with her teeth, revealing a tart, fleshy fruit like a lychee. *Zapote* was an oval, brown fruit that was not unlike a sweet potato, and Lucia advised Plum to use it in smoothies. Lastly, Plum purchased a thorny soursop, whose creamy flesh tasted like custard.

Lucia suggested that Plum purchase only the vegetables grown locally. That included fresh kale, cabbage, spinach, carrots, cauliflower, beets, garlic, onions, plantains, and potatoes. Soon Plum had so many items that she had to switch from a basket to a grocery cart.

"Those are perishable. Are you sure you can eat all of that?" Lucia asked when she saw the pile of goods that Plum had gathered.

"I hope so. I can make soup if things are about to expire," said Plum with the confidence of someone who had actually made soup before.

After produce, they moved on to the pantry section and picked up bags of rice and beans, coconut milk, meat, chicken, and a variety of spices. Plum bought fresh-squeezed *chinola* (passion fruit) juice that Lucia recommended for breakfast, as well as local honey and yogurt. Plum was energized. This was so much more inspiring than the grocery store at the resort or even the grocery store in her neighborhood in New York. Maybe she would really learn how to cook? She instantly conjured up an image of her making a gourmet meal for Juan Kevin. He would be ecstatic at her prowess in the kitchen and her ability to make local Paraison favorites.

In the checkout line, a short middle-aged man with bushy eyebrows stood behind them and greeted Lucia. She introduced him to Plum.

"This is Charlie Mendoza; I think you talked to him about resort entertainment," said Lucia.

"Yes!" said Plum. "So nice to meet you in person."

"You too, Plum. And I haven't forgotten about you. I'm working on that thing you asked me about now."

"Thank you!" she said.

They chatted as they checked out before taking their bags and convening in the parking lot. Charlie and Lucia were comparing notes on grandsons, outlining the boys' abilities to wrap their grandparents around their fingers. Plum listened to the amiable conversation until she was distracted by a figure across the street.

"Excuse me, but is that Carmen Rijo?" Plum asked Lucia.

Both Lucia and Charlie turned in the direction of Plum's gaze.

"Yes, I believe so," said Lucia.

"She looks rather dramatic," said Plum. Carmen was wearing all black as well as a black headscarf.

"She's going to have her cards read," said Lucia. "A woman who calls herself Priestess Pepe has a store there. She is not Paraison, and no one knows where she is from, but she now has a following."

"Is she legit?" asked Plum.

"No," said Charlie quickly. "Just like Carmen."

"What do you mean by that?" asked Plum.

Charlie shook his head. "I shouldn't say anything."

Plum waited, unblinking. It was a trick she had learned from her former boss. Say nothing and people will continue to ramble. If Plum had said, "I get it," Charlie would not have clarified what he meant.

"Carmen is a very cunning person," said Charlie. "I have to be careful because I work at the resort, but I am loyal to Alexandra, the first Mrs. Rijo. I saw firsthand how Carmen manipulated Emilio and presented herself as a sweet, naive girl. But there is nothing naive or sweet about Carmen. She is calculating."

Plum nodded. "I can believe that."

"Be careful of her," warned Lucia. "She's dangerous."

"I will be," Plum promised.

Lucia had to pop by the bank to deposit checks for the business. Plum took the opportunity to garner a closer look at Priestess Pepe's establishment. The storefront had no signage except for a poster of tarot cards against a red curtain. The door was open, the scent of incense wafting out to the street. Plum poked her head in. There was no one in the dimly lit sitting room. The stifling room was meagerly decorated with a sunken couch and a side table occupied by a lamp with a tasseled shade. She could make out voices behind a velvet curtain that separated the reception area from the back, and Plum moved stealthily to see if she could hear Carmen and the priestess.

"I was prepared," whispered Carmen.

"I know," said a voice Plum assumed belonged to the priestess.

"You showed me that Tower card, and I knew that evil was coming. I took care of it."

"You must use the cards to your advantage to prepare against your enemies. You had the Three of Swords card last week. Some people believe it only represents heartbreak or loneliness, but you knew it was a warning against betrayal and rejection."

"Yes. I had to crush the enemy before I was crushed," said Carmen.

Plum was leaning closely against the curtain, straining to hear.

"Everyone wants something from you. Only trust me," warned the priestess.

"I know," said Carmen, who started to whisper.

Plum tried to make out what she was saying. She leaned so close to the curtain that she lost her balance and fell down into the room. Two surprised heads jerked in her direction.

"I'm so sorry!" squealed Plum. She lifted herself off the floor.

Carmen glared at her. The priestess—a chubby, middle-aged

woman who looked vaguely East Asian gave her a curious look. They were both seated at a table with the tarot cards spread out in front of them.

"I'm with a client now," the priestess said. "You can come back in half an hour."

"Okay, yes, thanks," said Plum. "Hi, Carmen."

"Hello," said Carmen evenly. Plum thought she could decipher a suspicious tone in the widow's voice.

"I just picked up some groceries at the store across the street, and I thought I would see what this is all about," said Plum, as if they had asked for an explanation. "I've got to run now, but I will be sure to come back another day."

They watched in silence as she dusted herself off from her floor jaunt and left the store.

Lucia was standing by her car and witnessed Plum make her exit. When Plum reached her, she gave her a shake of the head.

"Why did you go in there?"

"I wanted to see if Carmen would say anything, you know, incriminating."

"Like what?"

"I don't know. Maybe she would confess to murder?"

Lucia didn't reply but opened her car door and got in. Plum followed suit. When she pulled out of the parking lot, Lucia spoke.

"You have to be careful, Plum. Charlie and I were not kidding when we said that Carmen is dangerous. The Rijos are powerful. You don't want to get mixed up with them."

"I know," said Plum. "It's just that Juan Kevin seems so enamored with Carmen that he won't even conceive of the fact that maybe she had something to do with Nicholas Macpherson's death."

"Why are you so sure she does?"

"She didn't tell us she had gone back to Casa Mango with him."

"She's private."

"It would have been useful."

"Only if you wanted to incriminate her."

Plum was about to protest but had to concede that Lucia was correct. "I think Carmen has a dark side."

"That's what I've been telling you. Stay away if you want to have a future here."

CHAPTER

23

PLUM WAS EXCITED TO UNPACK her groceries. She couldn't remember the last time she'd had a stocked pantry or robust refrigerator and wondered if she'd ever had one. In recent years she had relied on take-out delivery or dinners at restaurants. To be fair, the tiny galley kitchen in her New York apartment hardly inspired culinary creativity. But now that she had more space and excellent produce, she could become the next Julia Child.

After everything was put away, Plum opened the refrigerator and stared at it. She wasn't sure what to make. Her eyes scanned the cupboard shelves as if she would find a cookbook there, but as she had never purchased one in her entire life, it did not magically appear. Her internet was still spotty, so it took her a long time to research recipes with the ingredients she had. As soon as she would find one that appeared hopeful, she would be frustrated to discover she was missing several key ingredients. Her soup ambition was thwarted by a lack of any sort of chicken or vegetable broth or bouillon (and her inexperience did not allow her to conclude that she could make her own chicken or vegetable broth). She had neglected to buy any sort of cooking oil, which presented a problem. And she was saddened to realize she only had a few dull knives in the drawer. Cross and exasperated, Plum stomped out of the kitchen having eaten nothing.

She took a long shower (she had no choice; the water pressure was abysmal—like a slow tinkle from a toddler) then wrapped her hair up in a towel and put on her bathrobe. She applied aloe to her face and decided that she would feel a lot better if she had a glass of wine. And perhaps some alcohol would get her creative juices flowing and she would conjure up a delicious meal.

When Plum walked through the living room, she saw a white envelope had been slipped under her front door. She had a fantasy that a Chinese-delivery worker had left a menu, but her hopes were quickly dashed. Her name was written on the front in block letters. She opened the envelope, and a white piece of paper came fluttering out. Plum picked it up and read.

STOP INTERFERING OR ELSE

She quickly opened her front door and stepped outside. Her eyes scanned the street, but it was void of activity. No one was lurking in the bushes as far as she could see, and no one was waiting to kill her. She shut the door and locked it, her heart beating fast. Should she be scared? Probably.

Plum hastily dialed Juan Kevin's number.

"I've just been given a warning to stop interfering or else," she said without bothering to greet him hello.

"Once again, please?" asked Juan Kevin.

"Someone left me a note telling me to stop interfering. It was put under my door while I showered."

"And I'm assuming you didn't see anyone or a car or anything," he said.

"No! Should I be worried? Who do you think did it?"

"I don't know."

"I recently saw Carmen Rijo. She seemed pretty annoyed. I think she thought I was following her."

"Were you?"

"Yes, but that's not the point. I wouldn't put it past her."

"I don't think Carmen would do that."

"I know, your favorite Carmen wouldn't do anything bad..."

"That's not what I mean," he interrupted. "I think it would be risky. She's very conspicuous around Las Frutas. Even if she wanted to give you a warning, she wouldn't hand deliver a letter. Not to mention she has other, better ways to get rid of you."

"Like what?"

"She can ban you from the resort."

"She can't do that..."

"Of course she can. Emilio left her half of the resort. She's my boss."

Plum paused. That had never occurred to her. "Then who do you think wrote it?"

"Let's see. It could have been Deepak or Jason. Or Kirstie Adler. Damián, maybe. Leslie Abernathy is a long shot, but she could have been annoyed. The list is long and growing."

"That's disconcerting."

"I think you should be cautious. I can make sure my security team does extra rounds on your block tonight."

"Okay," said Plum meekly.

There was a heavy pause. Juan Kevin finally spoke. "Do you want me to come over to make sure it's safe?"

"That would be great!" said Plum. "See you as soon as possible."

Plum changed into a long, white skirt and a striped T-shirt while she awaited Juan Kevin. She also squirted some perfume on her wrists and put on some mascara. *What the hell*, she thought. May as well. She also dabbed some lipstick on her chapped lips. She was about to attempt to straighten her hair, but then she shrugged and decided to leave it au naturel.

Juan Kevin performed an exhaustive search of Plum's town house. He checked her closets and even under her bed. He also walked around the property outside until they were both satisfied that his inspection was thorough.

"Can I get you a glass of wine?" asked Plum.

"Sure," said Juan Kevin.

Plum noticed that he was not in his usual blue blazer and khakis but instead wore jeans and a polo shirt. "I didn't take you away from anything, did I?" she asked, handing him the glass.

"No. I had just showered at the gym."

"Oh, so no hot date?"

He smiled. "Not tonight."

She wasn't thrilled with that answer. "I was going to whip something up for dinner; are you hungry?"

"Sure," said Juan Kevin. "What are you cooking?"

"Well, I went to the grocery store and bought lots of things," she said, waving toward the bowls of fruits on the counter as if she were a mannequin on a game show displaying the prizes.

"That looks great. I didn't realize you cooked."

"Yes, well, I eat," said Plum.

"Me too."

"Do you cook?"

"I do," said Juan Kevin. "My mother is an excellent cook, and she taught me how."

Plum sighed. "Okay, then maybe you can help me. The truth is, I forgot to pack up my cookbooks, and I am hopeless without them. I am really one of those people that needs to follow recipes."

"Sure."

For the next forty-five minutes, Plum watched as Juan Kevin made braised chicken in a garlicky broth with lots of fresh herbs. He served it alongside rice, black beans, and mashed plantains. He was not deterred by her lack of oil and instead used butter, an improvisation that she found logical but confounding.

"This is delicious," said Plum.

The evening was warm with only a hint of a gentle breeze, so they set the table on the balcony. The sun had set, and a dark, starry night stretched out as far as the eye could see. Plum put the pair of candlesticks from the sideboard on the table and lit them.

Juan Kevin examined the warning letter while they ate.

"This is amateurish," he remarked. "I don't think this is from the killer. Although I do want you to remain vigilant."

"The only person that I know who knew where I lived was Robert Glover. Have you been to see him yet, by the way?" she asked.

Juan Kevin sighed. "I don't want to again contribute to your criticism of the way my country does things, but he has been moved from the jail in Diego to San Jose, the capital city. The American embassy is there, and I think he reached out to them. Now it is all mired in red tape, and the police keep shifting him around. Therefore, I have not yet had the opportunity to talk with him and verify if it was Leslie kissing Nick."

Plum shook her head. "I won't say anything, but it's absurd that the cops are so inept."

"That's saying something."

Plum didn't want to argue, so she dropped it. "You know, Robert Glover was hired by Jonas Adler, Kirstie's dad. That would mean he was in communication with him. Maybe he told Jonas where I lived, and he told Kirstie."

"It's possible. She did tell you to stay away from her and her fiancé."

"She did. Maybe she's the killer and she wants me to stop investigating."

"I have a hard time picturing her killing Nicholas. Like Deepak said, she's so tiny, and he was a big man. I don't see how she could overpower him."

"He was drunk, and maybe she had the element of surprise," said Plum.

"I suppose. What has bothered me from the beginning is that everyone seems to be withholding information."

"I agree. And you know, someone said something to me that I didn't pick up on, and I can't remember what it was, but it was meaningful."

"Who said it?"

"I can't remember that either."

"It will come back to you."

The nocturnal creatures had started to make themselves known. There was a particularly loud species that Plum had been unable to identify.

"What's that noise?"

"Those are the coquis, a type of frog. The males make calls at night to attract the females."

"I feel like I'm at the Metropolitan Opera every evening. They're so loud."

Juan Kevin laughed. "Yes, the male enters a rival's territory and challenges him, and they engage in a singing duel. The first to falter in keeping up with cadence is declared the loser and needs to leave the territory."

"It's like nature's version of *American Idol.*"

"Yes."

"You don't get that in New York."

"No," agreed Juan Kevin.

"Have you ever been there?"

"Yes, several times. It's not for me."

"Why not?"

"I like open skies and open space. Also, a slower pace, which I know infuriates you."

"I'm adapting," said Plum. She realized that was true. "I'm starting to prefer open skies and space as well. I never thought I would say that. I grew up with a lot of it in Upstate New York, but there, it felt oppressive and sad. To me, it was as if I was missing out on everything in the world, and I couldn't wait to get to New York City. But I don't feel that way here."

"Maybe you were lonely."

She was about to contradict him, a knee-jerk defensive response to admitting any sort of vulnerability, but decided against it. "I guess I was," conceded Plum.

"Paraiso can be a wonderful place to live. It is an adjustment, but if you're in the mindset that you're not on vacation, and if you don't compare it to other places, you can enjoy it for all it has to offer."

"Yeah. I guess I should do that."

"My advice is for you to resume the hobbies and normal extracurricular activities that you did in New York. It will help you fall into a routine."

"The only thing I did in New York was work."

"What about the weekends?"

"I was so tired that I generally did nothing."

"Do you play any sports?"

"Not really."

"Huh, well, maybe you can find something of interest here."

Plum suddenly felt desperately shallow and boring before remembering something that might make her not seem so pathetic. "There was one thing I did every now and then…" began Plum. "I really love animals, so when I could, I would volunteer at the rescue shelter walking the dogs. I traveled so much, I couldn't have my own…"

"That's great!" said Juan Kevin. "There is a shelter in Estrella where my sister works. When things are settled at work, you can volunteer there."

"Maybe…"

"No, it will be great. I will bring you myself and introduce you to everyone."

"Great."

"They will be thrilled to meet you."

Plum smiled. "I appreciate you giving me a second chance. After seeing how Kirstie behaves, I can imagine I came off sort of rude."

Juan Kevin brushed off the comment. "Let's start over. I'm happy you are here in Paraiso."

They lingered over their dinner, and Plum's mind became filled with sultry fantasies about how the night would end. This was not a date, but it felt like one. Juan Kevin's eyes sparkled in the gauzy candlelight, and Plum's heart swelled with romantic thoughts. They would kiss, she was certain. But would anything else happen?

"Uh-oh, looks like I have to go," said Juan Kevin.

Plum had been staring into space and didn't even notice he had received a text and was glancing at his phone.

"What's up?"

"Our friends Kirstie and Jason were caught yet again trying to leave the country. Her father sent a helicopter to take her to the airport where the private jet awaited them. My security guy stopped them at the heliport. They're making all sorts of threats. I need to go."

"I'm coming with you!" said Plum, running to get a light sweater without waiting for an answer.

※

They could hear Kirstie yelling before they even entered the heliport control tower. A long string of expletives erupted from her small, puckered mouth. She was berating a young security guard who was cowering from her verbal abuse. Jason sat on a bench, staring blankly. There were stacks of expensive luggage surrounding him.

"Miss Adler, please refrain from addressing my colleague in that manner," said Juan Kevin.

"I'm an American. This is unconstitutional. I need to return to my country," she snarled.

"The police have requested that you stay," said Juan Kevin.

"I'm sick of this," she snapped before turning her attention to Plum. "You better get us out of here."

"Nothing I can do about it," said Plum.

"I googled you. You were fired from your job," said Kirstie.

"The magazine closed."

"You'll be fired from this job also."

"Let's not make threats," Juan Kevin interjected.

"Tell her, Jason," commanded Kirstie.

He glanced over as if he had been awoken from a dream. "Tell her what?"

"That this bitch better help us get home."

"That's enough," said Juan Kevin gallantly. "You will not talk to people like this. Go back to your hotel room. You are in a beautiful country, not prison. You will be home soon."

Kirstie screamed at the top of her lungs then stormed out of the building.

Jason stood up.

"Where's Deepak?" asked Plum.

"His room, I guess," said Jason.

"You were just going to leave him?" she asked.

Jason shrugged. "Yeah."

"That's kind of an awful thing to do to one of your best friends."

Jason nodded. "Yeah, you're right."

He followed his fiancée out of the building. Plum heard a car screech off.

"These people are unbelievable," said Juan Kevin.

The cowering security guard shook his head. "I am sorry to call you, boss, but she is very difficult."

"It's okay, Louis. You did the right thing."

"She also made a scene when she arrived last week," said Louis.

"So she did arrive through the heliport," said Plum.

"Why didn't you register her?" asked Juan Kevin. He was not pleased his security had been breached.

"We tried to," said Louis. "But she wouldn't let us take her picture. She kept hiding her face with her hands and telling us we had no right. We called her villa broker, and he said it was fine, he would vouch for her."

"Damián Rodriguez said that?" asked Plum.

"Yes," said Louis. "He said it was no problem."

Plum shot Juan Kevin a knowing look.

"I hope I didn't get him into trouble," said Louis. "I have worked with Damián for years. I thought he was okay."

"We need to stick by the rules, Louis," said Juan Kevin. "Everyone photographed, passport scanned, or they don't enter the resort."

"Yes, sir."

They were about to leave when Louis spoke. "She looks much better as a brunette."

He had their attention. "Who?" asked Plum.

"That angry woman."

"What do you mean?" asked Louis.

"When she arrived, she was blond. I don't know, maybe it was a wig, because I don't think she could change it all the way back to brown that fast. My sister once tried to do that…"

Juan Kevin interrupted him. "You're saying that Kirstie Adler had blond hair a week ago?"

"Yes."

"Why does it matter that Kirstie had blond hair?" asked Plum when they were outside the heliport. The area was completely dark, and there was no sign of activity.

"Maybe it wasn't Leslie Abernathy that Robert Glover saw kissing Nick. He told you he saw a blond neighbor. But maybe he assumed it was Leslie because she had come in through the bushes that way. But maybe it was Kirstie in her wig?"

Plum wanted to protest. But he had a point. "Possibly. And she and Nick were having an affair?"

"We assumed that Kirstie was eager to get Jason off the island and going to all these great lengths to protect her fiancé. Maybe she is protecting herself," said Juan Kevin.

"She definitely seems like the type who puts herself first," agreed Plum.

"It's a pity you don't have a better relationship with Damián. Maybe he discovered something in the villa she rented."

"I wouldn't ask him for any sort of favor. He wants to get rid of me so badly, he would probably feed me false intelligence."

Juan Kevin nodded. "True."

"What now?" asked Plum.

He sighed. "It's late. I'll drop you at home. We can regroup in the morning."

Plum was disappointed that the romantic element had been fizzled by Kirstie and Jason. *Oh well*, thought Plum. Hopefully there would be more opportunities ahead. She drifted off to sleep with the sounds of the coqui chirping their little heads off trying to woo a mate. How nice it would be to be able to skip formalities and have males battling it out for her, their naked passion laid bare.

CHAPTER

24

SEEING AS NO ONE EVER arrived at the office before ten, Plum knew she would have the place to herself when she opened the door at nine a.m. She flicked on the lights and glanced surreptitiously around the room, as if a surprise party were about to pop out from under the tables.

Plum casually walked over to Damián's desk. He had a stack of manila files in his outbox, and she quickly flipped through them. She wasn't sure what she was searching for, but maybe there was something about Kirstie or her father, Jonas Adler, that would be incriminating. Perhaps Damián had discovered a murder weapon at the villa that she had rented. Plum knew it was absurd, but she was fueled by her hatred of Damián and her motivation to please Juan Kevin.

After finding zero of interest in the files, she turned on Damián's computer. It felt like an eternity before the old desktop model booted up. Plum sat down in his chair, tapped her fingers impatiently, and scanned the office. Her heart was thumping. She was doing nothing wrong, she told herself.

Plum clicked on the icon that said *Clients* and scrolled through the Excel spreadsheet. Jonas Adler was listed as renting the villa, but other than his address and the confirmation of the wire transfer, there was no additional information to suggest homicide or controversy. Plum was disappointed. She was about to turn off the computer when she decided to click on the trash icon. There was a document that had recently been printed but had no name on it. Plum opened it.

STOP INTERFERING OR ELSE

It had been Damián who left her the letter! Plum was seething. How dare he intimidate her? What a pathetic turd. Emboldened, Plum opened Damián's emails. There was nothing of interest in his inbox, so she decided to check his old emails. She found his back and forth with his clients as well as exchanges with tour operators abroad. There was spam from clothing websites, airlines, and restaurants. She was amused to find out that he subscribed to HairClub and tucked that knowledge away for the future. She had almost lost hope when she saw one from three weeks prior with *Casa Mango* in the subject line.

When Plum opened the email, she was horrified. It had been a query about renting Casa Mango, and it included a reply from Damián that the villa was already rented. This was way before she had confirmed the bachelor party. Why had it gone to Damián? She clicked down and was aghast to discover there were further queries about the property—and many before she even dropped the price! Somehow Damián had rerouted them so they went to him instead of Plum! There had been interest in the villa for the busy holiday weekend, and Damián had interfered to ruin her.

"What are you doing?"

Plum had been so immersed in her reconnaissance that she didn't hear the door open. Damián rushed over, pushed her out of his chair and stood in front of his computer, blocking her view.

Plum staggered back, having lost her balance, but pulled herself up. "You threatened me and sabotaged me! How dare you?"

"You have no right to search my computer!" he roared.

"I can't believe that you would tell my potential clients that Casa Mango was rented! And then you have the nerve to leave me that threatening letter!"

"You are a liability!" he shouted.

The yells became louder, with both Damián and Plum accusing one another of criminal mischief, deceit, sabotage, and trespassing. Neither of them heard Juan Kevin enter the villa. He tried to get their attention, but they were fighting so actively that they didn't pay him any attention.

"This man is egregious." Plum fumed.

"This woman is a catastrophe." Damián seethed. "I want her arrested for invading my private property."

"And I want him arrested for leaving me that note! I found it on his computer!"

Damian turned and gave Plum a scathing look. "It's the *firm's* computer."

Plum scoffed. "You had no right," she said before turning back to Juan Kevin. "Damián also lied and impersonated me."

"Relax!" commanded Damián.

The yelling continued until Juan Kevin put his fingers to his lips and blew a whistle. They stopped and stared at him.

"Damián, what you did was wrong. Threatening someone is a very serious crime here in Las Frutas."

"It was a joke," said Damián, shaking his head as if he were dealing with idiots.

"I'll be watching you," warned Juan Kevin.

A triumphant smile appeared on Plum's face, and she folded her arms dramatically. "I want to wait and tell Jonathan," she said.

"I passed him earlier this morning, and he said he was off to a polo match. We have some time," said Juan Kevin. "Let's go get some coffee."

"Fine," said Plum, before turning to Damián. She wagged a finger at him. "You are dead meat."

He bristled. "Jonathan loves me. I have nothing to worry about."

"Let's go," urged Juan Kevin.

There was a coffee truck that parked by the main gates to the resort. Most of the staff purchased their second cup of brew there (always having the first one at home), and the general consensus was that it was the best coffee on the island. That said, Plum had already heard so many Paraisons making different claims of which was the best coffee, it was hard to keep track. Paraison coffee seemed to be a source of patriotic pride.

"That guy is awful," said Plum as they stood in line to order. "I knew there had to be other interest in Casa Mango. On that front, I feel vindicated. But the fact that he left me that note is evil."

"Yes," agreed Juan Kevin.

"Jonathan will be enraged," said Plum.

Juan Kevin didn't respond.

"What?" she asked.

"Do you think so? Is Jonathan Mayhew an ally of yours?"

"Well, no, but that was a terrible thing to do."

"It was," said Juan Kevin. "I only wonder if it was something that Damián would do without his boss's permission."

"You think Jonathan wanted to send me that letter?"

"Not overtly, but maybe there was tacit permission. The friction in your office is not unknown."

"Who said there was friction?"

"Plum, it's a small island and an even smaller resort."

"Humph," said Plum. But Juan Kevin was correct, she had to admit. Jonathan was not on her side. She once again had to look out for herself professionally. It was exhausting.

They ordered their coffees, and Plum also asked for a guava

tart, which was full of cream cheese as well as fruit. She'd sampled one when Lucia brought them to the office, and she had regretted it ever since. They were delicious and addictive.

After they paid, Juan Kevin said hello to a sporty blond woman who was in line behind them. She was in her late twenties, with prominent green eyes and a swinging ponytail. She wore a golf outfit that accentuated her good legs.

"Plum, this is Cindy Snather. She's Tony Spira's fiancée," said Juan Kevin.

"Are you a golf pro also?" asked Plum.

"No, I work in the golf shop. Sometimes I help with the kids' camp if they are interested in whacking the ball around, but I'm usually setting up tee times and selling clothing and clubs," said Cindy. She had a cheerful Southern accent.

"It's great to meet you," said Plum.

They said their goodbyes and started to walk away before Juan Kevin turned over his shoulder and addressed Cindy.

"By the way, happy birthday!" he said.

"Thanks, but it's not my birthday," said Cindy with surprise.

"Oh, well, belated. It was this week, right?" asked Juan Kevin.

"My birthday's in August," said Cindy. "But thanks anyway!"

They continued walking.

"That's odd," said Juan Kevin.

"What was that all about?" asked Plum.

"Don't you remember that Tony said he couldn't have dinner with Jason, Nick, and Deepak because it was Cindy's birthday?"

Plum jogged her memory. "You're right, that's weird."

"Maybe it's nothing," said Juan Kevin. "Anyway, are you feeling any better?"

"Somewhat."

"Good. I'm heading over to Estrella to finally interview Robert Glover. I'll let you know what happens."

"Great."

He glanced up at the sky. "Looks like it's going to rain, so be careful. It rarely rains, but when it does, it comes on strong."

Plum stared at the sky and thought Juan Kevin might be losing it. The weather was perfect. In fact, the humidity was not overwhelming, so Plum decided to take the time to walk back to her office. The more time away from Damián the better. It was also a good opportunity to walk off that guava tart.

She ambled along the path underneath the coconut trees, which were weighted down with their fruit, before turning to the path that snaked through the links course. She passed two men on a tee box preparing to drive and watched as one sliced the ball into the pond. He shrugged and hit another shot. Plum tried to reconcile how that could be a fun activity.

Plum heard voices behind her and saw two ladies in their sixties speed walking. They were clad top-to-toe in colorful spandex outfits, each had a large visor on her head, sunglasses with polarized lenses, and thick coats of makeup on their skin and lips. They wiggled their butts as they moved—as speed walkers do—and kept their fists clenched and pumping the air as if grasping imaginary ski poles. Plum moved aside to let them pass and happened to overhear their conversation.

"Leslie doesn't really like Carmen, but she was in a fight with Alexandra, so she invited Carmen to Piñas and Penises instead of Alexandra," said the brunette with curly hair.

Plum's interest was instantly piqued. Were they talking about Leslie Abernathy and Carmen Rijo? They had to be. She sped up, breaking into a trot to continue eavesdropping behind the women.

"Alexandra Rijo is just as tricky as the new Mrs. Rijo," said the other woman, a heavyset woman with platinum helmet hair. "Frankly, best to avoid all of them. Too much drama."

"I agree," said brunette. "I don't think Leslie will be inviting Carmen again."

Plum was panting, and the women turned and gave her side-long glances. "Can we help you?" they asked.

Plum wanted to ask them for more information, but she thought it tactless, not to mention fruitless, as she doubted they would divulge their conversation.

"No, sorry," Plum said and slowly fell back.

This was an interesting update. Leslie made it seem like she adored Carmen. But maybe it *had* riled Leslie that Nick preferred Carmen to her. Something to consider.

❧

A livid Jonathan Mayhew ushered Plum into his office when she returned to the office. His normally unruffled demeanor was absent, and a look of pure fury was on his face.

"This is not working out," he said.

"What do you mean?" asked Plum.

"I just received a call from a boorish man named Jonas Adler who said that his future son-in-law and his friends were being held prisoner at our resort and it was the responsibility of Jonathan Mayhew Caribbean Escapes to liberate them. Furthermore, he said that he will press charges and use all of his connections to destroy my business."

"Sounds like a jerk," said Plum.

"That is not the response I would like to hear from you," said Jonathan.

"Don't worry, as soon as they arrest someone for Nick's death, they are free to go."

Jonathan folded his long fingers and gazed at Plum with hostility. "At whose cost are the men remaining at the resort?"

"Um, I'm not sure."

"The rooms at the hotel are not inexpensive."

"Fine, you can take it out of my commission."

"Do you think they will still pay after their friend was murdered? Jonas Adler already told me he would like a refund for the deposit they placed."

Plum hadn't considered the financial ramifications of the murder.

"I'll cover it," she said.

"You will," he agreed. "And Damián has informed me that you broke into his computer and were casting around for some sort of information with which to blackmail him?"

"Categorically untrue. He left me a threatening letter telling me to stop interfering."

"He said he did it because you had been snooping on his computer and he asked you to stop."

"Lies. Did he mention that several people had actually wanted to rent Casa Mango before the bachelor party and he told them it was unavailable?" she said, triumphantly.

"Yes. He told me he did background research on them and found them to be unsavory. Something you should have done with the bachelor party."

"And you believe him?" asked Plum, aghast.

"He's worked for me for several years and has been a complete success. You haven't even worked for me for a month and have been a total disaster. Who shall I believe?"

"Me."

"Additionally, I do not have faith that you have made any progress with the article in the *Market Street Journal*. In fact, I think you were lying about that. Therefore, before you incur any more damages and completely ruin the business that I have worked for decades to build, I am terminating your employment."

It was fitting that for the second time that Plum had been fired, it started pouring as she made her disgraced journey home. Juan Kevin had been correct. He was a regular Al Roker. And, like all tropical rains, it happened so abruptly and virulently that it sent golfers and bathers scattering to find shelter. The wind had col-laborated with the rainfall and was flinging it sideways, straight through Plum's sluggish golf cart. Her entire back was soaked. At least she didn't have a soggy box of belongings to lug this time. She was the only soggy element.

Although she was mortified, she took solace in her reaction to her dismissal. She didn't grovel, accuse, or beg. She stood up word-lessly and exited. A victorious Damián had been at his desk—no doubt he had been alerted earlier and only showed up to watch her humiliation—but she refused to make eye contact with him. Lucia had tactfully made herself scarce, and Plum was grateful. A sympathetic look from Lucia would have made Plum weepy.

Plum knew she had made mistakes. She directly defied her boss's orders not to rent out the villa to a group. And in the end, it was the worst case scenario: murder. She couldn't deny she was somewhat responsible. It was a horrible feeling.

When she entered her town house, Plum opened the sliding glass doors in the living room and stepped out on the balcony. The sky had darkened and was a bruised shade of purple. An extended flash of lightning speared down over the Caribbean followed by growling thunder. *So, this is it*, Plum thought. Her little Caribbean experiment was over. It was strange to think that she would be returning to New York and leaving Paraiso. It had been her plan, yet…other than the whole murder fiasco, she felt that she was get-ting into her groove at last. But now there was nothing for her here.

Plum retreated into her bedroom and took off her damp clothes, throwing them in a ball into the hamper. She felt chilled by the oscillation between warm and wet weather and put on a cozy, fleece nightshirt and slipped under her bedcovers. After turning off her phone, she fell into a deep sleep.

CHAPTER

25

IT WAS PITCH BLACK OUTSIDE when Plum woke up. She was disoriented and had no idea what time it was or where she was. She picked up her phone and saw that it was only nine forty p.m. She had several missed calls from Juan Kevin, who had also left a voicemail. She didn't even want to listen to it. If he had heard from Lucia that she was fired, he was calling to commiserate, and if he hadn't, she would have to break it to him. Either conversation was unappealing. The rain hadn't completely abated, but it had softened into a dulcet pitter-patter.

Jonathan had given her a week to pack up and head back to New York. She wasn't sure she would stay in Paraiso the entire time—what was there for her here? But at least she didn't have to hop on the next plane. It was funny, because at the rate she was going, she would probably be allowed to leave before Jason and Deepak.

She lay back and put her head on her pillow. Her mind drifted to the murder and all the potential suspects and motives, and the same questions floated in her mind. Why had Nick been killed? Had it been impulsive or premeditated? If it was the latter, it would have to be someone who had a grudge against him and had carefully planned this, like Nick or Deepak or Kirstie. Or even Kirstie's powerful father. If it were impulsive, it would be Martin or Leslie or Carmen. She would love for it to be Carmen. The merry widow had a dark side, and maybe she had been spurned by Nick. Hell hath no fury like a woman scorned. Like Leslie, who had possibly been seen by Robert Glover in an embrace with Nick and was angry that he chose Carmen over her at the end of the night.

Something was niggling at Plum, and she couldn't figure out what it was. She had questioned so many people that week that she'd barely had an opportunity to process the information she gleaned. Yet she had a strong feeling that something of importance was either exposed or alluded to. Who had revealed a clue? Suddenly, she shot up out of bed. She remembered. It had been subtle, but there was an edge to the statement that required further questioning.

Plum pulled her hair into a ponytail and quickly dressed in jeans and a long-sleeved shirt. She had a yellow windbreaker with a hood; she threw it on over her shirt. There was a debate as to what footwear to don. She hadn't brought rain boots and her brand-new designer sneakers were more for style than sport and would get drenched. Flip-flops were appealing because they didn't become waterlogged. But they were hard to move quickly in. She went with the sneakers.

The streets were slick with rain, and very few cars were on the road. The pokey little golf cart's headlights were weak and only illuminated a small patch of about two feet ahead, where raindrops danced. The resort instantly felt shadowy and menacing. Plum knew she probably could have called, but the person she wanted to talk to had been so evasive that a phone call would not have garnered any intelligence.

There were signs of life at the hotel, and she pulled in between a car and a very souped-up golf cart that had plush seats and a radio. She'd had no idea that was even an option. Plum waltzed past the front desk and pressed the button for the third floor. She was counting on Deepak being in his room.

The third-floor hallway was quiet and dimly lit. Plum knocked on the door marked 322 and waited. There was no response. She knocked again and pressed her ear to the door to see if she could hear a television or any conversation.

"Deepak? It's Plum Lockhart."

She couldn't be positive, but she thought she heard a thud from behind the door. Then there was a definite sound of something falling down hard.

"You okay, Deepak?" she asked.

Plum pushed the door, not expecting it to open but it did. She stepped into the dark room, her eyes adjusting to the blackness. She moved to turn on the light and blinked around the room. It was empty, the bed unmade, the television on low volume. There was a room service tray on a table next to the bed, the hamburger and french fries half eaten. It appeared as if someone had just stepped out. The doors to the balcony were wide open, sheer curtains fluttering in the breeze. She slowly moved towards the balcony and noticed that a chair was overturned.

"Deepak?"

She saw him on the other side of the bed, motionless. Deepak's face was twisted at an angle, his eyes closed. Blood was trickling from his forehead toward his neck.

"Deepak, are you okay?" said Plum. She dropped to her knees and took his pulse. He was alive, warm to the touch. His diaphragm was rising slowly up and down, but he was unconscious. Plum reached for the phone by the bed and was about to dial reception when someone shoved her hard from behind, thrusting her down. The phone flew out of her hand, and she careened into the side table, banging her head on the sharp edge. Momentarily confused, Plum opened and closed her eyes several times in order to regain focus. She finally looked up and saw the door was now wide open, and whoever had attacked her had fled.

Plum shot up and was about to give chase, when she decided that Deepak needed immediate medical attention. She fumbled for the phone receiver and dialed zero.

"Las Frutas Resort. I hope you are enjoying your pleasant stay. How can I assist you Señor Gupta?" cooed the voice on the other end.

"Señor Gupta needs immediate medical assistance. Please call the doctor now!" Plum shrieked into the phone.

"I'm sorry to hear that Señor Gupta isn't feeling well. We do have a doctor on staff that I could send up…"

"You don't understand, this guy is dying. He's been attacked. Please send someone now. And security. Call Juan Kevin Muñoz. Tell him Plum said it's urgent."

"I will do that right away, Señora Plum. Is there anything else I can assist you with?"

"Just do it."

Deepak was still out cold, but Plum had to try and find out who attacked him—and her, for that matter. She went to the threshold of the door and peered both ways to make sure the attacker wasn't lying in wait. When she saw the hall was empty, she ran toward the elevators. She pressed the button several times, becoming increasingly impatient, but it looked as if it were stalled on the second floor. She had no time to waste, so she fled down the stairs to the lobby.

There were people milling around, a young family checking in, and couples returning from dinner. She didn't see anyone dressed like a killer, though she wasn't sure how they would be dressed, but they would probably be skulking away. She rushed to reception and pushed past the people in line.

"Excuse me, there's been an accident. Not an accident—an incident. I need immediate medical help in Room 322," she said to the attractive receptionist whose name tag said *Ava*.

"Are you okay? Do you know you're bleeding?" Ava asked with concern.

Plum's hand flew to her forehead where a bump was growing. "I'm fine. Just please send an EMT to 322."

A tall concierge came over and stood behind Ava. He was young and had a solemn face. "Is everything okay?"

"She's asking for medical help in room 322," replied Ava.

"Yes, ASAP," demanded Plum.

"You need medical help?" asked the concierge.

"Oh my God, I don't have time. I called the operator and want to make sure it goes through. Medical help and security up to 322. And you go up there now, Mr. Concierge. Make sure nothing happens to the man. And today, not *mañana*!"

She left them and rushed to the front door of the hotel lobby and walked outside. Her eyes scanned the parking lot. Maybe the killer had driven away. It was pointless, this was a big hotel. She needed Juan Kevin. She quickly shot off a text to him with her shaky hands.

Plum spun around to reenter the hotel and almost bumped right into Martin Rijo. She stepped back, and her eyes narrowed.

"It's you," she said.

"You been drinking?" he asked. "You need to watch where you are going."

"What are you doing here?" she asked, noting that he was clad in black jeans and a black shirt—a perfect outfit for an intruder or killer.

"You're asking me what I am doing here? I own the place."

Was Plum imagining it, or was he sweating profusely? As if he had just been running and attempting murder. "You just tried to kill me, didn't you?"

Martin gave her a surprised look. "Lady, I don't know what the hell you are talking about."

"I don't believe you."

"I don't care if you don't believe me."

"What do you have against Deepak Gupta?"

"No idea who that is. Now get out of my way, I am done talking to you."

"The police will find you," warned Plum.

He brushed by her and held up his middle finger in the air. She stood watching him in the rain, wishing she could make a citizen's arrest. He got in the driver's seat of a Porsche and leaned over and kissed the passenger. Plum squinted. It couldn't be…Carmen? She walked toward the car hoping to get a better look, but Martin sped off. Carmen wouldn't be kissing Martin, would she? Plum must be mistaken. As she contemplated her next move, an ambulance arrived, and Plum gave them the information about Deepak.

Plum returned to the front desk. She found Ava again.

"Can you tell me if you noticed anyone running out of the lobby before I saw you?" asked Plum.

"I didn't notice," said Ava, apologetically. "I was helping the tour group."

"Okay, thanks."

Plum was about to walk away when Ava stopped her. "It might not be anything, but there was someone…a woman who came from over by the elevators. She rushed out very quickly."

"What did she look like?" asked Plum eagerly.

"She had her hand in front of her face when she passed reception."

"Oh," said Plum with disappointment.

"But I recognized her."

"You did? Who?"

"She has a villa here, I believe. I do not know her name, but her face is…very…she has had surgery."

"Leslie Abernathy?" gasped Plum.

"I do not know her name. But she is blond and from Texas."

Plum mused how someone could vacillate from being so useless to so useful in a matter of minutes.

"That's her! Thank you!"

One more person connected the dots with Leslie. Plum wished she could go confront Leslie, but there were more pressing things to attend to.

The next couple of hours were stressful. Juan Kevin arrived, and Plum filled him in, but he was called away upstairs to assess the situation. Plum remained at the hotel and informed Jason and Kirstie about their friend. She was subjected to an intense amount of verbal abuse, which she took in silence. They were right. If she hadn't suggested that this was murder and just let them write Nick's death off as an accident, Deepak wouldn't be in the hospital. She calmed them down until Captain Diaz arrived, and then Kirstie went ballistic again. Plum gave his deputy her statement then hitched a ride with him to the hospital to check on Deepak. He was still unconscious, but they were hoping for the best. She waited in the hospital for updates, but the doctor told her there would be no pressing news, so he suggested she return home and come back in the morning. She took a taxi and finally fell back into bed at two a.m.

CHAPTER

26

DURING THE EARLY MORNING HOURS, the rain ceased, and the clouds were blown away by a western wind. The morning was clear-skied and tranquil, with a mossy scent in the air. The grass and trees were still damp from the showers, but the sun was steadily rising with an unbridled heat that would swiftly parch everything.

Plum dragged herself out of sleep at seven a.m. She padded into the bathroom and stared at her reflection in the mirror. The bump on her head was now a magnificent robin's egg, with bruises that matched the color of the bags under her eyes. Her sunburnt skin was peeling and patchy. The "Botticelli curls" on her head were contorted and made her appear like Bozo the Clown's sinister sister. She looked dreadful.

Plum quickly showered and did her best to appear like a human and not a Halloween costume. She had a text from Juan Kevin that instructed her to meet him at his office as soon as she was awake, and she sent him a thumbs-up emoji before downing a cup of coffee. She put on a casual linen dress and didn't bother with heels, instead slipping into comfortable sandals.

Steam was coming off the pavement, and birds were bathing

in quickly evaporating puddles. The dew on the grass glistened in the morning sunlight. *That was the beauty of the tropics*, thought Plum. There may be rain, but the next day is always a fresh start. She would miss this place.

"You look tired," said Juan Kevin when she entered.

"Never say that to a lady!" she reprimanded. "You don't know how much effort I put into myself this morning."

"Sorry," he said. She had found him slouched over his desk reading something, a giant cup of coffee in front of him.

"You don't look so good yourself."

"I think we both had a rough night. How's your head?"

"I'll live. Any update on Deepak? I need to go see him."

"I spoke with the doctor, and he said he'll be fine. He was lucid this morning, but the doctor needs to do more tests and doesn't want us to come until later today."

"Okay," Plum said as she collapsed into the chair in front of Juan Kevin. The lack of sleep suddenly hit her. "Have they made an arrest?"

Juan Kevin shook his head. "Not yet. Why did you go see him last night?"

"I remembered he had mentioned something to me when I accused him of murder. He said, 'You're barking up the wrong tree.' I didn't think anything of it at the time, but then it gave me pause. It was the way he said it, his tone—he knew the right tree to bark up. I've felt that he's been cagey with us the entire time, and I wanted to confront him again."

Juan Kevin nodded. "I wish you had called me. I would have gone with you. It's lucky you weren't brutally attacked as well."

"I was trying to lay low. Jonathan fired me yesterday."

"I heard."

"I'm embarrassed."

Juan Kevin looked thoughtful. "It's a pity, but I think you said this was only temporary."

"True, but I didn't want to go down in flames."

"I think you need to take one thing at a time. We need to solve the crime."

"Yes, that being said, I think it's Leslie Abernathy. She was seen rushing out of the lobby, and then we have Robert Glover, the detective, seeing her make out with Nick."

Juan Kevin shook his head. "You didn't listen to my voicemail? I finally interviewed Robert Glover, and he said he only told you that he saw Nick making out with a blond. He never said it was Leslie."

"That's not true..." said Plum, but then she stopped. Had he said Leslie, or had she assumed it? "I was sure he said Leslie, but maybe you're right. But she is still a suspect. I guess that means Kirstie is also. Not to mention Martin. I saw him coming out of the hotel as well. All sweaty."

Juan Kevin sighed. "I wouldn't put it past him. He's intractable. But why would he beat up Deepak?"

"Deepak said I was barking up the wrong tree. Maybe he knew it was Martin and Martin found out. Maybe Deepak was black-mailing him?"

"I think the blackmailing is far-fetched, but the other part is possible."

"I also think I may have seen Martin kissing Carmen."

"That can't be," said Juan Kevin quickly.

Plum put her hands up in surrender. "I admit I'm not sure. But it did look like her."

"Lots of women look like her."

Plum decided to drop it. "What's the plan now?"

"I think we should do a 'welfare check' on Jason and Kirstie," said Juan Kevin. "I want to make sure they haven't left the island."

"Good idea. We can find out more about Kirstie's days as a blond."

When they arrived at the hotel entrance, a large tour bus full of grizzled retirees had just arrived. They were meekly exiting their air-conditioned bus and peeling off sweaters and coats that they had worn from a colder place of embarkment. Waiters with bamboo trays of tropical drinks were proffering their libations to the suddenly sweaty and grateful travelers. Bellboys placed luggage and golf bags on carts under the watchful eye of additional torpid hotel staff who seemed to have no other responsibility besides bearing witness to the process. An upbeat Paraison song was being streamed through the discreet speakers. The sliding doors to lobby were swishing open and closed as the guests flowed in to reception.

On the other side of the bus, AJ and Lila were watching their suitcases being hauled into a minivan. They were both wearing travel clothes—long sleeves and long pants as well as closed-toe shoes—and were departing with nice tans.

"Hey," said AJ when they approached.

"You're leaving?" asked Plum.

"We are getting out of here now," said Lila. "Supposed to leave tomorrow, but did you hear what happened to Deepak? I don't feel safe."

"Yes, it's unfortunate," said Plum.

"Security is very tight at the hotel," said Juan Kevin.

"That's what you said last time," AJ replied. "We don't want to hang around to have you proven wrong again."

"Do you mind taking our picture before we go?" asked Lila, thrusting her smartphone into Plum's hand without waiting for a reply.

"Sure."

"It's for my Instagram," said Lila. "You should follow me."

"Okay," said Plum, knowing she would not.

It took several minutes for Lila to find the perfect location for the photograph, which was on an incline under the shade of a palm tree with sweeping views of the golf course and the sea in the backdrop. Bougainville dripped over the adjacent walls like a flowery waterfall. She asked Plum to take several pictures while she changed expressions and angles, sucked in her cheeks, pouted her lips, jutted her hips out. In some she was draped around AJ, and in others they were just next to each other while she gazed at the camera in a seductive manner. He appeared to be used to this experience and didn't complain. Plum couldn't imagine many men would be that patient.

When Plum handed Lila back her smartphone, she glanced up and noticed that behind the palm tree, several feet away, was Martin Rijo, glowering at her. He quickly walked away.

"Did you see Martin?" Plum asked. "He was lurking in the background."

"No," said Juan Kevin. "But let's go find Jason and Kirstie."

They wished bon voyage to AJ and Lila, the latter of whom barely glanced up from swiping through the pictures Plum had taken. AJ thanked them, and they all walked back to the entrance. Plum and Juan Kevin bypassed the crowds and made their way to the elevators. As they stood waiting, Plum happened to glance to her right and noticed the entrance to the hotel spa was adjacent.

"Hang on a second," Plum commanded.

She walked to the spa and pushed open the door, where she was accosted by the robust smell of lavender and other aromas. There was a small fountain in the center of the reception area, the soft tinkle of water making its way down the maze of rocks. Soothing, instrumental, New Agey music was being pumped into the room. A plump, white sofa and armchair surrounded a coffee table that featured health magazines fanned out atop. Two urns of water—one with lemons and limes bobbing in it—were on a side table. An attractive receptionist in a white uniform greeted Plum in melodious tones.

"Are you here for a spa treatment?" she asked.

"Not today. I have a question. Do you offer any services other than massage or a facial? I mean medical services, such as Botox and fillers."

"We do." The woman reached for a pamphlet and slid it across the counter. "Here is a list of our complete services. I would be happy to discuss our procedures and go over any information with you. I think you are probably looking for something for your eyes?"

"It's not for me."

"Oh. You may consider."

Plum's eyes skidded down the list. It was possible to schedule any sort of face altering appointment, from lasers to micromanipulation.

"Do you know if my friend Leslie Abernathy was here last night?" Plum asked. She knew she would probably not receive a confirmation, what with all those medical privacy laws, but worth a shot.

"Yes, Leslie was here," said the woman brightly. "She had a chemical peel and some dermo fillers as well as some sculpting on her stomach."

So much for privacy laws, thought Plum. They must not have them in Paraiso. "Thank you, that's very helpful."

"She comes here all the time," said the woman.

"Thank you."

When Plum left, she felt refreshed and salubrious just from having been in the spa. Maybe she would book herself a massage before she left town. Juan Kevin was leaning against the wall outside, glancing at his phone. He looked up when she came in.

"I think Leslie was hiding her face because she'd just had a procedure," said Plum.

"That would make sense as to why she wouldn't want anyone to see her."

"Yes," said Plum.

When the elevator door opened on the third floor, there was

a security guard standing in the hallway, and Juan Kevin briefly conferred with him before explaining to Plum that he had one stationed on every floor now. When they reached the door of Jason and Kirstie's room, the golf pro, Tony Spira, was exiting. He greeted Juan Kevin and Plum warmly.

"I wanted to check on Jason and his fiancée and make sure they were okay," he said.

"That's what we're doing too," said Plum.

"Do you have any idea who did that to Deepak? Or Nick? Any clues?" Tony asked eagerly, his eyes moving from Juan Kevin to Plum's faces.

"They are working on it," replied Juan Kevin.

"But they still don't know?" asked Tony.

"Not as of yet," said Plum.

"I'm sure it will be resolved quickly," said Juan Kevin.

Plum looked at Tony curiously. He appeared awfully interested in the case. "Do you have any ideas? Did anything come back to you?"

"Me?" he exclaimed. "No, I don't know anything. I only hope this will be over. I must run now; I have a lesson."

He was about to leave when Juan Kevin detained him.

"Quick question," said Juan Kevin.

Tony stopped.

"Why did you tell Jason and those guys that it was Cindy's birthday?"

Tony's eyes moved from Juan Kevin to Plum before he responded. "It was an excuse. I use it when I don't want to go out with clients or guests. People ask me all the time, and I can't burn the candle at both ends. They take it better when I say that it's my fiancée's birthday."

"I see," said Plum.

When he was out of earshot, Plum whispered to Juan Kevin, "Was he acting fishy or am I paranoid?"

"Normally I would say you were acting paranoid, but these days I don't know who to trust," said Juan Kevin.

Once again Kirstie and Jason were not thrilled to see them. Jason snorted a contemptuous hello and Kirstie gave them a nasty look.

"I'm not even bothering to talk to you," said Kirstie. She was wearing one of those rompers that children wear but are also fashionable with skinny adults. Jason was in jeans and a long-sleeved shirt with the cuffs rolled up.

"That's fine," said Juan Kevin. "We came to make sure you were okay."

"As my friends are all dying or being attacked, that question is redundant," snapped Jason.

Kirstie held up a finger at Jason. "Don't even listen to them. Pretend they aren't here."

"We need them to get us out of here," said Jason. He sat at the table, tapping his foot nervously and drinking a cup of coffee. He appeared jumpy, and his face was drawn.

"Daddy will do that," she said.

Plum noticed there was a large scratch on Jason's forearm. He saw where she was looking and quickly rolled down the sleeves of his shirt.

"What happened to your arm?" asked Plum.

"Nothing."

"It looks scratched."

"It's not," he said. He glared at her.

"Can I see?" asked Juan Kevin.

Jason sighed and pulled up his shirt. There were definite scratch marks there. "It's from golfing. My ball landed in the bushes, and I got a little scraped up recovering it."

Plum didn't say anything, but she wasn't buying it.

"Why did you wear a blond wig when you arrived?" asked Juan Kevin.

Kirstie rolled her eyes. "I always experiment with new looks. Why do you care?"

"When you spy on your fiancé?" asked Plum.

"What's this about?" inquired Jason, confused.

"Ignore them," Kirstie repeated. She began flipping through her phone. "Oh, this is darling, Jasonie. Lila posted a picture down by that cute tree. I want to take one of us there."

"I took that picture," said Plum.

Kirstie rolled her eyes at her and didn't bother to respond. The conversation had deteriorated, and there was nothing they could do.

"We will leave you to it," said Juan Kevin.

"Whatever," said Jason.

When they were in the elevator, Plum pulled out her own phone and went to Instagram. Lila had said her handle was @SomethingVeryWhite, and Plum quickly found it. She clicked on the first picture to admire her own photography skills. It was a nice picture, despite the fact that Lila was not a good person. She used her fingers to enlarge the photo, and then suddenly her stomach dropped.

"Juan Kevin, do you see what I see?" she asked.

She showed him the picture.

"Yes, that's Martin in the background."

"That's not what I'm talking about. Lila is wearing an engagement ring."

"Right. It's very big," he said, examining the large, emerald-cut diamond adorning her slender finger.

"But she wasn't wearing one before."

"Maybe they got engaged here?"

"It appears so."

"What are you implying?"

"You remember what Carmen told us? She said Nick was currently pulling a prank on his friend who was very mad because it would call off his engagement. We assumed she was talking about Jason and Kirstie. But what if he was talking about AJ and Lila?"

Juan Kevin nodded. "It's possible."

"And remember Joby, the chef from the restaurant, said that he heard Nick saying to his friend that there was no way the wedding would take place. And the friend said that Nick was just jealous, that he wanted the girl for himself."

"And then they almost got in a fight," added Juan Kevin.

"That could have been AJ," said Plum.

"I think you're on to something."

The elevator doors opened, but Plum pressed three again, and they began to ascend. "We need to ask Jason and Kirstie about them."

Once more, they were received with repugnance when they knocked on Jason and Kirstie's door.

"What is it now?" he asked somberly.

"What was Nick's relationship with Lila and AJ?" asked Plum.

"I don't know," said Jason. He ran his hand through his tousled hair.

"Think," demanded Plum.

"Nick and Lila used to date. Like briefly. He broke up with her, and then she started dating AJ."

"Was she still interested in Nick?" asked Juan Kevin.

"I don't know. I mean, she seemed kind of flirty with him at the bar that night, but I didn't really think anything of it," said Jason.

Kirstie came and poked her head out from behind Jason. "They got engaged while they were here, so I hardly think she was pining for Nick," Kirstie said.

"But maybe she was, but then Nick was dead," said Plum.

"Is it possible that Nick was kissing Lila? That she came back to Casa Mango on the night of Nick's death?" asked Juan Kevin.

Jason started to shake his head but then stopped. "You know, Deepak told me he thought the voice he heard when Nick came home late at night was Lila's, but I told him he was insane."

"Why didn't you tell us that?" Plum blurted out. "It would have been very helpful."

"You think Lila killed Nick?" asked Kirstie.

"No. I think AJ killed Nick. And then AJ tried to kill Deepak because he knew what he had done," said Plum.

On the elevator down, Plum swiped through Lila's Instagram again. There was a picture of her a few days earlier wearing the dangling turquoise earrings. Plum held it up to Juan Kevin.

"We need to go now," said Juan Kevin.

They raced out of the hotel, with Juan Kevin alerting his staff through his walkie-talkie and telling them to notify Captain Diaz and the police. He described the minivan and told them to get the license plate number from the hotel. Plum sat shotgun while Juan Kevin drove. They flew out of the resort gates in hot pursuit of AJ. As luck would have it, the narrow road that led from the resort to the highway was clogged with cars and foot traffic. In front of them was one of those old, gas-guzzling trucks that would fail an emissions test in the United States. It was stacked with chicken coops in the back.

"Honk," commanded Plum.

"What's the point? They will just stop and get out of the car and come over to find out what the deal is. It will slow us down."

They waited until they had cleared the small road—after having to refuse peddlers selling warm bottled water, bananas, and sliced melon. Juan Kevin gunned the accelerator as soon as they reached the highway. He was an adept driver, although Plum felt as if she were a passenger in a video game as they nipped in and out of traffic. She clung to the handle above the passenger door, silently praying. When Juan Kevin came dangerously close to going head-on with an oncoming motorcycle, she thought she might lose it.

"Let's slow down. Honestly, we can detain them at the airport."

"I don't want them to clear customs. Then they are officially out of the country. I need to catch them before they get there."

"And you don't trust the airport police?"

"They can be a bit...lackadaisical."

"Ah, the *tranquilo* approach."

"Exactly."

Juan Kevin pulled his car right up to the front of the busy departure terminal of the international airport and put it in park. He pulled a placard that said LAS FRUTAS SECURITY out of his glove compartment and placed it on his dashboard.

"That means you can park here?" asked Plum skeptically.

"No one will question anything that looks official."

"You won't even get a ticket?"

Juan Kevin shook his head. "No. Paraisons don't like to make a fuss. They are very straightforward people. If you say you can park there, they will not question."

"Good to know."

They ran into the airport terminal and scanned the area, with Plum looking to the left and Juan Kevin to the right. He motioned the airport police to come over and spoke to them briskly in Spanish.

"There!" she said, pointing.

AJ and Lila were at the first-class Air Paraiso counter. He was talking to the customer service agent, and Lila was taking selfies. Plum and Juan Kevin went running toward them, the newly arrived police following. AJ glanced over and saw them then instantly took flight. He jumped over his luggage and then knocked over the poles that separate lanes before attempting to flee. Lila turned, as if in slow motion, and then for no apparent reason, let out a bloodcurdling scream at the top of her lungs. This sent the crowd into panic mode. People quickly dispersed—some jumped behind counters for cover, and others lay down on the ground with their hands over their heads.

AJ ran toward the exit, the sliding glass doors opening in time, and started running through the incoming traffic. Juan Kevin and Plum followed him out to the parking lot. He began dodging behind cars, with Juan Kevin yelling at him to freeze. The police spread out, and they finally cornered him by the ticket booth in the lot.

"Clearly a man without a plan," muttered Plum.

"Don't shoot!" said AJ, putting his hands in the air.

"It's okay, we don't carry guns," said a young police officer.

"Don't tell him that!" hissed Plum. "He'll run away."

"You need to surrender, AJ," said Juan Kevin. "I'm coming toward you. I need you to get on your knees with your hands behind your back."

AJ did as he was told. Juan Kevin motioned for a police officer to handcuff AJ.

"Why?" Plum asked AJ.

"I didn't want to kill Nick," he said. "That's not true. I did. He was arrogant. He didn't care who he hurt. He knew I loved Lila, but he had a hold on her, and every time he beckoned, she came running."

"Maybe it's Lila you should have killed," deadpanned Plum.

Juan Kevin gave her a disapproving look. "And why did you attack Deepak?"

"Because he knew. When we were at the bar, Nick was flirting with Lila. I overheard him telling her that she should dump me. I was planning on proposing to her that night. I confronted Nick, but he just laughed at me, said Lila could do better. Lila and I left, and I heard her sneak out at night. I followed her. She went to meet Nick. I saw them kissing. When she left, I killed Nick. He deserved it. And then Deepak started to put two and two together later. He knew I had been mad at Nick. He said he heard Lila in the house. I had to get rid of him too. But then you came in."

"Why didn't you kill me?" asked Plum.

"I thought maybe Juan Kevin would be coming. I needed to get out of there."

"Did Lila know?" asked Plum.

"No," said AJ. "She had nothing to do with this. She's the most perfect thing in my life."

"She's shallow and vain. Not to mention that I'd have fired her if she worked for me. I don't think she's worth life imprisonment," said Plum.

"Oh yes, she is," he said, thrusting his lantern jaw into a defiant setting. "She's an angel."

27

AFTER THE INITIAL EXCITEMENT, THE next couple of hours were full of tedium. In movies, once the killer has been caught, it cuts to a scene of everyone celebrating over a pint of beer or champagne, with the dubious police captain reluctantly congratulating the rogue civilian who apprehended the criminal. In reality, it was a lot of waiting around and red tape.

Plum and Juan Kevin had to remain in the stifling heat of the diesel-fumed parking lot until Captain Diaz and his team arrived. They had given their statements ad nauseum, but then some other official with an unclear role would appear and demand a rehash. The only sliver of entertainment was when Lila was detained by the police and brought outside. Once she observed her betrothed handcuffed in the back of a dented police car, she unleashed a rant directed at him full of expletives that would make a grandmother blush. AJ hung his head. At first the police and airport security watched Lila's tirade with unease that manifested in paralysis. But when she became a broken record, they took her to a secondary location, where no doubt she would be forced to sit through hours of inane questioning. Plum hoped she would take some selfies in police headquarters. She made sure to follow Lila on Instagram.

"I told you this was murder," grunted Captain Diaz when he arrived.

"No, you didn't," protested Plum. "*I* told *you* it was murder."

This led to a ridiculous back-and-forth that Juan Kevin ultimately kiboshed.

"No more murders," Captain Diaz said, wagging his finger in her face as he went to interview AJ. "I don't want you stirring up trouble in Paraiso."

"That won't be a problem." Plum sniffed. "I'm leaving town."

He nodded. "Ah, that's a shame. But I suspected you would have a hard time adapting to a place like Paraiso."

"What's that supposed to mean?" she said, riled.

"You want things snap, snap, snap," he said, snapping his fingers to show her what he meant. "But life here is slower. We like to enjoy the moment."

"I enjoy lots of moments," said Plum, but as she said it, she fathomed it wasn't true. She had spent years looking ahead, always pushing to ascend the corporate ladder. But had she enjoyed herself? Or was she more like Kirstie, who snapped her fingers to get what she wanted? To silence people? Or Lila, who was always looking at her phone trying to stage the moment rather than experience the moment? It made her shudder. "You know what? Perhaps you're right."

Captain Diaz's eyebrows shot up in surprise. "You agree?"

"Yes," conceded Plum. "I think I do need to…mellow out a bit."

Captain Diaz nodded. "You will be surprised at how much pleasure you will get out of life with a new perspective."

"That would be a refreshing change," she said.

Juan Kevin murmured his agreement.

Plum persuaded Juan Kevin to drive to the hospital to check on Deepak. He was sitting up, a bandage on his head but otherwise intact. Kirstie and Jason were by his bedside.

"How are you feeling?" asked Plum.

"I'm better," Deepak said, his voice raspy. "Thanks for saving me."

"It's the least she could do," snapped Kirstie. "She's responsible for you being here. Plum almost had you killed."

"That's not true, Kirstie," protested Jason.

Kirstie glared at him then turned to Plum. "It's absolutely true. You're as inept at being a travel agent as you were at being an editor."

"Villa broker," murmured Plum.

"Whatever, you're pathetic," sneered Kirstie. "I can't even believe you ran a magazine. I don't know anyone in publishing who would be caught dead with that hairdo and in those sandals."

"Hey…" said Juan Kevin.

"That's really rude, Kirstie," said Jason sharply. "I don't think you should talk to her like that."

Kirstie put up her finger to silence Jason. He stopped talking and gazed at her. Then he raised his hand and slowly pushed her finger down.

"You know what, Kirstie? I don't like the way you talk to me either. You're very rude."

"What did you just say?" she exploded.

"You heard me," said Jason. "You're a spoiled brat. And I'm sorry it took all this for me to realize that. I don't want to marry you. Give me my ring back."

Kirstie's jaw dropped, and her eyes darted between Jason, Plum, Deepak, and Juan Kevin. She appeared about to say something but then snapped her jaw shut like a crocodile who has just swallowed a gnat. "Whatever. You'll regret it. I'm a catch."

"You may be a catch, but I feel like the one with a hook in me. I'm ready to throw you back into the ocean," said Jason.

"Fine. Well, say goodbye to all my connections. Say goodbye to living a one-percent lifestyle."

"Goodbye," said Jason defiantly.

"And say goodbye to flying private! I'm calling my pilot and telling him to go wheels up. Good luck getting a plane home!" she screamed.

"Actually, there is a flight to New York twice a day," said Juan Kevin.

Kirstie let out a wail then yanked her engagement ring off her finger and threw it at Jason. "I didn't like it anyway! It was a measly two carats!" she exclaimed before she stormed out of the room.

They remained in stunned silence for a moment before Jason broke the tension. "Guess you'll have to book me and Deepak a flight home," he said with a smile.

"I'm on it."

"I'm looking forward to going home," said Deepak. "We need a proper funeral for Nick."

"Deepak, did you know all along it was AJ who killed him?" asked Plum.

"No," he said, shaking his head. "But I began to sort it out when I ran into AJ and Lila at the hotel pool. He grumbled to me about how Lila had ranted that she thought Nick was such a fabulous guy when he was really a scumbag. It allowed me to connect the dots."

"Why didn't you tell us?" asked Juan Kevin.

"I was going to, before he came into my room and attacked me. You really saved my life, Plum. Thank you."

"What now?" asked Juan Kevin as they drove from the hospital to Plum's town house.

"I guess I need to pack up. Find a place to stay in New York. A job…" Her voice trailed off. "I don't even know where to start. I am completely aimless for the first time in my life."

"Stay a few days," he suggested. "Don't do anything hasty. I bet you barely even went to the beach while you were here."

She was about to protest, but then she realized he was right. "Okay," she relented.

Plum glanced at him as he drove and once again marveled at how handsome he was. Maybe, now that this murder investigation was finished, they could go on a date? Would it be possible?

"Or maybe we can go to the rescue shelter after you get off work tonight?" she asked brazenly.

"I would...but I can't tonight," he said cryptically.

"No problem," she said quickly.

"I have an old friend coming in from out of town. Tomorrow?"

"Sure," she said, masking her disappointment. She wondered if the old friend was a woman, and she instantly conjured up a sexy Carmen-like figure in her mind; she already loathed this imaginary woman. "Ah, brunettes."

"What?"

"Nothing."

"Did you say brunettes?" asked Juan Kevin.

Had she said it out loud? "No. I said *barrettes*. I need to get some barrettes for my hair. This humidity makes it wild."

"I quite like it," he said, giving her an admiring gaze.

The compliment was enough to make her day.

❦

After showering and changing into a fresh outfit—an ikat-print linen tunic over white capris—Plum rode her lagging golf cart down to her former office. The pretext was to book flights for Deepak and Jason, but that could have been done with a phone call to Lucia. She wanted to let Jonathan Mayhew know the crime had been solved, and she was completely vindicated.

On her way down, Plum paused at a stop sign and noticed a Porsche to her left. It was Martin Rijo. He turned and glared at her. Plum leaned forward and glanced at the pretty woman next to him. She looked a lot like Carmen, but it wasn't her. *I guess I was wrong on that one*, thought Plum.

Lucia and Damián were both at their desks when she entered. Plum noticed her desk had already been pushed against a wall in the back, as if awaiting removal. Just as they were awaiting her removal.

"Juan Kevin told us what happened. Are you okay?" asked Lucia sympathetically. "I've been calling you."

"I'm fine," she said. "Just a little bruise."

"I heard you are responsible for catching the killer! Well done!" said Lucia.

"Thank you," said Plum modestly.

Damián sat back in his chair and rested his hands behind his head. "Americans coming to my beautiful homeland to kill each other. Such a shame," he said.

"It is," agreed Plum.

"And you were responsible for bringing them here," he sneered.

"Not the homicidal one. The victim."

"When are you leaving?" he asked. "The cold New York streets are waiting for you. It will no doubt be difficult for you to find a job. You will not be getting a reference from Jonathan Mayhew. We are happy to see you leave."

"I'll let Jonathan tell me that himself, thank you very much," said Plum.

"Jonathan left for the day. Told me to tell you that," said Damián.

Plum was dismayed. She had wanted one last moment with Jonathan to apologize for her mistake but also to share her victory.

"Ignore him," Lucia advised.

"Will do," said Plum.

"He is very confident today," said Lucia. "Thinks he will secure a big account."

"I don't think I will, I know I will," said Damián.

"That's wonderful, Damián. I could not be happier for you," said Plum sarcastically.

"It is the best property on the island. The owner is eating out of my hand. Needs some cash for legal fees, and I suggested she rent her house for a couple of weeks and make some major money. About to close the deal."

Plum paused. "Is this Carmen Rijo you're talking about?"

"Yes, the one and only," he said smugly. "You have heard of the property."

"I have," said Plum, her brain racing. "And I've met Carmen."

"A woman who looks and acts like a woman. Nice, meek, submissive," he said.

Plum had an idea. "Maybe that kind of woman wants to have a woman rent out her house? Perhaps I should talk to her."

Damián smiled wickedly. "Good luck with that."

"Maybe we can make a bet? Like we did for Casa Mango?"

"You don't even work here," he sneered.

"Well, if I secure the rental, maybe Jonathan will give me my job back."

"An easy bet. Sure," said Damián.

He rose and went into the bathroom. When the door was closed, Plum stood outside it and said in a loud voice, "Lucia, remember you gave me those delicious *coconetes*?"

Lucia gave her a quizzical look. "Yes…"

"They are so delicious. I know they're Carmen Rijo's favorite cookies. Do you mind baking some for me so I may bring them to her?"

"Sure, no problem."

When Plum heard the toilet flush, she rushed back to where Lucia's desk and leaned over her shoulder, staring at the computer screen.

"Yes, let's book them flights at five p.m.," she said.

Damián strode out of the bathroom and glanced around. Plum looked up.

"I'm leaving now," he said. "I have an appointment."

He grabbed his phone and quickly departed.

"What was that about?" asked Lucia.

"You'll see."

"Plum, did you receive any of my messages? Someone named Gerald Hand has been calling you. He wants you to return his call as soon as possible."

Plum rushed to the phone and dialed Gerald's number.

"Beg us to come and then play hard to get?" he chided when he picked up.

"I'm sorry…there was a lot going on."

"We land at three tomorrow. The house better be amazing."

"You're coming?"

"Of course. I know it was you who had the resort book Leonard's dance troupe. It was a crafty ruse to get me to come down and cover Las Frutas. But I could use a vacation; the weather has been abysmal."

It had worked! Once she heard that Gerald had reconciled with his on-again, off-again choreographer boyfriend, Plum had called Lucia's friend Charlie Mendoza, who handled all of the resort entertainment, and implored him to hire Elite Feet to perform for several nights. She said she would cover housing and expenses. It was a last-ditch attempt to bring Gerald down to Paraiso.

"I can't wait to see you. The house is beautiful. A marquee property. You will love it here."

"See you tomorrow."

When Plum hung up, she turned and looked at Lucia. "I'm going to need your help."

Lucia nodded. "I stand ready."

CHAPTER

28

PLUM BORROWED LUCIA'S CAR AND parked in a shaded patch outside Carmen Rijo's mansion, tucked behind a thicket of large trees. She was sure she was safely concealed. She watched as Damián drove up and chatted with the guards. He held up a pastry box and then went through the gates, his cocky demeanor evident even from a distance. He was such a scoundrel. Fortunately, Plum didn't have to wait long. Within ten minutes he sped out of the gates, barely waiting for them to open, then floored it down the road.

Plum put the car in gear and drove up to the security check. "I'm here to see Mrs. Rijo. Tell her it is Plum Lockhart and I need to see her at once, as I have had a terrible premonition."

The guard said something into the walkie-talkie, and Plum quickly gained access. She parked the car then took a fast look at herself in the rearview mirror before taking a deep breath. "This is it," she told herself.

When the maid opened the front door, Plum rushed in frantically. "Where is she? Where is Mrs. Rijo?"

"Out here, by the pool," said the maid.

Plum hastily made her way to the pool. Carmen was standing,

her head in her hands, discarded cookies scattered around her. She glanced up in shock when she saw Plum, her red lips contorted.

"Carmen, forgive me for coming uninvited, but I had a terrible premonition about you, and I needed to make sure you were okay," lied Plum.

"What? How?" exclaimed Carmen.

"I had a vision of *fukú*. A *brujo* was coming to kill you. He would bring you something sweet that would kill you. Thank God I got here in time!"

"He did come!" said Carmen, grasping both of Plum's arms. "He brought me *coconetes* and said they were my favorite. I am allergic to coconut! He wanted to kill me."

Plum nodded. "You didn't eat them?"

"No, I threw them away!" she said, pointing to the ground.

"Then he was stopped. That's very good. I'm glad I got here in time."

"Me too," said Carmen, not fully realizing that it wasn't Plum who thwarted the attack, and she hadn't in fact been there in time.

"I think he was sent by your stepson. I think he conspired with him," said Plum.

"Yes! What shall I do? Martin is trying to kill me!"

"I have an idea… Is it possible for you to get away for a week?"

"Yes. I can go home to my village," said Carmen. "Or I could go to Paris. It's couture week. I need new dresses."

"Very good. You will need to leave as soon as possible. I will personally oversee the spiritual cleansing of your house. I have two friends from New York, they are experts in driving out evil. I will have them stay here, if they are available, and we will restore your home to the sanctuary it was."

"I'm so grateful."

"Just think of me as your *azabache*. I ward off evil," said Plum, who was never more thankful for Google. She had done a quick search on Paraison black magic in the car while she waited.

"You will be rewarded for this," said Carmen.

Plum was feeling celebratory but became disheartened when she realized she had no one to celebrate with. Juan Kevin was essentially her only friend, and he had plans. But as luck would have it, when she called Lucia to tell her about securing Carmen's house for Gerald and Leonard, Lucia insisted on taking her to Coconuts to applaud her success.

"It's pretty busy here," said Plum when they settled into their barstools. "But I guess it's happy hour."

"It's always happy hour here," said Lucia.

"Thanks for meeting with me. What about your grandson?"

"I had his mother pick him up today," said Lucia. "Sometimes an old geezer like me needs to have some fun."

Lucia ordered something called a Paradise Fairy, which was the official resort drink. Plum was about to order her usual white wine but decided to branch out and ordered the Paradise Fairy as well. She wasn't sure what it was but was pleased when it turned out to be a sweet, blended concoction with all sorts of stabbed fruits on toothpicks jammed into it. It had hints of strawberry and passion fruit, and the alcohol was undecipherable but went down smoothly.

"Yummy," said Plum.

"The best," concurred Lucia.

Plum became conscious of the fact that she knew very little about Lucia and spent the next hour asking her questions all about her life. She learned Lucia had spent several years working in her family's hardware store, ultimately taking it over when her father died. During her tenure there, she did everything from overseeing the locksmith department, the knife sharpening counter, and the garden supplies center to ordering and managing inventory and staff as well as the warehouse and the store property. She had sold it seven years ago to a larger chain and taken the position as office manager at Jonathan Mayhew Caribbean Escapes because she was tired of being her own boss.

"My grandson was a baby, and my son and daughter-in-law moved near me, and I wanted a lower-pressure job with great health insurance," she explained. "Plus, my husband was tired of me talking about the store all the time; he would get jealous."

"You're married?" asked Plum with surprise.

"Of course."

"I just…you've never talked about your husband."

"Really? Maybe because Alfonso and I have been married forty years, and I assume everyone knows that. He's a professor of horticulture at Paraiso University."

"Interesting."

"Yes. He's an encyclopedia when it comes to anything plants, trees, or flowers."

They talked more about Lucia's family before turning to Plum's future.

"I really have no idea where I should go or what I should do," confessed Plum. It was the first time she was totally candid with someone, but Lucia was so easy to talk to that she dropped her guard. It was her eyes—she had those big, owlish eyes underneath her glasses. She appeared as wise as she was.

"I think you should stay in Paraiso and open your own villa broker agency," advised Lucia.

"Me? No, I couldn't do that."

"Why not?"

"I…I don't know. I don't have the temperament."

"I disagree. You get things done. Jonathan Mayhew has been resting on his laurels for a long time. He has no competition, and he is old-school. I was very excited when he told us he was hiring you, but then I don't think he did anything to help you be successful. Nor did Damián."

"Damián impeded me every step of the way."

"Yes. It's a man's world at that office…but it doesn't have to be."

Plum shook her head. "I don't see this as my vocation. It was a nice experiment that illuminated what I need to do."

Lucia shrugged. "I think you would be great."

Plum glanced behind Lucia and saw that Juan Kevin had entered the bar. She put up her hand and waved, and he gave her a nod and a small wave. She assumed he would come over and say hi, but instead, he followed the maître d' to a table on the other side of the restaurant. Her eyes moved from Juan Kevin to the woman following him, and a pang of jealousy enveloped her body. She saw an attractive brunette with a clever face and clear, tanned skin. Her figure under her effortlessly chic, patterned wrap dress was the type admired by almost anyone with a pulse, and her excellent legs ended in high heels that Plum knew retailed for four hundred dollars. It was with increasing dread and repulsion that Plum watched as Juan Kevin waited for his date to sit down and pushed in her chair before sitting across from her. He did not look back at Plum.

"You look like you've seen a ghost," said Lucia.

She turned around to follow Plum's gaze, and her eyes landed on Juan Kevin. She turned quickly back to Plum.

"It's getting late; I should probably head home. And you are probably tired as well from so much drama the past few days," said Lucia. She motioned for the waiter to give them the bill.

"Do you know who that is?" asked Plum.

"Who?"

"The woman with Juan Kevin."

"No."

"Did you even look at her?"

Lucia glanced quickly behind then back at Plum. "No. I can't see very well."

"You're wearing your glasses."

"I need a new prescription."

"Is that his ex-wife?"

"I don't know," said Lucia. She refused to turn and look around again but instead began fumbling in her pocketbook for her wallet.

"Don't worry, drinks are on me," said Plum.

"Thank you. Just to remind you, the car will pick you up at two forty-five and take you to the airport to meet your friends…"

"Lucia, I think you are avoiding the topic. You've never told me about Juan Kevin's ex-wife."

"I didn't? Oh, well, I know very little." Lucia gave Plum her blandest expression and put on a fake smile.

"I don't believe you."

"I only know that she is the older sister of Carmen Rijo."

"What?" gasped Plum with astonishment. "Wow. And I thought he was in love with Carmen."

"He is protective of her. And he feels guilty because it was through him that Emilio Rijo was introduced to Carmen."

"It's all making sense now."

Plum was about to ask Lucia more questions, but then she heard laughter across the restaurant and saw Juan Kevin's date had her head back and appeared very amused at something he was regaling her with. *Forget him*, thought Plum.

"I guess it is time to go," said Plum.

It took every ounce of her willpower, but Plum did not look at Juan Kevin when she exited the restaurant. She felt foolish for having harbored romantic dreams of him when it was evident he thought of her merely as someone he worked with to solve a crime. Oh well. In fact, she felt embarrassed that she had asked him to take her to the animal shelter at all. How could she have been so naive?

That night, Plum lay awake in bed for a long time, preoccupied with Juan Kevin and their relationship as well as her future. Was he the reason in the back of her mind that she wanted to stay in Paraiso? That was absolutely preposterous, she decided. She could not allow her future to be swayed by the possibility of love.

She tossed and turned, clutched her pillow, threw off her blanket, unable to sleep. Finally, she picked up her phone and quickly sent Juan Kevin a text:

> Can't do dinner tomorrow, friends from out of town arriving.

Then she switched off her lights and went to bed.

Plum was surprised at how excited she was to see her off-and-on nemesis Gerald Hand. Perhaps it was the connection with the past and her "real world," or maybe it was nice to meet up with someone she had known for years, even though it was often rancorous. Her new outlook on life was to be positive, and she wanted to forget her acrimony with Gerald and treat him like a beloved brother, albeit one you verbally spar with and ungraciously dismiss from employment.

Gerald and Leonard exited the airport with a porter pushing an absurd amount of monogrammed luggage, as if they were setting off on a round-the-world voyage on the *Queen Elizabeth* circa 1950. They were a funny pair: Gerald was short, balding, somewhat pointy, with a hint of a stomach, and Leonard was tall, lithe, with dark skin, broad features, and the poise of a dancer. Plum embraced them both.

"Welcome to Paraiso! We are thrilled to have you here!" she squealed.

Gerald looked at her askance. "Are you on drugs, Plum?"

"Me? No, what are you talking about?"

"You seem so…happy," said Gerald incredulously.

"Yes, I've never seen you smile," added Leonard.

"I suppose I am happy. Happy to see you, happy to be here. I'm living in paradise—what is there to be unhappy about?" she asked.

Gerald and Leonard exchanged skeptical looks. "Whatever you say," said Gerald. "We are thrilled to be out of New York, although the plane ride was from hell. Screaming babies everywhere!"

"Why would you bring babies on a plane?" asked Leonard.

"It's just rude. They need an adult section at the very least," said Gerald.

"And airplane food should be illegal."

"Who even eats it?" asked Leonard.

"No one. But the scent of boiled beef wafting through the cabins..."

"And the rows of people getting on in wheelchairs. They just want to cut the lines and go first. Then they have a miracle on board and regain the ability to walk. And not just walk but run. They are first off the plane," said Leonard.

"They're fakers," agreed Gerald.

Plum listened to them bitch and moan with amusement. Not so long ago, she had been exactly like them. It was strange to realize that her cynicism was slowly slipping away. During the van ride to the resort, Plum chattered on about the island. She pointed out flora and fauna that she had learned the names of and described the mystery of why the woodpeckers only pecked on the south side of trees. She could tell that Gerald and Leonard were becoming somewhat bored, but her enthusiasm was blooming.

When they entered the gates of Las Frutas, both men perked up and began burbling about all the arrangements they had for lounging on the beach. Leonard would have to rehearse with his troupe and perform for two nights, but they wanted to make sure they swam and rode Jet Skis. The entrance to Carmen Rijo's villa further impressed them, and when they alighted from the van, they gazed around her estate with admiration.

"Plum, you have outdone yourself!"

"Villa Platano is the most coveted residence on the island of Paraiso."

"Fabulous," said Leonard.

He strolled through the capacious house and marveled at the pristine views and tropical gardens. Plum and Gerald followed, the latter plopping himself down on a chaise by the sparkling pool, allowing the bright sunlight to caress his Vitamin D–deprived body.

"This is the life," said Gerald, after a maid brought them all Paradise Fairy drinks.

"I agree," said Plum, lying down on the chaise next to him. There was no longer any remnant of the coconut cookie massacre, everything having been cleaned up to immaculate perfection by the staff.

Plum's phone pinged, and she glanced at the screen. It was a text from Brad Cooke.

> The in-laws are a go for renting out the house. I hope
> you will represent it for us. Thanks! Brad

Plum couldn't believe it. She was about to write him back and tell him she was out of the business, but then she decided to wait. She took a sip of her fruity cocktail and kicked off her sandals.

"For the article, what do you want it to say, that rentals are available through Jonathan Mayhew Caribbean Escapes?" Gerald asked.

"Yes," said Plum.

"Sounds good. I'm going to do a fabulous article."

Plum's mind drifted. A gentle breeze blew softly through the air. She could smell the mango trees. She felt content. And relaxed.

"No," said Plum.

"No, you don't want me to do an article?" asked Gerald, surprised.

"No, I mean, don't say that rentals are available through Jonathan Mayhew Caribbean Escapes. Tell them to refer to me for rentals. Plum Lockhart Luxury Retreats."

"For real?" asked Gerald.

"For real," said Plum. "I'm here to stay."

"I didn't know you were starting your own agency! When is this happening?"

"*Mañana,*" said Plum.

**Please turn the page
for a sneak peek of
Something's Guava Give,
the next book in the
Trouble in Paradise!
series.**

CHAPTER 1

PLUM LOCKHART STEPPED THROUGH THE narrow door and felt heavy gray cobwebs wrap around her shoulders. As she squirmed to brush them off, she inhaled a strong stench of mildew. The air was stifling, heavy with heat and ripe with neglect. She squinted through the darkness, afraid someone might be lurking in the corners, but could see only murky shadows. Her heartbeat quickened.

She spun around, unable to see the person who was behind her.

"Hello?" Plum asked, her voice echoing around her. "Anyone there?"

"Yes," came the whispered response.

"What godforsaken place have you taken me to?" Plum demanded of her colleague Lucia, who had accompanied her into the dilapidated villa. "I can't see a thing, and if I hadn't known you were following me I would have assumed I was being hunted down by a serial killer."

"*Cálmese,*" retorted Lucia, who flicked on the light switch. "There. Better?"

Plum blinked and glanced around the foyer, which had a grimy linoleum floor and mushroom colored walls that might have originally been a cool white. The light fixture above them was coated with a dense layer of dust and a cracked mirror hung over a small console table that had a broken leg.

Plum shook her head at Lucia, who was giving her an assured look from behind the thick lenses of her glasses.

"Decidedly not better," said Plum. "This place is horrible."

Lucia clucked and broke into a wide grin. "We both know that if anyone can improve and renovate this villa it's you. And besides, you always love a challenge."

Plum didn't disagree. She was incredibly competent. But she had always considered this a secret strength, like a superpower, and yet this small sixty-year-old grandmother had discovered it despite the fact that they had only been acquainted for four months. Perhaps Plum was more transparent than she had realized.

Plum sighed. "All right, show me around."

Lucia smiled mischievously. "I thought you would never ask."

As the tall redheaded American followed the short gray-haired Paraison through the unkempt villa, Plum marveled at how much her life had changed. At this time last year she had been Editor-in-Chief at the glamorous *Travel and Respite Magazine*, jet setting around the globe on fabulous trips to five star hotels, and based in New York City. When that all came crashing down, she made what she assumed would be a temporary move to the small Caribbean Island of Paraiso, taking a job at Jonathan Mayhew's eponymous travel agency at the Las Frutas Resort. But life wouldn't stop throwing curveballs, so the previous month she had ultimately (and impulsively) launched her own villa broker agency, Plum Lockhart Luxury Retreats.

"This place is a dump, Lucia," marveled Plum, peering out a filmy bedroom window that overlooked an overgrown courtyard. The shaggy ground was littered with rotten guava that bore deep brown spots. The neglected gum tree's bark sported a creeping fungus and the drooping leaves were curled in an anemic way.

Lucia shrugged. "We need inventory. It's April, one of the

busiest months here. We have three new clients very eager to find a place for Easter break."

A splashy article in the *Market Street Journal* by Plum's former coworker and on-and-off friend Gerald Hand had generated hundreds of queries, and she was now furiously working to secure more properties to manage, hence the visit to the squalid house, marketed as Villa Tomate.

"I suppose it is a good problem to have," said Plum, taking in the fractured surfaces and peeling paint.

"It is," insisted Lucia. She pulled out a notebook and began jotting down a 'to do' list.

"The name is kind of pathetic," said Plum. "All of the villas have fruit names and this one has tomato?"

"Tomato is a fruit."

"Technically. But most people consider it a vegetable."

"I consider myself a twenty-five-year-old blond with an hourglass figure, but that doesn't make it true," replied Lucia.

Plum smiled. When she started her agency last month she had been thrilled that Lucia agreed to join her (especially since it riled their former unappreciative employer, Jonathan Mayhew, and his deputy, Damián Rodriguez, who was Plum's nemesis.) She had even offered to make her a full partner, but Lucia had owned a hardware store for years and had no interest in incurring the headaches that came along with running a business. Instead, she accepted a role as "Director" (Plum was big on titles) and would work for a salary with commission. The arrangement suited both of them perfectly, as Plum did enjoy the glory of being the boss. But she also fervently admired her colleague's clarity of thought, decisiveness and clear outlook.

"We're going to need to send in those people who clean up crime scenes in order to get this place ready," said Plum.

"Don't be dramatic."

"Never dramatic, always practical."

"Hurry up and tell me what you think you will need. We have a three o'clock meeting with Giorgio Lombardi back at the office."

"What?" yelped Plum. "Why is that at the office? We've only just moved in, the place has boxes everywhere, it's like we are living out of it…"

"You *are* living out of it."

"I know that, but it's about images and perception," explained Plum. "We need Giorgio Lombardi to support our agency, and if he thinks we are some Podunk low-rent operation run out of a townhouse, he will be dissuaded."

"We *are* a low-rent operation run out of a townhouse," said Lucia. "But don't worry. He knows it is temporary, that you lost your housing when you left your previous employment and that this was all we could find for both office and residence at such short notice."

"Why couldn't we meet him at a restaurant?" moaned Plum. She folded her arms.

"Because we don't have the budget for all these fancy meals right now," Lucia admonished.

"That's what people do in New York."

"We're not in New York."

"No, we are certainly not," lamented Plum. "And the town-house is a disgrace."

"Don't worry, he's a man. He won't even notice the decor."

ACKNOWLEDGMENTS

I'm very grateful to the team at Sourcebooks: Anna Michels, Jenna Jankowski, and Shauneice Robinson. Thank you to my literary agent, Christina Hogrebe, and my film/TV agent, Debbie Deuble Hill. Vas, James, Peter, Nadia, Mom, Dick, May, Laura, and Liz for the support and distractions.

ABOUT THE AUTHOR

Photo by Tanya Malott

Carrie Doyle is the bestselling author of multiple novels and screenplays that span many genres, from cozy mysteries to chick lit to comedies to YA.

A born and bred New Yorker, Carrie has also lived in Russia, France, England, and Los Angeles. A former editor-in-chief of the Russian edition of *Marie Claire*, Carrie has written dozens of articles for various magazines, including countless celebrity profiles. She currently splits her time between New York and Long Island with her husband and two teenage sons.